# Mad Love

## SUZANNE SELFORS

Walker & Company
New York

First published in the United States of America in January 2011
by Walker Publishing Company, Inc., a division of Bloomsbury Publishing, Inc.
Paperback edition published in January 2012
www.bloomsburyteens.com

For information about permission to reproduce selections from this book, write to
Permissions, Walker BFYR, 175 Fifth Avenue, New York, New York 10010

The Library of Congress has cataloged the hardcover edition as follows:
Selfors, Suzanne.
Mad love / Suzanne Selfors.
p.    cm.
Summary: With her famous romance novelist mother secretly hospitalized
in an expensive mental facility, sixteen-year-old Alice tries to fulfill her publisher's
contract by writing a love story—with the help of Cupid.
ISBN 978-0-8027-8450-6 (hardcover)
[1. Love—Fiction. 2. Authorship—Fiction. 3. Cupid (Roman deity)—Fiction.
4. Manic-depressive illness—Fiction. 5. Mental illness—Fiction.
6. Mothers and daughters—Fiction. 7. Seattle (Wash.)—Fiction] I. Title.
PZ7.S456922Mad 2010        [Fic]—dc22        2010023261

ISBN 978-0-8027-2354-3 (paperback)

Book design by Danielle Delaney
Typeset by Westchester Book Composition
Printed in the U.S.A. by Quad/Graphics, Fairfield, Pennsylvania
2  4  6  8  10  9  7  5  3  1

All papers used by Bloomsbury Publishing, Inc., are natural, recyclable products
made from wood grown in well-managed forests. The manufacturing processes
conform to the environmental regulations of the country of origin.

YA
SEL

SELFORS,SUZANNE

MAD LOVE

4/12

DATE DUE

PRINTED IN U.S.A.

*For my grandmother, Maxine McLauchlan*

# Mad Love

"Behold," the Queen of Romance
declared as she gazed upon her
baby girl's face for the very first time.
"I have given birth to a new story,
and I shall name this story 'Alice.'"

# Sixteen Years Later

♥

## MONDAY

WHEN you're sixteen, summer is supposed to spread before you like a magic carpet, waiting to carry you to new, exciting places. Paperback novel in hand, bare feet buried in speckled sand, long kisses with the boy in the kayak—that's what it's supposed to be about. Summer, with its coconut and pine-apple flavors, with its reggae rhythms, with its endless possibilities for adventure and romance.

But if you asked me on that Monday in July, I'd tell you that there was nothing exciting about my summer forecast. My magic carpet looked more like a plain, beige indoor-outdoor kind of thing and it was nailed solidly to the ground.

If Mom had been home we might have driven to the coast or we might have rented a cabin by the river in Leavenworth. If I'd had friends here in Seattle, I might have met them at Alki Beach or at Greenlake. But I'd left my friends behind when I dropped out of Welmer Girls Academy. And when they started asking way too many questions about why I left school, I stopped answering. It's really hard to have best friends when you're living a secret life.

So there I sat, on the beige living room carpet, with twenty paperback romance novels stacked in front of me. I opened one of the books to its title page: *Hunger of the Heart* by Belinda Amorous. A few weeks ago I'd promised autographed books for a bookstore event, figuring that my mother would be around to sign the books, no problem. But today was event day and Mom wasn't here. I gripped one of the midnight blue, fine-tip pens that she preferred. Call it what you might—identity theft, forgery, fraud—it had to be done. So, after a steadying breath, I signed her name, making the little heart above the *i* like she always did. Surely no one would figure out the truth. If a reader questioned the extra curl in the *d* or the slight tilt of the *s*, I'd just say that signatures change over time, just like people.

But what I wouldn't say was that my mother had changed so much, she could no longer sign her own name. Belinda Amorous, the Queen of Romance, could no longer do much of anything.

And that was the secret.

So I signed all twenty copies of *Hunger of the Heart*. It had been a bestseller three years ago. Its cover was typical—a painting of a shirtless, square-jawed man and a busty, full-lipped woman. Their hair was blowing in the wind and their faces were clenched in what I'm sure was the artist's interpretation of passion, but it kind of looked to me like the woman was about to hurl. Maybe that's how you feel when a really handsome, half-naked guy grabs you around the waist and tries to kiss you. I don't really know since I've never been held by a handsome, half-naked guy, or any guy for that matter.

With a sigh, I closed the last book.

Forgery complete, I dumped the books into a shopping bag and slid my arms through my favorite little backpack purse. That's when my phone buzzed. Two weeks ago I'd set its alarm for 9:30 a.m. And every morning for the past two weeks, after hearing the alarm, I'd rushed to the living room window. What was there to see out the window at 9:30 a.m.?

Him.

It's nice when you can depend on things. Like knowing that the newspaper would be waiting on the stoop, not that I read it, but it's nice knowing I could if I wanted to. And knowing that I had enough milk for cereal and that I could eat that cereal while watching reruns of this reality show about a bunch of rich girls who get million-dollar sweet sixteen parties. And knowing that at 9:30 a.m., the boy on the skateboard would glide by my window.

I held my breath and waited for that whoosh of black hair, white T-shirt, and blue jeans to speed by. I first noticed him two Mondays ago when I'd been checking to see if it was a long-sleeve or short-sleeve kind of day. It was one of those moments my mother always writes about—a rush of instant, powerful attraction. Sure, I'd experienced it before. Let's face it, the world is full of good-looking guys. But this hit me hard, like a slam to the chest. And I'd been going back to the window ever since.

A summer job must have kept him on such a precise

schedule. I never opened the window and yelled, "Hello." I never waved. Just watched. And I made up this story about him in my head. His name was Skateboard Guy and he'd just moved to Seattle. He didn't have a girlfriend and he worked as a lifeguard at Alki Beach. One day, in my story, I go swimming and even though I'm a good swimmer, I get pulled out to sea by a rogue wave and he saves me on his Jet Ski. Of course there's mouth-to-mouth resuscitation. I was considering adding a vampire element to the story but hadn't worked that out yet. But, vampire or not, I was fairly sure that if he held me in his arms, and if he happened to be half-naked, I wouldn't want to hurl.

While the shopping bag of signed books waited on the carpet, I waited by the window, straining to see down the sidewalk. And then he appeared, right on time, rolling along on his yellow skateboard with its red dragon. With each stroke of his foot against pavement he came closer, his cuteness exponentially increasing. When he was in perfect focus, a smile broke across my face and I leaned against the glass. *Skateboard Guy, where are you going? Will you take me with you?*

Then he passed by, disappearing around the corner. That was the extent of our relationship. I suppose I shouldn't use the word "our" since he had no idea we were even having a relationship.

Red and blue jeweled shadows fell across my arms as I closed and locked the apartment door. A giant stained glass window crowned our building's entry and when sunshine poured through it, the foyer looked like the inside of a kaleidoscope. When we first moved into the building I used to dance through the colorful shadows. But that's the kind of thing a five-year-old did. Forging my mother's name is the kind of thing I did these days.

Crossing the foyer, I slid on my sunglasses, turned the front door knob, and stepped into an unusually hot summer morning.

"Hello, Alice," a cheerful voice called down. Mrs. Wanda Bobot, who lived upstairs, stopped watering her Spanish lavender and leaned over her balcony railing. "Where are you off to?"

"Elliott Bay Books," I answered. "I've got some signed books to drop off. Mom signed them before she left."

"Oh dear." Mrs. Bobot set her watering can aside and tightened her bathrobe belt, hoisting her double Ds a few inches higher. "I completely forgot. Is that romance writer event today?"

I shuffled. "Yeah. I said I'd go in Mom's place. You know, just to answer questions. No big deal."

"Why didn't you tell me? Of course it's a big deal. Your mother would be so proud." Then Mrs. Bobot pursed her lips. "Is that what you're wearing?"

I glanced at my peach tank top, khaki shorts, and flip-flops. "Uh-huh."

"I'm just thinking, sweetie, you might want to dress a bit more appropriately. After all, you are representing your mother. Your *very famous* mother."

I suppose a sundress and heels might have been a better

choice for the daughter of a romance writer, but I wasn't a sundress-and-heels kind of girl. Dressing up meant styling my long hair and putting on makeup, two talents I didn't have. "There's no time to change."

"Do you want us in the audience?" Mrs. Bobot asked. "A couple of friendly faces? You never know how many people are going to show up at this sort of thing. It would probably help to have us there."

"No way," a sour voice called from inside Mrs. Bobot's apartment. "I'm not going. Romance novels suck. They're totally and completely stupid."

I clenched my jaw. Nasty comments about the romance genre were nothing new, and nasty comments from *that voice* were to be expected. It belonged to Realm, Mrs. Bobot's granddaughter, who spent a month with her grandmother every summer. Realm, by the way, was the name she'd given herself. There'd been some sort of ceremony in her cul-du-sac, during which she'd scrawled her birth name, Lily, onto a piece of paper. Then she'd torched the paper. It had broken into tiny flaming flecks and had drifted into nothingness.

Mrs. Bobot turned away from the railing and stuck her head into her apartment. "Must you be rude? Does it help anyone? Does it make you friends or make the world a better place?"

"Whatever," Realm replied. "I'm just expressing my opinion."

Taking Realm to a romance event would be like unleashing a killer bee at a garden party. "You don't need to come," I called, starting down the brick steps. "It's no big deal. I'll only be there for a few minutes, to hand out these books."

Mrs. Bobot returned to the railing. "You're sure you don't need us? You're sure we won't be letting you down? Come to think of it, I do have things to do. I was going to bake raisin cookies. And a woman is coming by to look at the vacant unit. But I'll come to the event if you need me."

"I'll be fine," I said, relieved. I didn't want Mrs. Bobot in the audience. It's easier to tell lies when there are no loving eyes staring back at you.

I told lots of lies.

Deception had become my life. It wasn't a compulsion. I didn't do it for some sort of thrill. I lied constantly because I'd promised my mother that I'd never tell anyone the truth about our situation. Lie upon lie upon lie, heaped into a great big pile. Like a dung beetle, I maneuvered that pile everywhere I went. And I was sick of it.

"Drink lots of water today," Mrs. Bobot called. "It's going to be a hot one."

Thirty minutes until the event started—just enough time to get from Capitol Hill, where I lived, to Pioneer Square. The bus ride was stuffy and filled with the usual assortment of the unwashed, the weird, and those of us who were just trying to get somewhere without making eye contact. I went over a little speech in my head. *Thank you for coming to Elliott Bay Books. This is my mother's and my favorite bookstore. Mom wanted to be here but she couldn't because she's overseas researching her next novel.*

My mother's readers would expect the Queen of Romance to be doing something glamorous like traveling overseas, or getting fitted for a ball gown, or training a new butler. What a joke.

If they only knew the truth.

THE bus turned down First Avenue, passing the crowded public market with its overflowing flower and vegetable stands. Passing the place where they made melt-in-your-mouth miniature doughnuts, and the corner newsstand that carried papers from all over the world. "Heat Wave Predicted for Seattle," a headline read. Nothing like pavement to bring out the best on a hot day. Everyone on the street walked slowly, as if in a daze. Scorching heat in Seattle was as rare as a straight man at a romance writers' convention.

A few stops later, I stood in the heart of Pioneer Square, Seattle's historical district. A sign hung in the big front window at Elliott Bay Books: MEET OUR LOCAL ROMANCE WRITERS: MONDAY, JULY 20, 10 A.M. Taped to the window were red paper hearts, paper cupids, and three author photos in which each writer posed like a show dog. My mother's photo was totally ridiculous. She lounged on a red velvet couch, a diamond tiara sparkling amid her blond curls, a pink evening gown clinging to her curvy figure. Belinda Amorous, the Queen of Romance. With a box of truffles and a Persian cat at her side, she looked like a spoiled hotel heiress. The marble fountain pen propped in her right hand was the only clue that she actually *did* anything. I hated that photo, which was plastered on the back covers of her novels. It was an image created by Heartstrings Publishers. Another lie. We didn't even own a cat.

Someone from Elliott Bay Books had stuck a sticky note below the photo: "Ms. Amorous will be represented by her daughter." I caught my reflection in the window. No one would recognize me as Belinda's daughter. The brown hair had come from the father I'd never known. The brown eyes and wide feet were probably his too.

Tom, the event coordinator at Elliott Bay Books and one-time boyfriend of my mother's, opened the door. "Hi." He ran a hand over his wiry beard. "We've got a full house."

"Great," I said through clenched teeth. Crud! Lots of people meant lots of questions, which meant lots of lies.

"How's your mom?" Tom asked. "Did she get a chance to sign those books?"

"Yeah. She came home for a few days but she's off again."

"Lucky lady to be out of the city. It's supposed to be blazin' hot all week."

I took off my sunglasses and followed Tom downstairs, through the coffee shop where customers sat at little wooden tables, and into a rustic basement room. Folding chairs had been set up in rows. Happily chatting women filled the chairs and a dozen more stood along the wall, forming a colorful mural of handbags, iced-coffee drinks, and lipstick. My heartbeat doubled. I'd been to tons of these events with my mother over the years, but never on my own.

I wiped my sweaty palms on my shorts and followed Tom to a table. The other two romance authors were already seated. I'd met them before but couldn't remember their names. Each wore a sundress and heels. I tugged at my tank top, making sure it covered the top of my low-rise shorts. Then I set the shopping bag under the table and sat in the empty chair. Folding my hands on the table, I tried to look confident but I'm sure everyone could see my heart pounding beneath the peach-colored cotton.

"How's your mother?" the nearest author whispered. Her name tag read "Nessa Van Nuys" and she'd gained at least a hundred pounds since her author photo.

"Fine. She's overseas."

"Oh. That's nice. You know, she was my inspiration to start writing."

The other writer smiled and fiddled with her string of pearls. "I always thought that photo of her was so beautiful. I wanted a life just like that." Her name tag read "Cookie Sparrow."

I chewed on my lower lip as Tom introduced us to the crowd. He explained that I was Belinda's daughter and would answer questions on her behalf. He did a sales pitch for our books, *The Greek Tycoon's Wild Bride*, *On Holiday with a Swarthy Scoundrel*, and *Hunger of the Heart*. When he opened the floor for questions, a white-haired woman with cat-eye glasses raised her hand. "Where's your mother?"

I cleared my throat. Was I supposed to stand? "Um, thanks for coming to Elliott Bay Books. This is my mother's and my favorite bookstore. Mom wanted to be here but she couldn't because she's overseas researching her next novel." My response sounded totally rehearsed.

"Where overseas?"

"Um, all over, really. She's seeing as much of it as she can."

"Oh." The woman smiled. "What an exciting life she lives."

I nodded. The woman's eyes glazed over as she sat, her brain clearly intoxicated by the myth of Belinda Amorous— the beautiful, glamorous, rich, adventurous romance writer.

The truth was, a nurse had probably helped my mother take a shower that morning. Then she'd been wheeled into the hospital's dining room where she'd picked at some scrambled eggs and stared out the window as if the grass had some sort of hypnotic power.

A pale woman in a sparkly pink blouse raised her hand. "I already read *Hunger of the Heart*. I've read all of Belinda's books. It's been three years. When will we see her next book?"

"Soon. She's working on it." My underarms felt sticky.

"Excuse me." It was a guy's voice, which was a bit of a surprise. One of the readers must have dragged her husband along. I hadn't noticed him because he sat in the back row, partially concealed by the big floppy sun hat that bobbed in front of him. He wore a black hoodie, its hood pulled over his head.

"Yes?" Tom pointed to him. "Do you have a question?"

The guy stood. "I have a question for Alice."

I tapped my flip-flops against the floor. Though his eyes were somewhat shaded by the rim of his hood, his gaze was intense. "Yes?" I asked.

"I have a love story to tell," he said. "And I need you to write it for me. When can you get started?"

A few women chuckled, then a long span of silence followed as the guy continued to stare at me. Was this a joke?

Tom cleared his throat. "You mean you want Alice's *mother* to write it? Alice is the Queen of Romance's daughter. Maybe you didn't hear my introduction."

"I know who Alice is," the guy said. "I want her to write my story."

The word "want" hung in the air, adding an eerie note to the atmosphere. I shifted in my seat. "Well, that's very nice and everything, but it's your story so you should write it yourself."

"I'm not a writer," he said. "But I lived the story, so I remember every single detail. All you have to do is read through my notes, then write it."

"I'm sorry," I said, realizing this wasn't a joke. "But I'm not a writer either. Good luck though." I forced a smile, then looked away.

Tom rescued me by calling on someone else, and the attention turned to the other two writers. The guy sat back in his chair, disappearing, once again, behind the sun hat. I slumped against my own chair, relief washing over me. I'd done what

I'd set out to do—protect my mother's secret. For a brief moment I felt proud of myself, but as Cookie Sparrow made a joke, and as laughter filled the bookstore, the familiar ache of loneliness pressed against my chest. It felt as if I'd been on my own forever, and in many ways I had.

Tom went upstairs to work the cash register. While the two authors signed books, I handed out the copies with the forged signatures. "This book doesn't have sex in it, does it?" a woman with a sunburned nose asked. "I don't like the ones with all that sex."

*Hello? It's a romance novel.* "Actually, there is some sex," I said, having long gotten over being embarrassed by my mother's sex scenes. *Her finger ran along his thigh. His tongue searched for hers. Her breasts heaved with passion.* Stuff like that.

The woman narrowed her eyes. "Hmmm." She drummed her fingers on the table. "Well, I suppose I could make an exception." She grabbed *Hunger of the Heart* and hurried from the room.

It was the last copy. I pushed back my chair, but as I stood to leave, something landed on the table. The other authors turned to look. The something was a big manila envelope. A strange odor filled the air—salty and muddy.

"My notes are inside," the guy from the audience said. He stood on the other side of the table. His hood still covered his head but I now had a clear view of his face. He was my age, maybe a bit older, with a square jaw and full lips. It was that James Bond kind of handsome. Greek God kind of handsome. Not cute. Cute did not apply to this guy. And he was unusually pale, which is saying a lot because I live in a very pale part of the world. But that's all I noticed because my gaze was pulled toward his dark eyes. My mother would describe them as "smoldering." Her leading men often had smoldering eyes. The word that came to my mind was "intense." He stared at me as if he knew me, or *wanted* to know me. Kind of creepy. I looked away.

Nessa and Cookie, forgetting they had books to sign, stared up at him.

"Read my notes and then we'll talk about the first chapter." He started to leave. Nessa Van Nuys grabbed my arm.

"I don't care how handsome he is, don't let him leave his notes," she whispered. "You don't want to get stuck with them. Believe me."

"Hey, wait," I called. The guy turned back. "You can't leave this with me." I pushed the envelope to the edge of the table.

He narrowed his eyes. "Why not?"

"Because I can't write your story. I'm not a writer. I'm just here to answer questions."

"You're here because your destiny is to write my story." He spoke quietly but with absolute confidence. "And we're on a tight schedule so the sooner you read my notes, the better." Then he walked out of the basement room. Just like that. Like he had given me an order and expected me to follow it.

"Hey!" I called.

"Those good-looking ones are always the most demanding," Nessa Van Nuys said, shaking her head.

"If I had a dollar for every crappy story I've been asked to read, I could wallpaper my house with them," Cookie Sparrow said.

"Hey!" I called again. I grabbed the envelope and ran out of the room, through the coffee shop, and up the stairs to the bookstore's main floor. A line of women stood at the cash register, their arms filled with copies of *The Greek Tycoon's Wild Bride*, *On Holiday with a Swarthy Scoundrel*, and *Hunger of the Heart*. I searched for the black hoodie, even ran out onto the scorching sidewalk, but no luck.

"I had a reader try to give me a puppy once," Cookie said when I'd gone back downstairs to get my purse. "It didn't smell half as bad as that thing. What's inside?"

She was right. The strange odor came from the manila envelope. Nervous about what it might contain, I dumped its contents onto the table. A bunch of papers fell out—lined notebook paper, plain white paper, note cards, stationery, even a paper napkin. Each piece was covered with handwriting. I picked up a note card and read a few lines that described a woman's long hair and the way it glowed when the sun shone through it. And how it was the same color as the honey she drizzled on her bread. I stopped reading because a dark feeling crept over me, like maybe the line would be followed by, "And then I chopped her into a million pieces," or something equally disturbing.

"What a mess," Nessa Van Nuys said, poking a finger through the paper pile. "Well, this explains the smell." She'd found a flattened can of Craig's Clam Juice. "Yuck."

I turned the envelope over. "There's no name or return address. What should I do?"

"Whatever you do, don't throw the notes away," Cookie said. "They're handwritten. They're originals. You'll get sued if you throw them away."

I glared at the pile. Great. Just great. The last thing my life needed was a lawsuit. But surely the can of clam juice could go, so I tossed it into a wastebasket. Then I slipped the notes back into the envelope, opened the shopping bag, and dumped the envelope inside. The scent of clams lingered in the air.

"Don't worry too much about that strange boy," Cookie Sparrow said. "Your mother will know what to do with his notes. I'm sure you can rely on her."

If only.

I slid my arms through my backpack purse straps and walked back upstairs, the basement's coolness disappearing with each step. A girl was taking down the window display, peeling the hearts and cupids off the glass. "Thanks for coming," Tom called as he plugged in an oscillating fan. "Be sure to say hi to your mom for me."

"Okay," I said, watching as one of the paper cupids slipped from the girl's fingers. Caught in the fan's breeze, it lifted into the air, flew over the sales counter, and, for a brief moment, hovered in front of me like it was checking me out. Then, as the front door opened, it flew out of sight.

SWEAT tickled the back of my neck as I walked up First Avenue. Except for getting stuck with the stinky envelope, things had gone well at Elliott Bay Books. No one seemed to suspect the truth. Everyone got a signed book and a promise that the next one was on the way. "Keep the readers happy," my mother always said. "Without the readers, where would we be?"

Reader or not, that guy in the hoodie had sure been weird. I should have been more forceful, should have shoved the envelope back into his hands—shouldn't have been so nice. My mother is always nice, which is one of the reasons why the Queen of Romance lives in an old four-unit apartment building and not on a country estate as her readers imagine. *You'd like to invest in a seaweed farm in Vermont? Certainly. You're raising money for orphaned bison? How much do you need?* If you caught my mother during one of her spells, you could convince her that anything was a good idea.

The sun beat upon my feet as I waited for the crosswalk light to turn. The shopping bag's handle pressed against my fingers. A group of tourists on the Seattle Underground Tour passed by. A cluster of homeless men sat on blankets, mangy dogs at their sides. I needed to stop by the post office before going home. And I hadn't done any grocery shopping in a week. The light changed. With a sudden craving for an iced mocha, I eyed the nearest espresso stand and headed straight for it. A UPS deliveryman almost tripped me as he charged down the sidewalk. Pushing a handcart stacked with brown boxes, he wove between a couple of chatting old ladies. Then, as he darted around a corner, a small box fell off his cart.

The little box lay in the middle of the sidewalk. No one grabbed it, no one even looked at it. I could have ignored it, could have bought my mocha and continued on my way. But little boxes can contain wonderful surprises and someone was probably waiting for it. The deliveryman had disappeared, so I picked up the box. Turning it over, I read the label and found, halfway up the block, its destination—Lee's Antiquities.

I hate antique stores. The mere sight of one nauseates me. It's a Pavlovian kind of thing. Why this reaction? Because whenever my mother said, "Come on, we're going antiquing," I knew she was heading into one of her spells.

That's what bipolar disorder is all about, these spells of super hyperactivity or disruptive depression. Often, just before she got all wound up and took on a speed-of-light intensity, she'd get this urge to collect. So she'd drag me to dusty, creepy antique stores to rummage for things to add to her assorted collections. I'd crawl beneath a sagging dining table and read from a crate of moldy *Life* magazines while she searched for the latest item she desperately "needed." Then I'd follow her home, carrying a box of china cups or a bag of costume jewelry or one of those stupid garden gnomes, knowing that over the next few days she'd be lost to me, her mind caught like a writhing fish in a net.

And then, one night, she forgot me, left me behind in the antique store as she rushed off to find the final blue teacup that would make her collection complete. Too ashamed to tell the clerk, I stayed hidden under the dining table until the shop closed. Once the owner left, I used the shop's phone and called Mrs. Bobot. After climbing out the back window, I waited in the dark for Mrs. Bobot's headlights to appear like rescue beacons.

That wasn't the only time my mother forgot about me. I try not to dwell on this fact but certain images cling to my memories, like long waits on the school steps, a locked door with no key left behind, an empty apartment with no note. A night all alone, not knowing where she was.

How's a kid supposed to sort that out? Days of cuddling and cupcake making, of laughter and bedtime stories, then days of suffocating silence and absence. My mother had lived most of her life undiagnosed, so, until a few years ago, we didn't have a name for what was wrong with her. Because there'd been no disease to blame when I was little, I came up with my own answer—I'd done something wrong. I hadn't made the bed correctly. I hadn't said the right things. I hadn't been pretty enough or smart enough or nice enough. It was my fault that I'd been left at the antique store.

Late that same night, after my mother had returned to the apartment, I crept to the doorway and watched as Mrs. Bobot gave her a scolding. "If the police had found Alice in that antique store, at such a late hour, they might have called Child Protective Services. For God's sake, Belinda, Alice might have been taken away."

*Alice might have been taken away.*

From that moment on, I told no one when my mother disappeared. "Mom's in the bathtub, she can't come to the phone," I'd say. Or "My mom's got a migraine. Can I take a message?" I told no one when my mother couldn't manage to make dinner or couldn't get out of bed. I learned to go grocery shopping. Learned to do the laundry. Learned how to protect us both.

I learned how to hide the truth.

So there I stood outside Lee's Antiquities on that sweltering day in July, holding that little box and a shopping bag with a manila envelope that smelled like clam juice. From the sidewalk, Lee's didn't look like the antique stores of my childhood. The door was painted cherry red, with a golden pillar on each side. And the shop's picture window held a colorful array of objects—a suit of armor, a laughing Buddha, a medieval tapestry. The sun prickled my shoulders as I tried to decide what to do—leave the box on the front step and avoid the store altogether, or brave it.

And that's when I noticed it. Peering through the window, beyond the Buddha's stone head, a skateboard leaned against a counter.

A yellow skateboard with a red dragon.

**My** mother often uses the word "destiny" in her stories. Fate's invisible hand unites her hero and heroine, who've been searching for each other their entire lives. Like in *Hunger of the Heart*, the book I'd signed her name to earlier that day, Rachel Morgan is a beautiful and heartbroken chocolatier, and Tyler Daringwood is a handsome and arrogant nut factory owner. They meet because Rachel has run out of walnuts for her fudge and Tyler's delivery boy just happens to be sick, so Tyler has to deliver the walnuts himself. "They were destined to meet," my mother wrote on page three. And by the end of the story we know it's true, because Rachel and Tyler fit together like two pieces in a jigsaw puzzle. That's how it works in the romance genre.

Of course, that's the stuff of fiction. But there I stood, holding that little box, thinking maybe it had fallen off the cart on purpose. Maybe Fate had given the box a push because Skateboard Guy and I were supposed to meet.

Or maybe I'd read too many of my mother's books.

A feeling somewhere between nausea and thrill churned in my stomach. This was opportunity, no doubt about it. Would I seize the moment, walk into that shop, and meet the guy who was, in a clandestine way, already a part of my life? Or would I set the box in front of the door and go back to standing at my window every morning, daydreaming about my imaginary romance?

The cherry red door opened. Pushing his empty cart, the UPS man stepped outside. "Hey," he said, looking at the box in my hand. "You found it. Great." He held out his hand.

"Oh," I said, hesitating. Handing over the box was the safe option. Skateboard Guy would never know I existed and I'd go on living behind the window, imagining our story. But I wondered, what did his voice sound like? What was his real name? A simple "Hello" didn't mean we'd end up getting married. A simple "Hello" could be fun. I needed some fun. "I'm going into the store," I told the UPS man. "I'll deliver the box."

"Okay," he said, holding the door open. "I really appreciate it. I'm forty minutes behind schedule."

I took a deep breath and stepped out of anonymity.

There were no dark corners, ratty furniture, or piles of junk in Lee's Antiquities. A crystal chandelier cast a sparkling glow. Shiny glass cabinets held jade and soapstone figurines. Colorful masks adorned a wall and a squadron of wooden dragons hung from the ceiling. The usual antique shop smell of mildew and dust was replaced by the scent of cinnamon trailing from a lighted candle. A flute's melody floated above my head as if drifting in from a Peruvian mountaintop. I wandered through a forest of Roman statues, past an armless woman, a fig leaf–clad boy, and a thoughtful philosopher. Where's a toga when you need one?

Then I saw him. He sat behind a counter reading a newspaper. Mesmerized by the page, he hadn't noticed me. His plain white shirt glowed against his tan skin. His straight black hair hung over the rims of a pair of black hipster glasses. Okay, so he wasn't a lifeguard or a vampire, but he was real. Clutching the shopping bag and the little box, I stood next to the philosopher statue and stared. No pane of glass separated us. I'd become used to that pane of glass and I kind of missed it. Suddenly the situation felt too possible. He'd been a distraction, a fantasy. Did I really want to move beyond that to reality?

Skateboard Guy furrowed his brow and sniffed the air. He sniffed again. I cringed. *Clams*, I realized. *He's smelling Craig's freakin' Clam Juice*! I turned to leave but that's when he looked up. "Oh. Hi. May I help you?"

I set the shopping bag on the floor, straightened my tank top, then walked up to the counter. "I just bought some fish at the public market, so I left my bag over there, in case you're wondering about the smell."

"Did you go to the stand where they throw the fish?"

"Yeah."

"I watched them yesterday. How do they catch those things? They're slippery, you know?" Chandelier light twinkled in the lenses of his glasses. We were having a conversation, just like that. It wasn't so difficult. My stomach settled a bit.

He scratched the side of his neck. "What kind of fish did you get?"

"I don't know." I shrugged. "I don't really like fish."

His gaze swept over my body. Not in a rude way, but he was definitely checking me out. "You don't like fish but you went to the fish market?"

The tips of my ears started to burn. "I have a cat. She likes fish." Lying had become so habitual that I lied even when I didn't need to. And now my ears were turning red and that manila envelope was stinking up the nice antique shop.

*Why did I come in here? Oh, right.* I held out the little box. "I found this outside. It fell off a UPS cart."

"Oh. Thanks. That was nice of you to bring it in."

"Well, I wasn't really doing anything." That sounded pathetic. "I mean, I have things to do. I've got to go to the post office. And then I have other errands. You know, stuff. But I'm not doing anything right now."

He smiled. "You're talking to me *right now.*"

Yes, I was. And it was nice talking to him, far away from the apartment, far away from my life.

Skateboard Guy held out his hand. Newspaper ink had stained his fingertips. I gave him the box. When he opened it, Styrofoam peanuts stuck to his sleeve. "Good. It didn't break," he said, pulling out a porcelain figurine of a chubby toddler holding a bow and arrow. He set the figurine on the counter, then brushed the peanuts away. "It's the god of love."

"The god of love?"

"You know. Cupid." The guy leaned closer. Two freckles

dotted his right cheek. I hadn't noticed them from my window perch. "It's a replica. The original sculpture's in the British Museum. We get lots of figurine collectors in here. Do you collect anything?"

The last thing I wanted to do was collect. If the urge to collect ever reared its ugly head, I'd throw myself in front of the nearest train. Okay, my reaction wouldn't be that drastic but I'd definitely panic. You see, my mother's collecting hadn't been limited to blue china cups or costume jewelry or garden gnomes. She'd filled most of the kitchen drawers with old Baggies, rubber bands, and Tupperware "found" at potlucks. She'd filled pickle and mayo jars with pennies, candle nubs, and old lipstick tubes. "Jeez, Mom," I'd complained. "It's like we're living in the Depression or something."

So I'd come to live by the rule of three. Three of something was acceptable. More than three was a collection. Collecting was risky behavior. Collecting meant I was turning into my mother.

"I don't collect anything," I said.

He nodded. Then he narrowed his brown eyes. "You look kind of familiar. Have we met before?"

Familiar? I cringed. Oh God. Had he seen me watching him? Had he seen me standing in the window in my pajamas, chowing on a Pop-Tart? What about yesterday, when I'd been eating right out of the box of Cap'n Crunch? Had he seen me then? I imagined the worst, that he'd made up a story about me in his head. He called me Creepy Window Girl. My heartbeat doubled. "I don't think we've met."

"Yeah, you're right." He slid his glasses up his nose. "We just moved here. I'd remember if we'd met."

I tapped my flip-flops. He stared at me. I stared at him. The melody of the Peruvian flute skipped up my back and made me shiver.

"So," we said at the same time.

"Ladies first," he said.

"So, you just moved here?"

"Yeah. From Los Angeles. My dad owns this shop. He took a part-time job lecturing at the university. He teaches mythology. How 'bout you? You live around here?"

"Yeah."

"What's the high school like? I think I'll be going to Roosevelt."

Another lie rose in my throat and curdled on my tongue. "Roosevelt's okay. Normal, I guess. That's where I go." I didn't know anything about Roosevelt High. Since sixth grade, I'd attended Welmer Girls Academy, a prestigious boarding school in British Columbia, Canada, a three-hour drive from home. My life had been plaid skirts, choir practice, newspaper committee, and monthly dances with the Welmer Boys Academy. Being away at school had made things easier for both me and my mother. But everything was different now. Now I took classes online.

"I'll be a senior in the fall," he said.

"I'll be a junior."

A customer entered the antiquities shop. I didn't know what else to say. If I wasn't going to buy something, there was no other reason to hang around. "Well, I'd better get going."

"Yeah. You should probably get that fish into a refrigerator."

"Right."

"Hey." He slid off his stool. "I was wondering..." He glanced at the customer who was picking through some Japanese fans. Then he took a long breath, as if readying himself for a flu shot, and stepped around the counter. "I don't really know anyone around here. You want to go to a movie? Tonight?"

I froze. *Yes*, I wanted to say. *Definitely*. We'd sit side by side, sharing popcorn. Maybe he'd whisper in my ear. Maybe he'd put his arm around my shoulder. A walk home flashed before my eyes, another date, and then the inevitable questions. "Why can't I see your apartment?" "Where is your mother?" "Why haven't you been showing up at school?"

"I'm sorry. I'd like to but . . . it's complicated."

"Okay." He nodded, then returned to his stool. He didn't look at me. His cheeks turned a bit red.

That was it. With a single sentence I'd broken the spell. The serenading flute lost its charm. The fantasy was over. This had been my chance and I'd panicked and turned him down. The flute whined above my head as I grabbed the shopping bag and hurried toward the door. The cute guy with the freckles seemed miles away as I stepped back into the real world.

How do you make clam juice anyway? Do you dump the clams into a barrel and stomp on them with bare feet? Do you stick a spigot into their necks and drain out the juice? Or do you squeeze the life out of the little bivalves one at a time? And why would anyone drink a can of the stuff?

And how do you go on a date when you're scared to let anyone into your life? How do you smile and keep up the small talk and pretend that everything's okay? If you start a relationship pretending to be someone you're not, when can you stop pretending?

I wondered about all these things as I climbed the apartment's front steps and found Reverend William Ruttles blocking the doorway with his six-foot-six-inch frame. A canvas bag sat at his feet. "Hello, Alice," he said in his resounding preacher's voice. "How are you?"

"Fine." I unclenched my aching fingers. I'd stopped at the post office box on the way home so the shopping bag was heavy with bills and junk mail.

The reverend leaned on his cane, his knees weakened by his bulk. He lowered his voice, for secrecy thrives in hushed tones. "Are you going to visit your mother tomorrow?"

"Yes. Are you coming with us?"

"I'm afraid I'll have to miss this visit. I have a doctor's appointment." Reverend Ruttles was a member of my mother's inner circle so he knew the truth. Well, some of the truth. He lived in the first-floor apartment across from ours. The four-unit building had been one of my mother's many purchases in the days when she'd churned out books. But after a bunch of bad financial decisions, she'd been forced to sell the lake house. We'd moved into the apartment when I was five. The reverend and Mrs. Bobot had come with the place—built-in tenants who'd turned into trusted friends.

"Any word?" Reverend Ruttles asked. "Is she feeling better?"

"She's the same." I wanted to change the subject as much as I wanted to get out of the heat. "Where are you going?"

"I'm off to meet with the social committee. You're looking at the newly elected chairperson." Though retired from the pulpit, the reverend still volunteered at his Episcopal church. "We've got important matters to discuss, like coffee filters and diabetic cookies. There was a big hullabaloo last week about the price of doilies."

I carried his canvas bag down the front steps as he began his slow descent. "She will get better, Alice. You must have faith. Your mother is strong and nothing can keep her from you."

With all my heart I wanted to believe that.

At the bottom step, he took the canvas bag. "Thank you, my dear." He tapped the sidewalk with his cane and said, "Praise the Lord, what a glorious day." Then he hobbled off to the bus stop.

I hesitated before opening my apartment door, knowing the familiar ache that waited for me. Loneliness had moved into my apartment as if it had no better place to go. It rubbed up against me like a hungry cat when I stepped inside. Once the *click* of the door faded, silence filled the rooms. So much was missing—the smell of my mother's perfume, the sound of her tapping fingers as she wrote, the simple questions like, "How was your day?" Or "Do I look fat in this?" During my Welmer Girls Academy years I'd become used to the short separations between holidays and long weekends, but I'd never faced an entire summer on my own.

I kicked off the flip-flops, dropped my purse, then sorted through the mail. Catalogs, junk, a few bills, and a single fan letter. Why read it? It would be just like the others.

*When can I buy your next book?*

*When will your next book be out?*

*I'm so looking forward to your next book.*

Truth was, the letters used to come by the dozens. Now only a few arrived each week as hungry romance readers drifted to other authors. Romance readers are a unique group. They consume books by the armful and are fiercely loyal to their favorite authors. But even the most loyal reader can't be loyal if there's nothing to read. If my mother didn't write another book soon, a new writer would replace her on the bestseller list and Belinda Amorous would probably go out of print and her stories would drift into oblivion.

I pulled the manila envelope from the shopping bag and tossed it onto the kitchen table. One letter remained, from Heartstrings Publishers, my mother's publisher. Nothing good came from Heartstrings these days. They'd sent a series of letters and e-mails asking my mother when she'd finish her next manuscript. Because my mother wasn't around to answer, I'd pretended to be her and had replied, "I'm working on it." But she wasn't working on it.

Belinda Amorous was an inpatient at Harmony Hospital, an exclusive mental health facility.

When I was thirteen, after she'd emerged from a long depression, she sat me down at the kitchen table. "I went to the lawyer and had my will changed," she told me. "Mrs. Bobot is listed as your legal guardian if anything happens to me."

"Like what?" I asked.

"In case I ever get so sick that I can't take care of you. Do you understand?"

I didn't want to understand. "But that will never happen," I said.

But it did happen. Just over four months ago, I came home for a weekend visit and found her sitting in the corner of the bathroom, staring at the wall. She wouldn't move, not even to use the toilet. She sat there all day. Her doctor said she was in a sort of stupor and that she needed to go to Harmony Hospital, where her identity would be protected. "She can't go in an ambulance," Mrs. Bobot insisted. "It will cause too much of a scene." So Mrs. Bobot agreed to drive her. Just before they left, my mother managed to say a few words to me.

"No one can know. Don't tell anyone. Promise."

"I promise."

"She'll only be gone a few days," Mrs. Bobot assured me. "They'll give her some medicine and then she'll be fine."

A few days turned into weeks. I left Welmer Academy and finished my sophomore year online. She was still there.

No one at Heartstrings Publishers knew. Not my mother's editor, not her publicist, not anyone involved in the production of her books. At first I didn't answer the phone, but the message machine quickly filled. At first I just stacked the mail on the counter, but when I got a call from the power company that the bill hadn't been paid, I realized I couldn't avoid the entire world. I became my mother's voice and signature when the need arose. "Everything's fine," I'd say. "Mom's busy," or "on vacation," or "overseas." I kept up the facade as best I could.

And so I knew that the letter from Heartstrings Publishers would be another request for a finished manuscript. I wanted to toss it, unopened, into the recycle bin. I'd have to keep stalling, keep telling them that progress was being made. I opened the envelope.

Dear Ms. Amorous,

I am your new editor here at Heartstrings Publishers. Your previous editor, my aunt, has retired from the company.

Despite our numerous attempts to speak with you,
and despite our numerous extensions on your deadline,
you have still not turned in the manuscript for your
next novel.

We appreciate your long and successful
relationship with our company and we were looking
forward to another book. But we understand that
sometimes authors aren't able to fulfill their
obligations.

I've passed your contract to our attorney, who will
be in touch with you about collecting the $100,000
advance money that was paid to you. All future royalty
payments will be withheld until the $100,000 debt is
settled.

Of course, we would like to remedy this situation. I
am willing to grant you one final deadline. If I receive
the manuscript by the last day in August, then we will
happily pay you the rest of your advance and royalty
payments will resume.

Sincerely,
Prudence Heartstrings,
Editor in Chief

One hundred thousand dollars? I read the letter a dozen
times. I frantically searched through the stacks of papers
that surrounded my mother's desk until I found a copy of the
contract for an untitled work in progress. One hundred

thousand dollars had been paid upon signing the contract, another one hundred thousand would be paid when the book was written.

I searched the computer files for a work in progress. I searched the filing cabinet, the desk drawers, every inch of the apartment. During the last few years my mother hadn't been writing because she'd been taking a "much-needed" break. After all, Belinda Amorous had written thirty novels. She deserved a vacation. That's what she told me. But I didn't know she was *supposed* to be writing.

No manuscript. No story outline. Nothing.

Here's the problem. We didn't have one hundred thousand dollars to return to the publisher. Nor could we afford to have my mother's royalty checks withheld. That's what we lived on. Harmony Hospital cost a small fortune and my mother had no mental health insurance. Unless a magical beanstalk grew outside our window, I wouldn't be able to pay the hospital bills, and Mom would get shipped to a state mental hospital. The kind of place, I imagined, that you see in those old movies, where patients wear thin cotton nightgowns and bang their heads against the walls.

I flicked open my phone and pressed the first number in the contact list. "Hello, this is Alice Amorous. May I please speak to Dr. Diesel?" Generic music drifted through the speaker, wordless but rhythmic, something you'd hear on a movie sound track during a suspenseful moment. The music fit perfectly as I clutched the phone, my heart pounding with expectation. One minute. Two. "Dr. Diesel?"

"Hello, Alice. What can I do for you?" His voice always sounded hesitant, as if holding back bad news.

"Is she any better?"

Long pause. "No."

"What about the new medication?"

"We started it this morning. Any improvements should appear in a week or two."

"A week or two?" I slumped over the desk.

"This drug has shown remarkable potential in Swedish studies. I'm very hopeful about this one. Try to be hopeful, Alice."

"I'm trying." Tears filled my lower lids, turning the room into a watercolored haze. "I'm trying."

"Good. We'll see you tomorrow?"

"Yes." I closed the phone. Then I crumpled the letter, and threw myself onto the couch.

Honestly, a sumo wrestler could have sat on my chest at that very moment and it wouldn't have felt any worse than the suffocating panic that pressed me to that couch. Things weren't supposed to work this way. I was supposed to be swimming in Lake Washington with my old friends and making plans for my junior year at Welmer Academy. I'd be school newspaper editor by now. I'd have a solo in choir and maybe even a boyfriend. *Why me*? repeated over and over in my head. I even whispered it. "Why me?" But hearing those words drift from my mouth made me feel even worse. Because the things I missed, the aches I felt, were nothing compared to my mother's nightmare.

If Mom had been diagnosed with cancer, or if she'd suffered a stroke, or even had a plastic surgery disaster, there'd be no shame. There'd be no hiding. People would race to help. The publisher would understand. But no one writes get well cards for mental illness.

*Sorry to hear about the schizophrenia. Hope those voices go away soon.*

*Sorry to hear you've got multiple personality disorder. Hope all of you start feeling better.*

*Sorry to hear about your catatonic depression. Try to keep your sunny side up.*

I rolled onto my side and stared at the bookcase that lined our living room wall—filled with my mom's books. I'd read them all. As much as I'd been brought up on chocolate milk and peanut butter sandwiches, I'd been brought up on those love stories. There were times, too many times, when the only way I could feel close to my mother was to read one of her books, knowing she could always be found within the pages.

The air conditioner hummed its steady rhythm. Cars passed by the living room window. Out on the curb someone hollered for a taxi. I closed my eyes.

*Try to be hopeful, Alice.*

My thoughts drifted to the antiquities shop, to the scent of cinnamon and the sound of the flute. I imagined the cover of a romance novel—a painting of me and Skateboard Guy. Our hair blowing in the wind, our shoulders bare, our faces clenched as we looked hungrily at one another.

And then, as my eyelids grew heavy, I thought of the little paper cupid, set free, drifting out into the world on his own. Where did you go, little guy?

Can I go with you?

"ALICE!" a voice called, followed by pounding.

"Okay, okay." I bumped my knee on the coffee table as I rolled off the couch. That kind of annoying pounding could only come from one person. After stumbling down the hall, I opened the door.

"I've been knocking for like ten minutes," Realm said. "What's your problem? You're late for dinner."

Was it dinnertime already? I leaned against the door's frame. "I don't have a problem. I was asleep."

"Asleep? What's the matter with you? Are you sick?"

"Nothing's the matter with me." So what if I'd slept away another afternoon? It was better than sitting around worrying about everything.

Realm narrowed her blue eyes. "Are you depressed?"

"No," I said. But I questioned my response the second it burst from my mouth. Depressed people sleep in the middle of the day and I'd been doing that a lot lately. Like manic collecting, excessive sleeping was a really bad sign. A sign that the dark beast had chosen its next victim. A sign that my mother's mental illness was waiting to be passed down like wedding china. Nothing scared me more than that. Nothing.

"By the way, just so you know, your apartment stinks like clams."

"I bought some fish," I said. Then added, with a jab, *"Lily."*

"Don't call me that." Realm turned on her bare feet and marched away. Pasty skin peeked through a rip in the back of her black leggings. Had those legs ever been exposed to the sun? She'd sheared her blond hair since her visit last summer, which, when combined with her bony frame, gave off a chemotherapy vibe. "Better hurry up. Grandma's waiting." Though one year younger than me, Realm always acted as if she had seniority in our summer-only relationship. "Unless you're too depressed to eat."

"I'm *not* depressed."

Mrs. Bobot's apartment was on the top floor, right above ours. *Homespun Magazine* could have photographed all their issues in Mrs. Bobot's place. There wasn't a craft project she hadn't tried. She'd embroidered pillows and crocheted blankets, she'd jeweled light fixtures and soldered stained glass lamps. Her homemade lace doilies had held some sort of lovefest because they covered everything, including the toilet seat.

On that night, the scent of sautéed onions filled the apartment, along with pipe tobacco. Though Mr. Bobot had been dead for a very long time, from lung cancer, Mrs. Bobot still burned his pipe to keep the place alive with his fragrance. I really liked the woodsy scent.

Mrs. Bobot stood at her stove, her long gray braid swaying as she stirred a simmering pot. Her air conditioner droned in the corner. "Hello, dear," she said. "How did the event go? Did you get a good turnout? You probably did, your mother's so popular."

While Mrs. Bobot had long watched over me, she now did so like a mother lion. She bought vitamins and made sure there was always fresh fruit on the counter. She trimmed my hair, took me to the movies, and even sat me down for a very detailed, very honest, very embarrassing sex talk. My real grandparents were long gone, victims of a chartered airplane crash. There were some second cousins, somewhere, but since my biological father had disappeared off the face of the earth, I had no other family. Mrs. Bobot became the grandmother upstairs.

"While you were gone, I managed to wash all my floors and I made two dozen raisin cookies for William. He loves my cookies. And I found a renter for the fourth unit. She owns a beauty parlor and has offered to give us free makeovers. Won't that be fun? And now your mom will have more rent money coming in. Isn't that good news?"

I smiled. In light of the latest letter from Heartstrings Publishers that was good news. But additional rent money still wouldn't be enough to cover the hospital bills.

"Taste this and tell me what you think." She held out a wooden spoon.

"Taste this" was an alarming request when it came from Mrs. Bobot. She thought of her meals as craft projects unto themselves, where color was more important than flavor, texture more important than digestibility. She'd been known to melt milk chocolate in her chili, put celery seed in her waffles, and concoct one-pot meals from whatever needed to be used up in the refrigerator. Mr. Bobot had always enjoyed his wife's cooking, but only because smoking had killed all his taste buds.

"What is it?" I asked, taking a step back.

"It's a sort of stew."

Realm leaned against the windowsill. "Something's burning," she said.

"Not again!" Heat blew across the kitchen as Mrs. Bobot opened the stove. Then, donning a pair of oven mitts, she lifted out a tray of singed rolls. "I'll just scrape off the burned bits."

Realm and I sat on opposite sides of the Formica table. Mrs. Bobot shook salt and pepper into the stew pot, then turned away and sneezed. "Oh, too much pepper," she said with a little laugh. She filled our bowls with the mysterious stew, then sat down. I recognized most of the vegetables and it turned out it wasn't half-bad. Realm picked at her meal, then went into the other room to watch TV.

"I'm worried about her," Mrs. Bobot whispered. "She barely eats anything. Don't you think she looks too skinny?"

"Well," I said, "she's definitely lost weight." Which was true. In the days when Realm had been called Lily, she'd been chubby. Okay, she'd been fat. Real fat.

Mrs. Bobot dabbed her mouth with an embroidered nap-kin. "How are you feeling, Alice? I know you're missing your mother terribly."

I swallowed and looked away. That loving tone could coax tears from a rock. My tears, however, didn't need any coaxing lately. They waited eagerly, like convicts, for any opportunity to escape.

Mrs. Bobot put her hand over mine. "I know it's taking a long time, but she's got the best doctor there is. We just have to be patient. She'll come out of it. She always does. Before you know it she'll be sitting right here, eating dinner, talking about her next book."

The gentle squeeze, the kind smile, the hopeful words—gestures appreciated but it was getting harder and harder to gift wrap the truth.

Mrs. Bobot pushed back her chair. "After we do the dishes, we'll try my new deck of tarot cards. Maybe it will make us feel better."

I cleared the table and wiped down the counters while Mrs. Bobot loaded the dishwasher. Then we went out to the living room where Realm sat sideways in Mr. Bobot's La-Z-Boy, channel surfing. I sat on the couch behind a stenciled coffee table. "I should have opened the deck before you came," Mrs. Bobot said, peeling off the plastic wrapper. "It's important to give tarot cards time to breathe."

"Card reading is bull—"

"Lily!" Mrs. Bobot interrupted, narrowing her eyes. "I don't approve of such language."

"For the millionth time, the name is Realm." Realm punched the remote. "And tarot cards are a joke. Why don't you tell Alice's fortune from the bumps on her head, which is also total bull—"

"REALM!"

It was the rare occasion when I agreed with Realm. I didn't believe that tarot cards needed to breathe, or that they could predict a person's future. But it was something to do, something that didn't involve sitting in my apartment worrying about the book deadline.

Mrs. Bobot reached out and turned off the television. "Watching everything is exactly the same as watching nothing. Why don't you join us?"

"As if." Realm wrapped her skinny arms around her legs and curled between the chair's armrests like a cat.

Once she'd settled on the couch, Mrs. Bobot shuffled the cards. "Remember that the cards represent the hero's journey—the hero, in this case, being you." She smiled at me. "Are you ready?"

I nodded. Realm snorted.

"I assume you want to know if . . ." Mrs. Bobot lowered her voice. "If everything will turn out all right? With your mother?"

I nodded again.

"What's wrong with Alice's mother?" Realm asked.

"It's none of your concern," Mrs. Bobot said.

Realm sat up. "Where is she anyway?"

"Overseas," Mrs. Bobot and I answered. Then Mrs. Bobot

swept a hand through the air. "Now close your eyes and focus on the question you'd like the cards to answer."

I closed my eyes. Because I had no faith in this card-reading thing, I didn't focus on my mother's situation. Instead, I thought about Skateboard Guy. Tomorrow morning he'd skate past. Maybe I'd take a shower extra early and get dressed. Maybe I'd go out to the porch and pretend to be reading the newspaper. I could act like it was a surprise to run into him. But why would I do that? After all, I'd turned him down, told him things were *complicated*.

But I couldn't stop thinking about him.

"Okay, let's get started," Mrs. Bobot said.

I opened my eyes. Realm leaned over the La-Z-Boy's arm-rest. Mrs. Bobot had laid the cards in a line. She flipped over the first card. The card's illustration was a naked man hanging by his foot.

"Hmmm." Mrs. Bobot opened the instruction pamphlet that had come with the cards. "It's the hanged man," she explained. "The first card in the formation represents you, Alice, and the hanged man represents a person facing a crisis."

"Give me a break," Realm said. "Her mom's totally famous and rich. That doesn't sound like a crisis to me."

Mrs. Bobot tapped a finger on the coffee table. "Shall we continue?"

I stared at the next card lying facedown on the table, its message waiting to be revealed. Suddenly the reading felt creepy, like a ghost story around a campfire or a séance in an old house.

"What's the matter, dear? You've gone pale."

"I don't know."

"If you're uncertain, I could take a peek at the last card," Mrs. Bobot suggested. "To see how your journey will end. How about I do that? If it's good, and I'm sure it will be good, then we'll look at the other cards."

"Isn't that cheating?" Realm asked.

"Shhhh."

"Okay," I said.

Mrs. Bobot peeked at the tenth card. Then, after referring to the instruction pamphlet, she smiled. "The end of your journey is very good." She turned the card over. "It's Apollo, the Sun God." A young, bronzed man held a shield and wore a wreath on his head.

"How come all these guys are naked?" Realm asked.

"Because these are Classical illustrations, dear. The Greeks and Romans appreciated the human body." Then Mrs. Bobot read from the pamphlet. "Apollo, the Sun God, represents a rosy dawn, which is rebirth." She looked up. "While you start in crisis, you end in rebirth. That's very good. I don't think you could end a journey in a better way. Let's turn over the rest of the cards to see about the journey itself."

One by one, she turned the eight remaining cards faceup. Each was identically illustrated with a naked guy holding a bow and arrow. "Curiouser and curiouser," Mrs. Bobot said, referring to the pamphlet again. "There's only supposed to be one Cupid in the deck."

"Weird," I said, remembering the little floating cupid and the cupid figurine. "I've been seeing cupids all day."

Mrs. Bobot picked up one of the Cupid cards and examined it. "I wonder what all these cupids could mean?"

"I'm no expert," Realm said, turning the television back on. "But I'd say that Alice has some *love* coming her way."

## TUESDAY

THE sun woke me. Its rays pierced the curtains and my eyelids, announcing another hot day in the Emerald City.

I'd been sleeping on the living room couch lately because my bedroom had started to feel small. As I stretched my legs, a bus drove past, a car honked, a man shouted. Some might find the city's sounds annoying, but I'd gotten so used to them it would be weird to wake up to silence. That's another reason why I'd started sleeping in the living room. The sounds outside the window reminded me that I was part of something bigger—that there was more to the world than my messed-up speck of space.

It was Tuesday, which meant our weekly trip to Harmony Hospital. Mrs. Bobot liked to do housework in the morning so we usually left for the hospital around ten. The manila envelope from yesterday's visit to the bookstore still lay on the kitchen table. I pushed the envelope aside, then grabbed a bowl, spoon, quart of milk, and a box of Cap'n Crunch.

The *Sweet Sixteen* reality show was on TV. That day's sweet sixteen was a brat from Austin, Texas, who wanted her friends flown in a private plane to Paris, where they'd rent the Eiffel Tower for a night of partying. She seemed blissfully naive that a problem-plagued world existed beyond her speck of space. As I watched her try on party dresses and scream at her stylist, I stuffed my face with Cap'n Crunch.

During a commercial break, I turned the manila envelope upside down and dumped its contents onto the table, still hoping to find a name and return address. Fortunately, the clam scent was gone. I unfolded a piece of notepaper that was covered in bold handwriting. It described an old man who was the father of the girl with the long, honey-colored hair. He had a deeply lined face, one missing eye, and a missing front tooth. I skipped to the bottom of the page where the description continued. Apparently the old man didn't bathe very often and he spent most nights at his neighbor's house, drinking himself into a stupor. I searched through the other pieces of paper, all covered in the same handwriting.

No name or return address anywhere. How could I get the envelope back to the guy from the bookstore?

After I showered and dressed, the clock read 8:35. Should I wait around for Skateboard Guy? He wasn't a fantasy anymore. He was a real flesh-and-blood person who worked in his father's antiquities shop, and I'd made it perfectly clear that my life was complicated and that I couldn't go out with him. But still, I really wanted to see him. Some people get up and crave that first cup of coffee. I'd come to crave the moment when he'd glide past. Tuesdays were tricky, though, because I usually brought bagels to the hospital because my mother loved them. If I left now, there'd be time for me to walk the two blocks to Neighborhood Bagels and get back to see Skateboard Guy.

The morning air was already sweltering—another day of record heat. The scent of freshly toasted bagels floated past. Good luck to anyone in my neighborhood who was trying to diet, because that scent will put you into a kind of trance and pull you down the sidewalk like the Pied Piper.

Inside Neighborhood Bagels I ordered Mom's favorite, blueberry. Then I sat at the window counter and sipped an iced mocha. There was still plenty of time before I needed to get back to my window perch at home. Sweat dampened my lower back just from the short walk. It would be terrible to live in a place that's always hot. Maybe that's why the sweet sixteen girl from Austin, Texas, was such a raving freak. But who was I to judge? One girl throws temper tantrums, another girl forges signatures.

One of the rules when I visited my mother at Harmony Hospital was that I wasn't supposed to mention anything stressful. Dr. Diesel had set this no-stress rule, and it made sense. So I'd never told her that I was forging her signatures. I hadn't mentioned all the letters from Heartstrings, the letters asking when she'd finish her next book. I kept thinking that she'd get well.

But this latest letter was too much for me to deal with. Mom needed to know that the publisher was going to stop sending royalty checks. She had to know. She'd have to pull herself together and start writing again, because we didn't have one hundred thousand dollars to return. Maybe, just maybe, this little piece of news would wake her up and bring her back to reality.

Bring her back to me.

"Hello." The guy from yesterday's romance writers' event took a seat at the counter, leaving an empty stool between us. Was he wearing the same black hoodie? And who wears a hood in the middle of a heat wave? "Did you read my notes yet?" he asked.

Paranoia crept up the back of my neck. If this had been a chance encounter he would have said something like, "Hey, how great to run into you." Had he followed me? I remembered that serial killer who'd easily convinced girls to get into his car because he was Greek-god handsome. I chose my words carefully. "Your notes are very nice," I said. "But you need to find someone else to help you. I'm not a writer."

He raised his eyebrows and they disappeared behind the rim of his hood. It's hard to get a clear impression of someone who's wearing a hood, but his gaze was as intense and hypnotic as it had been at the bookstore. The bright sunlight streaming through the window highlighted the slight reddish tint in his eyes. And his hand, which fiddled with a newspaper that was lying on the counter, was ghostly white. I couldn't quite put my finger on it, but something was wrong with him.

I took a pen and notepad from my purse and set them on

the counter. "If you'll write down your address, I'll mail your notes back to you."

"I knew this wouldn't be easy," he mumbled. Then he turned away. Sliding his knees beneath the counter, he folded his hands and stared out the window.

I pushed the notepad closer. "I need to get somewhere, so if you'll—"

"Alice, I want you to listen very carefully to what I'm about to tell you. Don't ask questions until I've finished."

I scowled. He sounded like a parent talking to a child. Who did he think he was talking to me like that? I wanted nothing to do with this guy.

"My name is Errol, but I used to be called Eros. Most know me as Cupid." He continued to stare out the window. "I wasn't named after Cupid. I *am* Cupid. The original, one and only Cupid."

Music and customer chatter competed with his statement, so no one turned to gawk or snicker. But I'd heard him. A pained smile spread across my face as I pretended to be interested. My suspicions were proven. Something was wrong with him and the last thing I needed was to be on his radar.

"There's only one thing I want," he continued. "And that is to tell my love story to the world. Not the version you find in mythology books, but the real story. The true story. I'm the only person who can tell it and I want you to write it." He sat perfectly still, his gaze focused on the other side of the street. Or maybe he was staring at his reflection in the window.

"I'm not a writer," I said slowly, calmly, hoping he'd actually listen this time.

He shook his head. "You say you're not a writer. But I believe that it's your destiny to write my story. We'll each benefit from this arrangement."

Arrangement? A prickly feeling covered my arms.

Then it suddenly made sense—he'd gone to a romance writers' event not because he'd been dragged there by his girlfriend or because he was a fan of the genre, he'd gone there because of the Cupid thing. If anyone could relate to Cupid it would be a romance writer, right?

There were plenty of people in Neighborhood Bagels so I wasn't worried that Errol might try to hurt me. But how could I get away without pissing him off?

One of the things you learn when you live with someone whose moods are unstable is the art of being agreeable. And that is why I smiled sweetly and nodded, as if I believed everything he was telling me. As if Cupid himself, in a black hoodie and jeans, sat next to me in a bagel shop.

He turned toward me and folded his arms. "You don't believe me. You think I'm insane."

"I don't think you're insane." I tucked the notepad and pen into my purse. Apparently, he wasn't going to give me a mailing address. "I'm sorry but I need to get going."

"You think I look nothing like Cupid."

"No. I don't think that." I swung my purse onto my back.

"I suppose you're just like everyone else in this century. You think Cupid is a child. A fat, pasty white cherub with wings."

That's exactly how I imagined Cupid, but I didn't tell him that. "Um, Errol, why don't I go and get your notes? I'll bring them here." Problem solved. I'd bring the notes to the bagel shop and then they wouldn't be my responsibility anymore. I could even give him the name of some local writing organizations. Maybe he'd find a writer willing to help. Wait, that wouldn't be a good idea. I'd simply be making his craziness someone else's problem. He narrowed his eyes as I slid off my stool. "You stay here. I'll be right back. Ten minutes."

Grabbing my iced mocha and the bag of blueberry bagels, I raced home, checking over my shoulder to make sure he wasn't following. Just my luck that the one guy who'd noticed me that summer had turned out to be delusional. What would it be like to date a guy who thought he was Cupid? Cupid was a god, right? So I'd be dating a guy who thought he was a god.

Maybe that's not so unusual.

Once I was safely in my kitchen I thought about ditching Errol, but that would only be a temporary fix. He'd find me, I sensed it. So, leaving my stuff on the table, I grabbed the manila envelope and hurried down our building's front steps. That's when my phone's alarm buzzed. Nine thirty. I spun around. Skateboard Guy came straight at me, a blur of white T-shirt and black hair. "Hey," he said, jumping off his board. "You're the girl who found our figurine."

Standing on the sidewalk, the sun beating on my face, I squinted at him. "Hi."

He stepped on the tail, tipping the skateboard upright.

The red dragon looked ready to leap off and fly away. "You live here?"

"Yeah." I turned off my alarm and shoved the phone into my pocket. My heart pounded. I took a few quick breaths as I tried to figure out what to say. Coming face-to-face with a fantasy boyfriend is freaky enough the first time. "Where do you live?"

"Up the hill," he said. Then he smiled and swept his hair from his face. One stubborn strand remained, hanging over his left eye. I imagined reaching up and pushing the strand aside, then sliding my fingers through the rest of his shiny hair. "So are you going somewhere?"

I held out the manila folder. "I have to deliver this."

"Where?"

"Neighborhood Bagels." I pointed down the block.

"I know the place. I go there all the time." He leaned against the front stoop's railing. "You know, I kinda owe you a favor. That figurine you saved was expensive. I could deliver the envelope for you. I'm going right past the place. Then you don't have to walk there in this heat."

I fiddled with the envelope. Maybe it would be best if I avoided any more contact with Errol. But I'd told him I'd be back. "That's okay. I need to deliver it in person."

"You mind if I walk with you?"

"No." A huge smile broke across my face and the worst kind of giggle, the kind that makes you sound like a little girl, shot out of my mouth. I managed to cover it with a cough.

He picked up his skateboard and we walked to the end of

the block without saying anything. I became aware of every inch of my body. Did I have underwear lines? Had I missed any hair when I'd shaved the back of my legs? Would he notice that my toenail polish was chipped? Did my breath smell like coffee?

"Is that your job? Delivering things?"

"No," I said. "I don't have a job."

"Oh. I'm saving up for college," he said as we started across the intersection.

"Where do you want to go to college?"

"I'm hoping for Stanford," he said. "My parents went there. But there are lots of good premed programs to choose from. What about you?"

This was it, one of those important questions that defines a person. Should I tell the truth, which was that I had no idea. Or should I make something up and try to impress him? "I'm thinking about premed too."

He smiled. Impression made.

"What took you so long?" Errol asked. He was waiting outside Neighborhood Bagels, his hood draped over his head, hands in his jeans pockets. Dazed by Skateboard Guy's smile, I'd almost bumped into Errol.

*Please*, I thought, *don't make a scene.* "Here it is." I held out the envelope.

Errol's upper lip curled as his gaze darted to Skateboard Guy, who stood next to me, leaning on his board. "You're giving it back?"

"Yes."

"You're not going to help me?"

"Errol, I told you, I'm not a writer."

"I had hoped you'd be . . . cooperative, Alice." After another searing glance at Skateboard Guy, Errol took the envelope from my hand. "I should have known better. I'll have to find another way."

A bead of sweat rolled down the back of my neck as I watched him cross the street. I thought about wishing him good luck, but that might mean starting up the conversation again.

"He was glaring at me," Skateboard Guy said. "Are you two—?"

"No!" I dismissed the notion with a snap of my hand. "I don't even know him."

Pedestrians stepped around us as we stood in the middle of the sidewalk. Skateboard Guy slid his glasses up his nose. "Well, I'd better get to work." He dropped the front of his skateboard. The wheels landed on the sidewalk. "So that's your name? Alice?"

I nodded.

"Well, see you later, Alice." With a push of his foot, he jumped onto the board and started down the block. "Oh, just so you know," he called. "I think your pink pajamas are really cute. And I like Cap'n Crunch too."

What? My mind raced to the other morning, my hand shoved into a box of cereal, my face pressed against the window.

Kill me now.

A fiery blush rose from the base of my neck to the tips of my ears. Fortunately, Skateboard Guy didn't look back. He swerved around a woman and her poodle, then darted around the corner.

And while I stood there, trying to figure out how long he'd known that I'd been watching him from my window, I realized that I'd forgotten to ask his name.

THE drive to Harmony Hospital takes less than an hour north on Interstate 5, then a short ferryboat ride to Whidbey Island, one of the many islands that dot Puget Sound. At first we visited my mother two or three times a week. But the ferry ride was expensive and the visits were totally draining. So somewhere along the way we settled into a Tuesday visit.

"I'm taking Alice to see a school friend," Mrs. Bobot told Realm. "So you'll be on your own this afternoon."

"Fine by me," Realm said, then asked for twenty dollars. "Don't expect me to eat that weird leftover stew."

"You know," Mrs. Bobot said, giving Realm a fierce hug, "I love you whether or not you eat my weird stew."

My plan that day was to tell my mother about the letter from Heartstrings Publishers, so I tucked it into my little backpack.

During the drive, Mrs. Bobot talked nonstop. I knew she wasn't simply passing time. She was filling the car with cheerful words, spinning a verbal cushion that would protect both of us as we made our way toward the sadness that was my mother. Despite her effort, anxiety bubbled in my stomach. Regular hospitals are bad enough. But mental hospitals, even those that try to disguise what they really are with pleasant names and fancy rooms, scared me more. After my mother got the diagnosis, bipolar disorder, I read as much as I could about it. That's when I discovered the term "genetic predisposition," which means that because my mother had the disease, I had a greater chance of getting it. Lucky me. I remembered that quaint term each time I stepped inside Harmony Hospital, each time I encountered a sedated and expressionless patient.

Doctors might understand the engineering that drives the heart and makes kidneys and livers work, but no one really gets how the mind works. The brain's as mysterious as a cosmic landscape.

"Tourists," Mrs. Bobot complained as the driver in front held up the ferry line by asking the ticket taker a bunch of questions. "Wasn't that odd to have all those Cupids show up in the cards? If I didn't know the deck was bad, I'd agree with Realm and say that you've got a lot of love coming your way." She fiddled with a fabric sunflower that she'd ironed to the front of her yellow shirt. "Just out of curiosity, have you met any nice boys lately?"

"No. Not really." I rolled down the window. The car's old air conditioner was close to exhaling its last breath and the black interior was heating up. "I think it's hotter today than yesterday." I plucked a rubber band from my shorts' pocket and pulled my hair into a ponytail. Had I met any nice boys? I cringed, once again reliving that moment on the sidewalk when Skateboard Guy had admitted to seeing me in the window. I tried to picture what I'd looked like from a sidewalk view. Day after day, pressed against the glass in my pajamas, that stupid goofy grin on my face. "What about you?" I asked. "Have *you* met any nice guys lately?"

Mrs. Bobot inched the car forward. "I know a very nice guy but he's not interested."

"You mean the reverend?" I asked.

"What?" She frowned. "Is it that obvious?"

It was so obvious, the way she was always baking for him, the way she smiled whenever she said his name. The only person unaware of Mrs. Bobot's feelings was the reverend himself. "What are you going to do? I mean, do you think you'll ever tell him how you feel?"

"Oh no, of course not." She fiddled with her sunflower again. "And don't you say anything." Then she pointed out the window. "Oh look. There's another cupid." A logo on the side of a van read: CUPID FLORISTS.

Another cupid. What was up with that? My mother once told me that whenever she started a new story, elements of that story popped up everywhere. A book about a cowboy meant cowboy boots and country music waited around every corner. A story about an apple pie contest meant that suddenly everybody was eating apple pie. Ever since my encounter with that little floating paper cupid, I'd been seeing cupids everywhere. When our senses are on the alert for something specific, we find it. But what didn't occur to me as I waited for the ferry was that sometimes it works in reverse.

Sometimes things find us, drawn by forces we can't see or comprehend.

During the ferry crossing I stayed in the car while Mrs. Bobot went upstairs to use the ladies' room. A lone seagull flew alongside the ferry, its breast feathers gently rippling as it matched the boat's speed. The gull turned its head and caught my eye. For a moment I felt its weightlessness and imagined being lifted into the sky—the sensation of pure freedom. Then the seagull soared out of view, rising above the world. Rising to a place where no secrets were needed.

The ferry landed. "Why don't they fill these potholes?" Mrs. Bobot complained as her car rattled up the hospital's long, winding driveway. The hospital had once been a private lodge, built by a lumber baron in 1930. He'd made his fortune cutting the massive cedars of the Pacific Northwest. In an ironic twist of fate, his wife was killed during a windstorm, flattened by a falling tree. Her death haunted the lumber baron and he came to believe that the trees had sought revenge and that they would kill the rest of his family if he didn't make things right. So he started replanting the forest. Every day he'd carry a bag of seedlings into the woods. Every night he'd return home fearing that he hadn't done enough. The fear consumed him. One night he didn't return to the lodge and his butler found him sleeping in a cave, a bag of seedlings clutched in his hand. He refused to go home because there was so much planting to do, and he ran off, never to be seen again. Some think a bear got him, others say he fell over a cliff. A few think the trees ate him.

When his estate ran out of money, a corporation bought the lodge and turned it into a luxurious mental health facility—a place where movie stars and moguls went to recover from nervous breakdowns. A place where the rich could seek treatment in private.

My mother wrote a novel called *She Loved a Lumberjack*. It was one of her biggest hits. She could even make a sweaty guy with an ax and wood shavings in his beard seem sexy.

Once inside, Mrs. Bobot waited on a bench while I paced. The lumber baron's portrait loomed on the far wall. A stocky man with wavy red hair and a red beard, his wild eyes followed visitors around the lobby. I'd looked into those eyes many times, wondering about his death. If I were his biographer, I'd choose the ending where the trees ate him. It was much more poetic. It was also the most rational explanation, because if he'd died in the woods, then he'd decomposed there as well. His body had fed the forest.

"Hello?" A young woman holding a file folder approached. "Are you Belinda Amorous's daughter?"

"Yes."

"We haven't met yet. I'm Mary, from patient accounts. Would you step into my office for a moment?" I followed her. We stood just inside her open doorway. "It says in the records that you're the contact person for your mother's account."

"Yes."

Mary opened the file and pulled out a piece of paper. "An automatic payment system was set up through your mother's bank, but last week's payment was not met and when I tried again this morning, the bank said there were insufficient funds."

The moment had come sooner than I'd expected. I took the bill from Mary's hand. The list of expenses seemed endless—all sorts of stuff I'd never seen before like massage therapy, hydrotherapy, and a pedicure. Mrs. Bobot hurried in. "What's going on?" she asked.

The room was stuffy and small. Mrs. Bobot pressed against me. Mary's perfume clotted the air. "We don't have enough money for the bill," I said.

"What?" Mrs. Bobot gripped her straw purse. "Are you sure?"

I stood straight and tall and looked into Mary's eyes. "My mother gets a royalty check in October. We'll be able to pay the bill then." *But only if Mom turns in a book,* I thought.

Mrs. Bobot nodded. "Yes, they can pay in October." I hadn't told her about the letter from Heartstrings Publishers. Why bother her with more of my troubles? She'd done so much already.

"October?" Mary removed a pencil from behind her ear and fiddled with it. "They have a very strict policy here about late payments. I'm sorry. I don't make the rules."

"You'll have the new rental income for the fourth unit," Mrs. Bobot said, clutching my arm. "Will that cover things?" Then she gasped as she looked at the bill. "Oh dear. The extra rent won't be near enough. And I'm afraid I don't have that kind of money either."

There was a long moment of silence as we stared at the amount due. "I'm a big fan," Mary said. "I've read most of your mother's books. I love her stories. I wish I could help you."

"Really?" Mrs. Bobot said. "Then why don't you put this bill in a drawer and ignore it? Just until October."

"I can't do that." Mary's neck reddened. "I'm sorry. I'd lose my job. I have to send out a ten-day notice. And there's something else you should know." She closed the file and set it onto her desk. "Your mother will be transferred out of the hospital if the bill isn't paid."

"Transferred?" I said. "To where?"

"That's up to you. If you can't afford private care there are a number of public hospitals."

Mrs. Bobot put her arm around my shoulder. "Don't you worry. Your mother won't need this place in ten days. She'll be better and she'll be home." Then she glared at Mary. "I intend to speak to your supervisor. We'll see about this."

Dr. Diesel met us in the lobby. He tucked a pen into the pocket of his white medical coat, which was tight across his middle-aged belly. "Hello, Alice. Hello, Mrs. Bobot." He motioned us into a private corner, then spoke softly. "I'm sure you'd like an update. The good news is that Belinda has not experienced any uncomfortable side effects from the new medication. I'm still very hopeful that we'll start to see some improvement in a week or so." He didn't finish with, "The bad news is . . ." He didn't need to.

"Dr. Diesel? Can you talk to somebody about my mother's account? Tell them that we can pay the bill in October. Tell them that they can't transfer her out of here just because of money."

"Money?" Dr. Diesel frowned. "I'm sorry, Alice. Certainly I can try, but the governing board is very strict, believe me. But I'll talk to them. I wouldn't want to see your mother transferred—especially in the middle of this new treatment." He tilted his head toward the hall. "She's in the library."

Mrs. Bobot stepped back. "Go ahead. I'll wait out here." She always let me go in first.

"Remember not to talk about anything stressful," Dr. Diesel said. "Stress would work against us at this point. We need to keep her calm. Try to be as upbeat as possible. Try to be hopeful. That's what she needs."

I started across the lobby. My backpack, with the letter tucked inside, felt as heavy as a bag of bricks. During the first couple of visits, I'd run across that floor, eager to fling my arms around my mother. But now dread slowed my steps. Because now, when I closed my eyes at night, I saw the woman she'd become, the woman who stared at me with empty eyes. I didn't want that image to replace the others. I wanted to think of her as she used to be.

All the clichés work when describing the way Belinda Amorous used to be. She was drop-dead gorgeous—a blond bombshell. She lit up a room and stopped traffic. She was comfy jeans and strappy sandals, strawberry ice cream, and freshly squeezed lemonade with a paper umbrella. She was the cat's meow.

People used to think of my mother as "eccentric," but in a way that was admired and accepted. She belonged to lots of social clubs. She planted dahlias with the Seattle Gardening Club, led the funding drive for the Seattle Art Museum's Impressionist wing, and marched in parades with the Daughters of the American Revolution. On Friday and Saturday nights she got dressed up and went to parties and auctions with men whose names I never knew. "Friday and Saturday nights are for grown-ups," she'd tell me. "But the rest of the week belongs to my little princess."

The rest of the week did belong to me, but only when I was very little. Mom would write in the mornings while I was at preschool, then we'd go on afternoon adventures. Trips to the aquarium, rides at the Seattle Center, dress-up parties in the backyard. And every night I fell asleep between the satin sheets of her bed. And so it was, in those early years.

Then the clouds came. The eccentric and enthusiastic public persona of Belinda Amorous remained the same, but at home she began to fight with her moods. During the upswings, one dozen cupcakes weren't enough, there had to be twelve dozen. Her costume jewelry collection wouldn't be complete without a red brooch, which had to be found that very night. All of the toiletries had to be reorganized alphabetically. Then she'd stay up all night writing, pumping out novel after novel to her publisher's delight.

Then came the downswings. Closed doors and silence. When I turned eight, Mom said I couldn't sleep with her anymore. She started taking sleeping pills, the only thing that brought relief. I'd wait for her to fall asleep, then I'd sneak into her room and sleep on the floor at the foot of the bed. She didn't seem to notice my despair. She'd journeyed into her own, mysterious world.

And that's when her colors disappeared. I've never told anyone this, but when I was very little I could sometimes see a cloud of colors swirling around my mother's head. I used to think it was magic. The colors sparkled like fairy dust and coated everything that Mom passed or touched. I'm older now, so I know it had nothing to do with magic. It was just some sort of hallucination, a misfiring of a neuron—or maybe a sign that I had a "genetic predisposition" to craziness.

I stood in the doorway to the hospital's library. A lone figure in a terry cloth periwinkle bathrobe and matching slippers slept in the corner armchair, her blond hair fanning over her shoulders. Her hands folded in her lap, her head slumped, her breathing steady and peaceful.

*Remember not to talk about anything stressful. Stress would work against us at this point.*

I walked ghostlike into the library, then gently slid a fallen slipper back onto my mother's foot. The only hope I had was that the new medication would start to work. I would do whatever the doctor wanted. I would protect my mother from the truth, and keep her calm so that she could get better.

The letter from Heartstrings Publishers would stay in the backpack. The overdue bill from Harmony Hospital wouldn't be mentioned. I'd have to deal with these problems on my own.

I took the bag of blueberry bagels from my backpack and set it beside a reading lamp. Then I sat on the floor at her feet and looked up at her oval face. I wanted to tell her about Skateboard Guy, wanted to tell her how cute he was and how he'd asked me to go to the movies. Wanted to ask her if I was pretty enough for him and hear her say that I was beautiful, inside and out.

A lifetime ago I would have been comforted by the sparkles that danced around my mother's head. But now all that surrounded us were bookshelves crammed with books that neither of us wanted to read.

What is more terrifying—the things we imagine or the things that are real?

"**How'd** it go?" Reverend Ruttles asked when we got home late that afternoon. He stood in the foyer, leaning on his cane.

As I searched for my key, Mrs. Bobot and the reverend spoke in hushed tones. "The doctor thinks the new medicine might work, but it needs time," Mrs. Bobot said. "But we got some terrible news." She told him about the conversation in the patient accounts office.

"Alice?" Reverend Ruttles took out his wallet. "Let me give you some money. I don't have enough to cover your mother's hospital bill, but you'll never go without. Not with us around."

"That's right," Mrs. Bobot said.

"I'm okay. Really. There's plenty for food and bills. There's just not enough for the hospital."

"Can you believe the cost of health care?" Mrs. Bobot folded her arms. "It's an outrage."

"Why don't we go to the bank tomorrow and help Alice apply for a loan?" the reverend suggested. That sounded like a great idea, and for a moment everyone's mood lightened.

"No, that's not going to work," Mrs. Bobot said, shattering the mood. "Alice is a minor. And Belinda can't sign for the loan."

"I could sign for her," I said, as innocently as possible. As if the idea of forging my mother's signature was brand new.

Revered Ruttles shook his head. "That wouldn't be right. That would be breaking the law."

"It wouldn't work anyway," Mrs. Bobot said. "They require a notary public for a loan. Your mother would have to be there in person."

Reverend Ruttles and Mrs. Bobot exchanged a fretful look. Then Mrs. Bobot took both of my hands. "Why don't you spend the night with me, like you used to? We'll pull out the sofa. There's always a nice breeze in my living room."

"Thanks," I said. "But I'd rather sleep in my own bed." I might have spent the night at Mrs. Bobot's if Realm hadn't been around. Her moodiness was the last thing I wanted to deal with.

"It's not healthy for you to spend so much time alone. We should do something fun," Mrs. Bobot suggested. "How about we go to the lake for a swim? It'll be good to get away from all this hot cement. We'll pack a picnic. Spend the day."

The lake did sound nice. Something to do that was summery. After Mrs. Bobot and the reverend ran through a list of doctor's appointments and church committee meetings, they agreed on Saturday. "Don't you worry, Alice," Mrs. Bobot said. "We will never allow your mother to go to a public hospital. It simply will not happen. She's sure to get better, I just know it." Then we all hugged and said good night.

The apartment's walls pressed in on me the minute I stepped inside. I hurried to the living room window and flung it open.

One of the reasons my mother bought the old four-unit building was because it looked out onto Cal Anderson Park. From the living room window I could see the park's focal point, a conical fountain made from stacked stones. My mother used to sit next to that fountain. Running water has a way of soothing the mind.

Twilight had settled and the park's lampposts glowed like liquid amber. Dog walkers strolled the gravel trails. A man with a guitar sat on a bench, strumming. A couple walked past, hand in hand, whispering secrets. Too often that summer I'd stood at that window, watching the evenings pass by. The lies that protected my mother had locked me up in solitary confinement. *What am I doing?* I thought. *Sitting around every night, hanging out with old people. I should have gone to the movies with him. Just one night. Just one movie.*

As I leaned against the sill, Dr. Diesel's words echoed in my head. *Be hopeful, Alice.* He was right. I needed to stick all my problems into Mrs. Bobot's stew pot and add a great big helping of hope. Because who really knows? Tomorrow could bring good news from Harmony Hospital that Mom was better. Or good news from New York that Heartstrings Publishers had burned down, along with the copies of all its contracts.

Tomorrow could bring anything.

But if tomorrow failed me and brought the same old stuff, then I'd have to figure out a way to make the hospital and the publisher happy.

*Be hopeful, Alice.*

## WEDNESDAY

I made my morning call to Harmony Hospital. Nothing had changed, except that the nurse forwarded me to the patient billing department and I got an "official" verbal notice from some guy that we had ten days to pay the bill. I told him about the October royalty check, but he didn't care. He repeated the official notice and told me that Harmony Hospital was not a charity organization. I squeezed the phone, trying to channel all my anger into that cellular signal so it would overload on the other end and the man's head would explode.

Cereal and a reality show followed. Today's sweet sixteen was throwing a fit because her father wouldn't buy her an elephant, which she wanted to ride to her party. He tried to convince her that they had no place to keep the elephant, but she had her head wedged so far up her butt, she didn't hear him. I was beginning to suspect that the show was rigged. These people couldn't actually exist, could they?

As I dumped my bowl into the sink, Realm pounded on the door. "Alice!"

When I opened the door, she shoved a thick stack of paper at me. "When your mom gets back from wherever she is, overseas or someplace, give that to her. It's my novel. I finished it yesterday while you guys were gone."

"Your novel?"

She tugged on her long sleeves until they covered her hands. "It's not a *romance* novel but I don't know any writers other than your mom. So I'm hoping she'll help me get it published."

"Sorry," I said, trying to hand over the stack. "My mom's too busy to read anything."

Realm folded her arms and glared. She wasn't going to budge.

"Look," I said, "people ask my mom to read things all the time. She almost always turns them down, unless somebody she knows recommends it."

"Then you read it and recommend it to her," Realm said.

"What?" The stack was enormous. "I'm not going to read this."

"Yeah, I think you will." Realm smirked. "Because that's the kind of person you are. You're *nice*. So read it, then tell your mom it's the best thing in the world so she'll send it to her publisher."

I'm *nice*. Nice people get stuck with manila envelopes full of scribblings and stacks of paper to read. *Not nice* people get elephants for their birthdays. "Fine. I'll read it," I lied.

Sure, I could have read it. My social calendar was totally empty. But the shallow truth was, I didn't want to help Realm get her book published. We'd never gotten along, not even in the old days when she'd still called herself Lily. She'd come to visit her grandmother and we'd all go out for ice cream and then swim at the Edmonds pool. Her visits always made me feel bad about myself because of the things she said.

"You think you're special just because your mom's a famous writer."

"You think you're better than me because you go to a private boarding school."

"You think you're prettier just because I'm fat."

I'd never thought those things, but Lily always said I did. Then she transformed herself into Realm, cutting her hair, losing the weight, covering up every inch of skin, and refusing to go out for ice cream or to the pool. And her comments got nastier. A bigger, darker cloud settled around her. I had enough dark clouds in my life.

My phone buzzed its 9:30 a.m. alarm. No way was I going to stand at the living room window in my pajamas. That would be just like taping a sign to my chest that says, I'M TOTALLY IN LOVE WITH YOU. But he wouldn't be looking for me in the foyer window. I could sneak a quick glance.

"My story's called *Death Cat*," Realm said as I turned off the alarm. "It's about this cat whose owners force her to be in one of those stupid cat shows. You know, where they wear costumes and sleep in decorated cages. Totally humiliating." She pulled on her sleeves again. "Anyway, after the cat show, the cat kills her owners. Then she decides to kill all the people who organized the cat show. It's a horror story."

Holding the stack of papers against my chest, I crossed

the foyer and peeked out the window. A sun-drenched sky saturated Cal Anderson Park so that all the colors seemed washed out. Where was he?

Realm stood right behind me. "Horror's not easy to write, you know. Not like romance. I mean, *anyone* can write romance. It's not brain surgery."

Under normal circumstances I might have snapped at Realm. I might have told her to get lost or I might have shoved her manuscript into her snotty face. Because common courtesy dictates that if you're asking a writer to help get your book published, you shouldn't insult that writer's genre. At the very least, you should proclaim your love for everything that writer has written.

But instead, I stood very still, sensing something on the horizon, the way a hound might stick his nose into the wind and sense an approaching fox. At that moment an idea was born and it flitted before my eyes like a moth outside a window. I turned and looked at Realm. "What did you say?"

"I said horror's hard to write."

"No, after that."

She narrowed her blue eyes. "I said anyone can write romance. It's a stupid formula. Every story's the same. Everyone knows that. Anyone can write it. Anyone."

"Anyone?" I repeated.

A gong sounded. *Gonggggg*, like a Buddhist monk was standing right behind Realm. "That's what I said. Anyone."

"Anyone?" I asked again.

The gong sounded again. *Gonggggg*, clear and bright.

"Crap, that's my mother." Realm reached into her pocket and pulled out her phone. Then she argued with her mother about something, as her skinny legs carried her back up the stairs.

Forgetting about Skateboard Guy, I rushed into my apartment. *Death Cat* landed in the junk-mail box as I hurried to my mother's desk. I grabbed her publishing contract and read it again. The contract stated that the "untitled work in progress" was supposed to be an entirely originally work created by Belinda Amorous, but it didn't say, exactly, that Belinda couldn't have someone "help" with the process. Help with the typing, for example, or help with the proofreading. What if, during the typing and proofreading, an entire book should happen to get written? The contract didn't say anything about that.

Why couldn't I write *Untitled Work in Progress* for my mother?

Being the Queen of Romance's daughter made me the Princess of Romance. I may not have inherited her Nordic bone structure, her sexy figure, or her naturally plump lips, but surely I'd inherited *something*. And maybe that something was the knack for storytelling. I'd gotten Bs in English. I'd been raised on the romance genre. It was such an obvious answer. And what else was I doing with my summer?

Nothing!

I could devote every minute of every day to the project. It didn't have to be a Pulitzer Prize winner, just something that Heartstrings Publishers would accept. This could work. It would work. It had to work. The hairs on my arms stood up, electrified by possibility. Like a resolution maker on New Year's Day, nothing was going to stop me. A goal was set and all that was needed was total commitment. *Yes, I'll do it. I'll start right away!*

I scrambled out of my pajamas, showered, then threw on a pair of shorts and a purple tank top. Then I sat at the computer, my fingers posed on the keyboard, and I sent a letter to Ms. Heartstrings, letting her know that there was no need to contact her lawyers. There would be no need to pay back the one hundred thousand dollars and no need to withhold the royalty checks, because the book would arrive in her office by its August 31 deadline. Then I signed my mother's name.

And I pressed "send."

Immediate regret. My hands flew over my mouth. What had I done? What had I been thinking? I was going to write a romance novel? In my mother's name? I chewed a fingernail, then another. I paced around the room. A happy voice drifted from the kitchen television. The sweet sixteen, who'd ended up getting everything she wanted, told the viewers that her life was great. I turned off the television and sat back at my mother's desk. This was no time to freak out. I could do this.

So I opened a new document and stared at the blank screen.

And stared, and stared, and stared.

How do you start a story?

I scanned my mother's bookshelves. She had dictionaries, thesauruses, memoirs of writers, but she didn't own a single book on how to write. The romance genre had rules, and though I was fairly sure I knew those rules, a how-to book might keep me from wasting precious time. So, after a check-in call to Mrs. Bobot, I headed for the library.

Despite the smothering heat, pride put a little bounce in my steps. I was *doing* something. I was gripping the proverbial bull by the horns. The master of my own destiny. No "official notice" or contract deadline was going to bring me down. My sole job had been to take care of things so my mother could recover, and I wasn't going to fail her. Not even a heat wave could ruin my mood.

I already knew the basics of the romance genre. Rule number one: regardless of the social or political climate, the story is about a man and a woman. Perhaps that will change in the future, but right now, that's the way it is. Rule number two: there has to be a happily-ever-after. A romance novel does not end with a divorce, or a fatal disease, or the hero and heroine getting murdered by their deranged cat. Rule number three: love conquers all because love is the most powerful force in the universe.

Eighteen minutes after leaving my apartment, I crouched on the industrial carpet of the Capitol Hill library, scanning the lower shelf in the writing section. My finger stopped on a yellow spine. *Writing a Romance Novel for Dummies.* Who was the dummy—the writer or the reader? Unsure, I grabbed it. Then my finger stopped on *Anyone Can Write a Romance Novel.* Just as Realm had declared. I grabbed it.

A snarky reviewer once wrote in her review of my mother's novel *Lassoed by Love* that romance novels are the cheese puffs of literature—fluffy, artificially colored, and deep-fried for the masses. "What would we do without cheese puffs?" my mother had said after reading the review. "Eat rice cakes and saltine crackers? I think not."

Next I found *The Rules of Romance* and, in a serendipitous sweep of a nearby table, I also found *Write a Romance Novel in One Month*. That meant I had an entire extra week. It could be done!

Bursting with empowerment, I carried the books to a window nook and settled onto the cushioned bench. Maybe Rome hadn't been built in a day, but imagine what the engineers might have achieved if they'd had a book called *Anyone Can Build Rome*, or *Building Rome for Dummies,* or *Build Rome in One Month*.

Each of the writing books began by congratulating me on pursuing my passion to become a published author. And each book overflowed with promises.

> *If you follow my directions, you will have a completed manuscript to submit to a publishing house by the end of the month.*

> If you follow my simple steps, you will write a romance novel that readers will adore.

> If you follow my advice, all your dreams will come true.

I eagerly flipped through the pages and here's what I learned. Books that tell you how to write are full of lists. Lots and lots of lists. According to these books, writing is an orderly process that can be mastered with easy, straightforward steps. I hoped this would be the case because it would sure make my life a lot easier.

"Hi, Alice."

My gaze darted up a plain white T-shirt and rested on a pair of black hipster glasses. I closed the writing book, then flipped it facedown. "Hi."

Skateboard Guy stood at the end of the window bench. "You look like you're doing some research."

"Sort of." I crossed my arms over the pile of books. "Not really, though. I'm just . . . hanging out."

He fiddled with his leather watchband. "Dad said I could come in a little late today so I thought I'd get something to read. I'm Tony, by the way." He held out his hand. "Tony Lee."

I held out my hand and his warm fingers pressed against mine. We shook. "I'm Alice Amorous."

"Amorous? That's a great name."

"Lee's nice too." We stopped shaking. I glanced at Tony's book—*The Metamorphosis* by Franz Kafka. "We had to read that last year," I said, slowly pushing my own books behind my back.

"My dad recommended it," Tony said, sitting at the edge of the window bench. Even though his glasses were kind of nerdy, nothing else about him was. His arms were tan and muscular, and he had high cheekbones and a big, confident smile. And those two freckles were adorable.

I nodded. He nodded. I chewed on my lower lip. He tapped

his fingers on his thigh. The silence might have been bearable if physical attraction hadn't been pulsating through me like a strobe light, magnifying every movement and breath. My mouth felt dry. I tried to think of something to say but what was the use? There was no time to get to know Tony, not with *Untitled Work in Progress* waiting to be written.

"Um, well, I have to go." As I collected my books, one fell to the floor. Tony picked it up and I braced myself for a snide comment.

"Write a romance novel in one month. Hey, you want to be a writer? I thought you were going premed?"

"I am. I'm going premed, definitely. These books are just for fun." Another book slipped from my arms.

"Here, let me help you." Before I could protest, he scooped up the rest of my books. "You're gonna check out all of these?"

"Yeah." If another neighborhood girl wanted romance-writing guidebooks, she'd just have to wait. I, however, couldn't wait and needed all the guidance I could get.

As we walked to the checkout counter, I felt kind of idiotic having a guy carry my books. But the attention, even if only for a few moments, was nice. Was Tony the kind of guy who held a door open and gave up his seat on the bus? The kind of guy that my mother and Mrs. Bobot always said was as extinct as a dodo? As he laid the books on the counter, pine and cedar drifted past—the scents of a guy's deodorant. I reached past him to grab a free bookmark, inhaling his spiciness. He smelled so good.

Smothering heat pounced on us as we stepped out of the

library's front door. "Can't believe this heat wave," Tony said, transferring the books to my arms, then grabbing his skateboard. "I thought it was supposed to rain all the time in Seattle."

"Not all the time," I said. "Just most of the time."

We walked down a ramp and stopped at the sidewalk. He took Kafka off the top of the stack and tucked it under his arm. "So, I'm just wondering . . ." He tapped his fingers on his board. "Are you sure you don't want to go to a movie or something? I mean, maybe you have a boyfriend. If you do, then just tell me and I'll stop asking."

I pictured myself sitting in front of the air conditioner all afternoon outlining a novel. Then writing that novel into the evening. And tomorrow and the next day and the next. All alone. I was about to tell him that I didn't have a boyfriend. I was about to tell him that I'd really love to go out. Anywhere. A movie, a coffeehouse, a corner bench at the park. This was what I'd been dreaming about! But as I pressed my lips together to form the first word, a creepy feeling tickled my neck. Someone was watching me.

Errol.

He stood across the street, looking right at me. Foreboding rolled over me, dark and sinister. If ever there was a time to run, it was then. But I didn't run. I couldn't. Like in a nightmare I stood rooted to the spot.

"Alice?" Tony touched my arm.

Errol's hood concealed most of his face, but his mouth was tight with determination. He held his left arm straight out.

Then he pulled his right hand to his chest. Something was going to happen. Something bad. I felt as helpless as a small creature caught in headlights.

And then, *BAM*!

Something collided with my chest. A jolt shot through my body, electrifying the tips of my fingers and toes.

THE next thing I knew, I was lying on the sidewalk staring up into the faces of strangers.

"Is she hurt? Did she faint?"

"Maybe it's the heat."

"Can she talk?"

Tony's worried face came into view, blocking the others. He squeezed my tingling hand. "Alice? Are you okay?"

I wasn't sure. Cement pressed against my spine. My legs were splayed like a discarded rag doll. "What happened?" I murmured.

"You fell backward," Tony said, helping me sit up. "I think you fainted. I couldn't catch you, it happened so fast. Good thing you had those books. They protected your head."

Sure enough, after flying out of my hands, the books had landed on the sidewalk a moment before my head. *Anyone Can Write a Romance Novel* had kept my skull from cracking open—a service its author hadn't included in her introduction.

"I fainted?" That didn't seem right. I'd never fainted before, though I'd come close during a frog dissection in seventh-grade biology. A splash of cold water on my face in the girls' bathroom had calmed the wooziness. But this wasn't a biology class. And it wasn't a Regency romance novel where girls faint all the time—except in those stories the girls always manage to land in a handsome man's arms, not spread-eagled on a sidewalk.

"Should I call an ambulance?" a lady asked.

"I'm fine," I said. "I don't need an ambulance." I felt the back of my head. No bump or sore spot. No blood.

"Are you sure?" Tony asked.

"I'm fine." *God, how embarrassing.*

"She's okay," Tony told the onlookers as he helped me to my feet. Dizziness swept over me, blacking out the world for a moment. As my vision cleared, Tony led me to a bus bench. I peeled a discarded coffee lid off my bottom, then sat. The crowd wandered away while Tony collected my library books.

"Where are my shoes?" I asked.

One of the flip-flops had flown down the sidewalk. Tony found the other behind a garbage can. "Weird. Look," he said, handing them over. The rubber soles were misshapen as if they'd melted, then solidified. It looked like I'd stepped into enormous wads of chewing gum. "The sidewalk must be really hot."

I stared at the deformed shoes. Nothing made sense. I'd fainted and my shoes had melted. And now my body tingled and my mind was fuzzy. Slipping my feet into the flip-flops, I tried to remember the moment just before falling. "I don't get it," I said. "Why would I faint?"

"Maybe you need to eat something. Maybe it's a blood-sugar thing."

"But I had breakfast." Then, like a windshield wiper brushing away mist, the fuzziness cleared. "Errol," I said, jumping to my feet. "Errol was over there." I pointed across the street, but Errol was gone.

"Who's Errol?" Tony asked.

"That guy from the bagel shop." I scanned the street, then rushed to the end of the block and looked up and down the sidewalk. A woman walking a bulldog, a couple of kids carrying ice cream cones, but no black hoodie anywhere.

Tony followed me. "You mean that guy at Neighborhood Bagels? The one you gave the envelope to?"

"Yeah. That guy."

"I don't see him. Are you sure?"

"I saw him. And then something hit me." My fingers flew to the point of impact, just below my left breast. It felt tender, a sure sign that a big ugly bruise was forming. "I think he threw something at me." Why would he throw something at me? What kind of a person does that? Even if he was pissed because I'd refused to help him, that was no reason to hurt me.

Tony shoved his hands into his pockets. "I was standing next to you, Alice. I didn't see anything hit you."

"*Something* hit me."

We walked back to the scene of the crime and searched

the sidewalk for something, anything, that might have been thrown across the street. But we found nothing.

"I really think you fainted," Tony said. "People faint all the time. You probably got too hot. I'm from LA and even I think it's hot today. Let's go back inside and get you some water."

"I don't need water."

"Does your head hurt?" He ran his hand over the back of my head. "You could have a concussion." He looked into my left eye, then my right eye, like he was practicing for medical school. "I had a friend who got a concussion skateboarding."

I stepped away. "I don't have a concussion."

If I kept insisting that Errol had thrown something, Tony would think I was crazy. I just needed to get home and lie down for a bit. Maybe take a cool shower. A Tylenol would probably make the aching stop. I scooped up my books.

"I'll walk you home," he asked.

"No thanks. I'm fine."

He adjusted his glasses. "I think I should, just in case you faint again."

"I'm not going to faint," I said. "I feel fine." I didn't, though. Something tugged at me. Just minutes ago, Tony Lee had asked me to go to the movies and I had almost said yes. Now I wanted nothing to do with Tony Lee. I wanted something else—but what? "Bye!" Books in hand, I hurried down the sidewalk, my mangled flip-flops making sucking sounds the entire way.

The early-afternoon sun beat mercilessly upon Capitol Hill, suffocating the breezes that usually drifted off Puget Sound.

Tiny puddlelike mirages spread across the pavement. The air was stale and thick with car exhaust and human fatigue. Ice cream vendor carts had sprouted like weeds all over the urban landscape, but I didn't stop to buy anything. I cut across Cal Anderson Park where every shady spot had been claimed. Shirtless men exposed rolls of belly fat. Women forgot about hiding their varicose veins and cellulite. Shoes lay strewn around the central fountain as people soothed their swollen feet. Kids of all ages splashed in the long ornamental pools. I might have joined them but a hollow, aching feeling had settled in the pit of my stomach. Like an Alzheimer's patient who wants something but can't remember the word, I struggled to define the feeling. Intangible, yet insistent. What was it?

It was Need.

I needed. But what, exactly, did I need?

Realm sat on the front stoop, defying the heat wave in leggings and an oversized men's denim shirt. A journal lay on her lap and music squeaked out of her headphones. "What are you wearing?" she asked, curling her lip as she looked at me.

"What?"

"Those shoes. They're all wrong."

I started up the front steps. "Whatever."

She yanked off the headphones and pointed. "Who's that guy?"

Tony Lee stood across the street, at the edge of the park. He'd followed me. "Just wanted to make sure you got home," he called, then jumped on his board and skated away.

Of course I got home. I wasn't an idiot. And I didn't have a concussion.

Realm smiled wickedly. "What's up with your freaky hair? You look like you got struck by lightning."

"Huh?" My reflection floated in the front door's pane. My hair stuck out as if I'd rubbed a balloon all over it. I grabbed a clump. It felt freeze-dried.

*Lightning?* I held my breath as a new possibility took shape. Fainting didn't cause a person's hair to stick up all over or shoes to melt. Or fingers and toes to tingle. As I brushed a lock from my cheek, the hair made a crackling sound. "Lightning," I said.

Rushing into my apartment, I dumped the library books onto the carpet and flipped open my phone. Directory assistance connected me to the local television station, where I was forwarded to the weather department. "Have there been any reports of lightning today?" I asked.

"No," a man answered.

"Are you sure?"

"Just a minute." He put me on hold for a few seconds. "Yes, I'm sure. No lightning."

"But I think I was . . ." I'd sound crazy. "My friend thinks she was struck by lightning in front of the Capitol Hill library. About a half hour ago."

"I don't think so. There haven't been any thunderstorms in weeks. We're in the middle of a heat wave, or hadn't you noticed?" The weather guy's voice brimmed with testiness, as if the last thing he wanted to do was talk "weather."

I snapped the phone closed, then tossed it onto a chair. That's when Realm stomped into the living room, waving the copy of *Death Cat.* "Thanks a lot," she snarled. "I just found this in a box of junk mail by your door. You said you'd give it to your mom."

"She's not home," I said, cursing myself for not bolting the door. Why did my chest itch? I reached under my tank top and scratched. My fingers stopped on a small bump. What was that?

Realm picked an empty bag of Cheetos off the floor. "I didn't know you ate junk food. I guess you can eat anything you want while your mom's gone."

I hurried to the bathroom, lifted my tank top, and pressed close to the mirror. An angry red welt glared back, just under my left breast. I examined the tank top. A tiny slit marked the spot where something had pierced the fabric.

Here was the proof that something had hit me. Should I tell Mrs. Bobot? We'd end up at the doctor's office where she'd discover that I hadn't gone in for my yearly physical, like I'd promised. And that would lead to a bunch of questions and she'd find out that I hadn't been to the dentist either. And then she'd snoop around and find out that I hadn't been taking my daily vitamins and that I'd been eating way too much junk food. "Just as I suspected," she'd say. "You're too young to take care of yourself." And she'd move into my apartment so she could supervise 24/7 and it would only be a matter of days before she found out that I was writing my mother's next book. "You can't write your mother's next book! What are you thinking?"

"What's up with the blue teacup collection?" Realm

hollered from the living room as she snooped around. "Did your mom really write all these books?"

I pressed closer to the mirror. The welt was the size of a dime, tender, with a small puncture mark in the center. Some cortisone cream and a Band-Aid were probably all I needed. And that tingling in my hands and feet had faded, which had to be a good sign.

"Why do you want to write a romance novel in one month?"

I bolted from the bathroom. "You need to go," I said, pushing Realm toward the door. "I'm really busy."

"Whatever. It's not like I want to hang out with you. But just because you got struck by lightning, that's no excuse for being so rude." She shoved *Death Cat* into my face. "Just read this. Okay?"

"I said I would."

As soon as I'd slammed and locked the door, I threw *Death Cat* back into the junk-mail box. Then I stripped off my clothes and stood in the shower, cool water tumbling over my shoulders. I worked a leave-on conditioner through my hair. The label promised to "fight the frizzies." But though the texture of my hair returned to normal, the unsettled feeling in my stomach didn't go away. It shifted, moving up through my torso.

Need. I need.

Cleaned and conditioned, cortisoned and bandaged, I sat on the couch. The air conditioner droned its refrain. The new writing books sat at my feet like eager puppies. *Read us, read us, read us,* they squealed. But reading was the last thing I wanted to do.

I really need.

Our brick building sits in the middle of the block. The Spanish lavender on the upstairs balcony and the stained glass window above the entry add splashes of color, but mostly the building is unexceptional. You might stroll past and not even notice it, eyes drawn to the Tudor next door or the pink stucco number around the corner. But on that particular day, at that particular time, while the exterior was as ordinary as dry wheat toast, the interior was a different matter altogether. For something extraordinary was happening inside one of the first-floor apartments.

When Franz Kafka's hero woke up in *The Metamorphosis,* he'd grown a pair of antennae. His entire body, as it turned out, had transformed into an insect. As I sat on the couch in a tank top and shorts, though my long brown hair and short legs were the same, something was changing.

A yearning, the likes of which I'd never known, grew and grew until it churned like a busy swarm.

*Errol, Errol, Errol, Errol, Errol, Errol, Errol.*

I wanted, more than anything, to be near Errol. Yes, that demanding, handsome guy in the black hoodie who believed he was Cupid and who had thrown something at me. That guy.

When I reached out, I wanted to find him standing there. When I listened, I wanted to hear his voice. When I inhaled, I wanted to inhale his scent. I didn't ask myself why I felt that way, didn't wonder why my thoughts had moved from Tony—who was clearly obsession-worthy—to Errol, who was clearly . . . weird. Wait. The old me thought he was weird. The new me focused on the beauty of his name. A strong name. A hero's name. I grabbed a notebook and wrote his name. Then I wrote *Alice + Errol*, the way you do when you're a kid. I wrote it a second time, bigger and bolder. I wanted to write it everywhere, so I ran into the bathroom and grabbed a tube of pink lipstick and wrote across the mirror, *Alice + Errol*. Across the wall, *Alice + Errol*. Across the shower, *Alice + Errol*.

That's when a scratching noise skipped down the hallway. Had Errol come for a visit? I threw the lipstick tube into the sink, stumbled down the hallway, and opened the door.

"Meow."

"Oh, hi, Oscar." A massive orange tomcat wound between my shins.

"Hello, Alice." Reverend Ruttles stood in his own doorway, across the foyer. He wore a white button-up shirt, as always, but his reverend's collar was reserved for church duties. "We've got chow mein," he happily announced, for the reverend loved few things more than Chinese food. "It's Wednesday lunch. Remember?"

Since my mother's hospitalization, I'd been eating Wednesday lunch at the reverend's. "I'm not hungry," I said, scratching my bandaged welt.

"Not hungry? Nonsense. It's Wednesday. Wanda will skin me alive if I don't feed you a healthy lunch."

"Alice, get your booty over here and eat," a melodious voice called from the reverend's apartment. Oscar the cat pranced toward the voice. "I made wontons especially for you."

My stomach growled but I didn't care. What was Errol's last name? How would I find him if I didn't know his last name? If I went back to Neighborhood Bagels and waited, maybe he'd show up. Maybe he was a regular and someone at the counter knew where he lived.

"Alice?" The reverend had hobbled across the foyer. He took my arm. "You're mumbling to yourself. Clearly you are in need of food."

"I need to go to Neighborhood Bagels."

"Bagels? Nonsense. Why would anyone choose bagels over chow mein?" Though weak in the knees, the reverend's grip was still as strong as a young man's and before I could explain, I was standing next to a table set for Wednesday lunch.

A clean, cheerful place, the reverend's apartment, but that had not always been so. There was a time when I didn't want to go in there because it smelled disgusting. Those were the months when he'd almost given up on life. Fortunately, someone had come along and had set things right.

I was ten years old when Mrs. Ruttles had her fatal heart attack. My mother held my hand when we stepped into the sterilized hospital room, which was sickly sweet with the scent of get-well bouquets. The reverend sat beside the bed, his head bowed. A machine stood nearby, bleeping with each worn-out beat of Mrs. Ruttles's heart. I watched the screen bleep and flash, bleep and flash—life itself reduced to an annoying noise.

"Is there anyone you want me to say hello to in heaven?" Mrs. Ruttles asked when my mother coaxed me toward the bed. The dying woman's eyes, once bright green, had faded to a mossy gray. Mrs. Ruttles, her voice barely a whisper, repeated the question.

"Lulu," I whispered back.

The reverend raised his head. "Lulu?"

"The dog we had when Alice was very little," my mother explained.

"My dear, dogs do not go to heaven," Mrs. Ruttles said, closing her eyes. "Pick someone else." Then she gasped for air.

My stomach clenched. I ran from the room with its poisonous stench and torturous noise, where death waited in the corner, ready to pounce. My mother found me outside and we sat on a bench beneath a broad oak. "Of course dogs go to heaven," she said, holding my trembling hands. "Don't you let anyone tell you differently. In fact . . ." She smiled cherry red at me. "Dogs run heaven."

Following Mrs. Ruttles's death, it came as no surprise that the reverend did not take well to living alone. The church ladies did their best, but after a year had passed they eventually stopped bringing salmon loaves and Jell-O salads. Grief sickened the reverend and he retired from his church. Day after day he shuffled to the mailbox in the same sweatpants, the sour odor of unwashed feet trailing behind.

"Enough is enough," my mother said, and she placed an ad for a roommate. The ad went something like this:

> Older, male roommate wanted for older, retired reverend. Must be quiet, clean, and have conservative values. Good references necessary and domestic skills appreciated.

Archibald Wattles, never Archie, was not what anyone had in mind when they pictured the perfect roommate for the reverend. In hindsight, he shouldn't have been such a surprise. Once a neighborhood of affordable rents and retired couples, Capitol Hill had slowly become the gay center of

Seattle. When Archibald, a legal secretary, stepped into the foyer in his perfectly creased slacks, polished loafers, and blow-dried hair, my mother whispered to Mrs. Bobot, "This should be interesting."

The reverend was asleep on the couch in a stained undershirt and sweatpants. "Poor fellow," Archibald said in a soft voice. He asked about the rent while collecting strewn socks and underwear. He asked me about school while beginning a wash load. While he and my mother discussed the lack of available men, he loaded up the dishwasher. While he and Mrs. Bobot discussed the benefits of using one's imagination while cooking, he whipped up a pot of cream of potato and onion soup from the meager ingredients in the reverend's pantry. The scent of the soup woke the reverend, who stumbled to the kitchen table and ate like a stray dog.

"Is this your wife?" Archibald asked, holding up a small, framed photo.

"Yes," Reverend Ruttles replied, wiping away tears. "She took such good care of me. I'm lost without her."

"My partner, Ben, died last year," Archibald said, wiping tears from his own eyes. "I'm lost without him."

"Partner?"

"Yes. My boyfriend."

My mother, Mrs. Bobot, and I stood quietly in the corner, watching as Reverend Ruttles absorbed Archibald's words. My mother wrapped her arm around my shoulder as we waited for the reverend's reaction. The silence felt endless. Then, soupspoon in hand, the reverend said, "This is the most delicious soup I've ever tasted."

Archibald moved in the very next day, along with his cat, Oscar. Soon after, the sound of vacuuming and bursts of Lemon Pledge filled the morning air. On Sunday nights, the reverend's apartment once again smelled like pot roast. Within a few months he was back on his feet, attending church and his community meetings, and greeting everyone with his usual, "Praise the Lord, what a glorious day."

And so it was, on that Wednesday at lunchtime, that the reverend gently pushed me into a chair. "Wonton?" Archibald asked, holding out a platter.

My mind still raced with Errol. The faster I got through lunch, the faster I could get out there and find him. I heaped food onto my plate. "Thanks."

"Can you believe this heat wave?" Archibald asked.

"Mmmmph." My mouth was already full.

"Don't eat so fast," Reverend Ruttles said. "You'll get acid reflux."

I grabbed another wonton. "I've got something to do," I said between doughy bites. A jittery current ran through my body as if I'd had too much coffee. Is it normal to be annoyed by a guy one day and yearn for him the next? I could barely remember a time when I hadn't felt the yearning, which seemed as much a part of me as the blood flowing through my veins.

"What do you have to do?" Archibald asked, smoothing the tablecloth.

"Just stuff." I scratched my bandaged spot, then plunged my chopsticks into some chow mein. What did Errol look like under that hood? Was his hair long or short, straight or curly?

"We can help," Archibald said.

"You can?" A clump of noodles slid off my chopsticks. "Do you know Errol?"

"Who?" Archibald asked. He'd taken to wearing Hawaiian shirts during the heat wave. That day's shirt was covered with an orange bird-of-paradise print. "Did you say Errol?"

I chewed like a gerbil. "Uh-huh. Hey, do you have clam juice? I'm thirsty."

The reverend sat back in his chair. "Did you say you want clam juice?"

"Um . . ." I screwed up my face. *Do I actually want clam juice?* Errol drank clam juice. "Yes, I do. Clam juice. Craig's Clam Juice would be nice."

"Sorry. Don't have any. But we have tea. How about some tea?"

"No, thanks." I snagged another noodle clump. It would be rude not to have any clam juice for Errol when he came to see me. I wanted to have all his favorite things, whatever they were.

*Errol, Errol, Errol, Errol, Errol, Errol, Errol.*

I was about to take a bite when someone at the table said my name. "Yes?" I answered.

The reverend looked up. He'd been struggling with a piece of celery, trying to trap it between the smooth wooden sticks. "Are you speaking to me?"

"You just said my name. You said *Alice.*"

The reverend set his chopsticks aside and stabbed the celery with a fork. "I didn't say *Alice.*"

"Nor did I," Archibald said.

"Oh." Having eaten as much as I could, I pushed my bowl aside. "I need to go," I said, wiping my mouth on a crisply ironed napkin.

*Alice.*

"Yes?"

"What?" the reverend asked.

"You just said my name again."

The reverend shrugged. "I didn't."

"Nor did I," said Archibald.

*Alice. Find me, Alice.*

Pressing my palms on the table's edge, I leaned forward. "Listen. Someone just said, 'Find me, Alice.'"

Reverend Ruttles and Archibald leaned forward and tilted their heads. For a few moments, we sat in silence. Then I heard:

*Alice, find me, Alice.*

Neither Archibald's nor the reverend's lips had moved. "There it is again," I said, jumping to my feet. My bowl wobbled. Where was it coming from? It was a man's voice, distant but clear, but not just any man's voice. I recognized it from Neighborhood Bagels and from Elliott Bay Books. Errol's voice was calling to me, telling me to find him.

Archibald and the reverend shared a long look. I knew that look. I'd exchanged it many times with Mrs. Bobot when my mother had spun into one of her moods.

My hands dropped to my sides and I stood very still. My gaze darted between the two men as they watched me, worry deepening the creases in their faces. Even Oscar the cat, who lay in the fourth chair, stared at me with unblinking green eyes.

*Find me. Find me. Find me.*

Again, no one's lips had moved. No one had flinched. Only I had heard the voice.

A shiver ran down my spine.

It wasn't the first time I'd thought I might be losing my mind. There'd been that time on the bus, last year, when a soft buttery glow had floated around a woman's head. And the year before that there'd been a man carrying flowers, streaks of watery blue radiating from him. On both occasions I'd turned away, refusing to acknowledge the visions. As a little girl I'd thought that the colors and sparkles that danced around my mother were real. Of course they were simply the result of an overactive imagination. Illusions. Nothing more, I'd often told myself. Imagination, not madness.

But never, never ever, had I heard voices.

*Find me. Find me. Find me.*

"I've got stuff to do," I announced.

Archibald reached out a hand. "Wait, Alice. You seem so tired. We can help you with whatever you need to do. We love helping you."

"Yes, yes," Reverend Ruttles said. "We love helping you."

"That's okay. I don't need help." I shuffled in place to hide my trembling legs.

"How about we open our fortune cookies?" The reverend cracked his. "Oh, look at that. 'Love thy neighbor.' Isn't that nice?"

"Thanks for lunch," I said.

I fled the worried eyes, the serious expressions. Once inside my apartment, I leaned against the bolted door and looked down the hallway. The walls pressed in.

I'd tell Archibald and the reverend that I'd been tired, that the voice had been music playing from the street. But even as I struggled to find a rational excuse, to keep my head above the waters that I feared, the voice threatened to pull me under.

It had followed me into the apartment and had grown louder. I tried to shut it out by putting my fingers in my ears. Why was Errol's voice in my head? Why was this happening?

*Find me. Find me. Find me.*

On that day, it wasn't loneliness that waited to pounce on me. Instead, terror sped toward me, rolling down the hallway like a tsunami, closer and closer until it swept me into its dizzying turbulence. I sank to the floor. *No, no, no, no, no. Please, no.*

In those articles about mental illness, the ones that mentioned genetic predisposition, hearing voices was a bad sign. A real bad sign.

My deepest fear had come true. I was losing my mind, just like my mother.

I don't know how long I sat there, my arms frozen around

my knees. But it was Mrs. Bobot's voice that broke through the trance.

"Alice, let me in this minute! Let me in or I'll go upstairs and get my key."

Slowly I stood, oddly disconnected from my body—like the time when Beau, a boy from Welmer Boys Academy, had given me that can of beer at the winter dance. When I unbolted the door, Mrs. Bobot rushed in, her face contorted with motherly worry.

"Realm just told me that you were struck by lightning. Why didn't you call me? Someone should have told me." She ran her hands over my head and neck. "What happened? How do you feel?"

I pushed the frantic hands away. "I'm fine."

Errol's voice sang in my ears. *Find me. Find me. Find me.*

Mrs. Bobot stepped back. "Did Realm make it up or did you get struck by lightning? Tell me!"

The memory was buried deep but I could see its edges—a stack of library books, two freckles on a cheek, and then the sun-drenched sky. I scratched the Band-Aid. Wasn't I supposed to be doing something—something for my mother?

"I don't see how you could have been struck by lightning. There's been no storm today." Mrs. Bobot pressed her cheek to my forehead. "You're not feverish, but you have a glassy look to your eyes. Why would Realm say such a thing? She nearly scared me to death. But you do look a bit pale. Maybe you're coming down with something."

The building's doorbell rang.

"Oh, I almost forgot. It's the new tenant." Mrs. Bobot took my arm. "Come and meet her and then we'll take your temperature, just to make sure." While leading me to the front door, Mrs. Bobot said, "She's very young and adorable. I think you'll like her."

"Hi." A young woman with short, strawberry red hair stood on our front stoop. A red heart-shaped gem sparkled at the corner of her right eye. Her hoop earrings swayed as she waved some papers. "Here it is. The rental agreement. All signed and everything."

"Hello, Velvet," Mrs. Bobot said, taking the paperwork. "I'd like you to meet Alice. She's the landlady's daughter. We're both watching over the place until her mother gets back from her trip overseas. I think you two will become fast friends."

"Hi." Velvet batted false eyelashes at me. "Here's the check for the first and last month's rent and the cleaning deposit."

Mrs. Bobot took the check. "And here's your key." She handed it over. "Velvet's only twenty years old and she owns her own business," she told me. "Isn't that impressive?"

"I had some trust fund money," Velvet said, smoothing her short skirt. The silver bangles on her arms made music when she moved. "And college wasn't my thing, you know?"

"College isn't for everyone." Mrs. Bobot examined the check. "Velvet's Temple of Beauty. Is that the name of your salon?"

"That's it. Velvet isn't my real name. My real name is Sara Smith but that's so boring. I mean, can you get any more

boring than that? Hey, you two can come to the salon anytime for free haircuts. We can do a whole makeover thing."
She reached out and touched my hair. "I've got this unbeliev-
able conditioner that will fix those frizzies." She leaned a bit
closer. She smelled like grape Kool-Aid. "And we do eyebrow
waxing too."

I might have been insulted, except that voice was still
bouncing around. *Find me. Find me. Find me.* I stuck a finger in
my ear and wiggled it, trying to loosen the voice, trying to set
it free so it would fly out the front door and into someone
else's head.

Mrs. Bobot cleared her throat. "So, when will you be
moving in?"

"I think he's moving in first thing in the morning," Velvet
said. She pulled a compact from her purse and drew on some
lip liner. "It's so hot out. Everything sweats right off."

"I'm sorry," Mrs. Bobot said. "Did you say *he*?"

"Uh-huh." She pulled out some gloss and applied it.
"Errol."

I pulled my finger from my ear and my body went rigid.
"Errol?"

"Yeah, my friend Errol. He's the one who's going to live
here, not me. I already have a nice apartment. But he's totally
broke and he needs a place where he can rest and get better,
so I told him that I'd rent an apartment for him. I'm lending
him some of my extra furniture. I've inherited so much furniture I don't know what to do with it. Well, guess I'd better be
going."

"What?" Mrs. Bobot's mouth fell open. "You're not the tenant?"

"I am, on paper." She shrugged. "I mean, I'll be paying the bills."

"Wait." I held out a hand. "Your friend's name is Errol?" It couldn't be the same Errol. "Does he wear a black hoodie?"

Velvet closed her purse. "All the time. Hey, do you know him?"

My heartbeat doubled. "Where is he?" I practically screamed. "I need to see him!"

"Alice," Mrs. Bobot said sternly, pulling my hands off Velvet's tan shoulders. Guess I'd been shaking her too hard. "Whatever is the matter with you?"

"Please tell me where he is," I said, scratching the Band-Aid like a dog scratching a flea. "He wants me to find him. I must find him. Please." My voice cracked with desperation. "PLEASE!"

Velvet's blue-shadowed eyes widened until she looked like a fish. "Oh, I get it."

"It's not what you think," Mrs. Bobot said, stepping between us. She pressed her hand to my forehead. "She's not well. Alice, come back into the apartment and lie down. I'm going to call the doctor."

"I'll say she's not well," Velvet said. "Now I see why Errol wants to move here. They're in love."

"What?" Mrs. Bobot gasped. "Alice, is this true?"

"Of course it's true. Look at her. She's a mess."

In love? I had a welt on my chest, a voice in my head, and

a raging yearning to see someone I barely knew. That wasn't love, was it? And yet I needed to be near Errol. I HAD to be near him, in the same way that a magnet is drawn to a refrigerator, I felt his pull. "Where is he?" I pleaded.

Velvet laughed. "Oh my God, you have it so bad. I used to be in love with him, ages ago. But it wore off. Now we're just friends."

Mrs. Bobot waved the rental contract at me. "Alice, this is *not* going to happen. You can't have a boy move in here. I'm going to tear up this check."

"NO!" I cried, grabbing it.

"Hey, you already agreed and I signed that lease. And you gave me the key," Velvet said. "Don't worry. Girls fall in love with Errol all the time, believe me. But it never lasts. She'll snap out of it eventually." She walked down the front steps.

Girls? What girls? Did Errol have other girlfriends?

"I think it's nice that he has a new girlfriend. Especially since he's so sick. Hey, come by the Temple of Beauty anytime." And then she walked off.

I was Errol's new girlfriend?

*Find me. Find me. Find me.*

"Alice, who is this boy?" Mrs. Bobot asked, trying to get the rental check, but I shoved it behind my back.

"Errol," I said. "He's Errol." And tomorrow he'd be moving in upstairs. We'd be together. Every day. Forever. I had to get ready. I had to pick out something special to wear.

"Alice!" Mrs. Bobot followed me back into my apartment.

"Exactly how did you meet him? And how old is he? And what did she mean when she said he was sick?"

Waiting until tomorrow morning would seem like an eternity. I set the check on top of my dresser, then opened my closet door and shuffled through the clothes. What looked best on me? Why was everything in my closet so plain?

"Alice!" Mrs. Bobot screeched. "Why are you ignoring me? Alice!"

Archibald and Reverend Ruttles peered into my room. "Hello? We brought some leftover chow mein," Archibald announced, clutching a Tupperware bowl. "Is everybody okay in here? What's all the commotion?"

Red blotches had broken out on Mrs. Bobot's wrinkled neck. "I don't know what I should be more worried about—the fact that Alice may have been struck by lightning or the fact that she's got a secret boyfriend who's moving in tomorrow."

Reverend Ruttles leaned on his cane and frowned. "Lightning?"

Archibald smirked. "Boyfriend?"

I pulled out a red shirt. "Go away," I said. "I need to get ready. Errol's coming."

"Go away?" Mrs. Bobot gasped. "Go away? Alice, how dare you speak to us like that?"

"Uh, I'll put this in the refrigerator," Archibald said, then he headed toward the kitchen with his Tupperware.

"Alice, you're not acting like yourself," Mrs. Bobot said. "We need to talk about this. If you got hit by lightning, like Realm said, then we should go see the doctor."

"What's going on?" Realm asked, sticking her head into my bedroom.

The red shirt was boring so I pulled out a black shirt. Errol liked black. He always wore that black hoodie. Did I have a black hoodie?

Archibald's voice called out, "Wanda? I think you should come in here."

Mrs. Bobot, Reverend Ruttles, and Realm hurried from my bedroom. Hopefully they'd go away forever. Really, why was everyone bugging me? Couldn't they see that I had important things to do? Couldn't they see that Errol was the only thing that mattered?

They gathered in the bathroom, right next door to my bedroom. The bathroom walls amplified their voices so even though Errol's voice still chanted in my head, I could hear their conversation perfectly. And here's how it went:

Realm: Holy crap! My mom would kill me if I wrote all over the walls.

Reverend Ruttles: Alice plus Errol? Who's Errol?

Mrs. Bobot: He's Alice's secret boyfriend.

Realm: Alice has a secret boyfriend?

Archibald: I don't know this Errol fellow but take it from me, most guys don't like it when you plaster their name all over your apartment. I learned that lesson the hard way.

Reverend Ruttles: Did someone say something about lightning?

Mrs. Bobot: Realm? Answer me and don't lie! Did Alice get struck by lightning?

Realm: I don't know. I wasn't there.

Mrs. Bobot: Writing all over the walls. Telling us to go away. She's not acting like herself.

Archibald: She wasn't acting like herself at lunch, either. She kept hearing a voice but we couldn't hear it.

Mrs. Bobot: Hearing voices? Oh God, no. This can't be happening. Please tell me this isn't happening. She can't be like her mother.

Realm: What do you mean? Is there something wrong with Alice's mother?

Archibald: I think we're jumping to conclusions. Alice is not her mother. She's just having a little breakdown from all the stress. I have them all the time. That doesn't mean I'm mentally ill.

Realm: Oh. My. God. Is Alice's mom *crazy*?

The word "crazy" ricocheted off the bathroom walls, then made a beeline for my bedroom. The word hit me full on. It cut through my daze and ignited a memory. I grabbed a photo off my bureau, taken on the Halloween just before we'd moved to the apartment. Dust coated its gold-painted macaroni frame. Mom had set the camera on the railing of our front porch—the beautiful lake house we used to live in. We'd both dressed as gypsies, with strings of glass beads and big hoop earrings that had pinched my earlobes. It had been a good day. We'd made popcorn balls, heating the corn syrup and butter so that the kitchen smelled like a candy factory. We'd wrapped the balls in plastic, tied them up with black and orange ribbons. I'd walked our neighborhood with a girl from school while Mom stayed home to pass out the popcorn balls. My mother had thought it best to avoid the neighbors. There'd been some "incidents" that year, so the neighbors didn't like her much.

But on the way back, just two blocks from the house, I passed a little ghost and his mother. The little ghost held one of the popcorn balls. "Don't eat that," his mother scolded, taking the ball away. "We don't know what that crazy lady might have put in it."

*Crazy.*

The photo dropped from my hand, scattering golden macaroni shards across the floor. As I took a sharp breath, the real world tumbled back. What was I doing? Wasn't I supposed to be working on something for my mother? Why did I care so much about Errol?

*Find me. Find me. Find me.*

As quickly as the real world had returned, it disappeared again and I scratched my bandaged wound.

"Alice?" Mrs. Bobot stood beside me. Everyone had returned to my room.

I sat at my vanity and opened a makeup kit my mother had given me last year. It came with twelve eye shadows, five lipsticks, and a row of gold-handled application brushes. I'd never wanted to use it until that moment. As I applied a heavy layer of Cherry Red to my lips, I mumbled, "Findhimfindhimfindhim."

"What's she saying?" Archibald asked.

"Findhimfindhimfindhim."

"She's freaking out," Realm said.

"She's speaking in tongues," the reverend said. "By God, Alice is speaking in tongues."

"That's ridiculous," Mrs. Bobot said. Then she gently touched my shoulder. "Alice?"

"Findhimfindhimfindhim."

Mrs. Bobot threw her hands in the air. "Something's definitely wrong with her. William, get my car!"

THE emergency room doctor clicked his ballpoint pen and wrote something in my file.

Even though I'd journeyed into a sort of trance, I knew enough not to mention the voice. It was one thing to have a third-year resident shine a light in my eyes, another thing entirely to be shut away for psychiatric evaluation.

When a technician slid me into a tunnel for a CAT scan, I told myself that everything was going to be okay because I was going to see Errol in the morning. And when I sat at the edge of the examination table, I forced myself to smile sweetly as the doctor discussed the results.

"She looks fine. There's no evidence that she was struck by lightning."

Mrs. Bobot folded her hands in front of her double Ds. "Are you certain? She's acting so strangely. Look how she's smiling."

The doctor shuffled through some papers. "No drugs in

the urine. Everything checks out. But you're right, she does seem dazed. Is she under any stress?"

"I'm fine," I said, a phrase I'd repeated throughout the visit. Then I scratched the bandaged welt.

The doctor stepped closer. "Alice? You keep scratching the same spot. Can I take a look?"

I pushed up my tank top and the doctor carefully peeled off the Band-Aid. "How long have you had this welt?"

I shrugged, forcing my mind to focus. "Today, I think. Maybe yesterday. I don't know. It itches." It didn't seem important. Why couldn't I just go home and get ready for Errol? I was about to be reunited with the person I yearned for, just like in one of my mother's stories. He was my soul mate. My destiny.

"It's not Ebola, is it?" Mrs. Bobot clenched her hands. "I've read terrible things about Ebola."

The doctor grabbed some stuff off the counter. "It's not Ebola. I think it's a spider bite. Probably a brown recluse. They're not deadly but their poison can have many effects. Dizziness, sleepiness, mild hallucinations." He dabbed the welt with some ointment, then applied another Band-Aid. I pulled down my tank top. "The venom will run its course. She should be fine in a day."

A relieved grin spread across Mrs. Bobot's face. "Yes, that's it. Oh, wonderful. It's only spider poison." She hugged me. "That's all. Nothing to worry about."

"The spider might still be in the house," the doctor said. "When you get home, try to find it and kill it. They're big and brown."

"I'll call Archibald right now and tell him to start looking," Mrs. Bobot said as she searched through her purse for her phone.

A big brown spider had bitten my chest? I didn't remember a big brown spider. On a normal day I would have been freaked about it lurking between my sheets or hiding under my bed, waiting to sink its fangs into my flesh. "Errol will kill it," I said, jumping off the bench. "He'll kill the spider. I know he will. He'll kill it!"

The doctor and Mrs. Bobot shared one of those worried looks. "She does seem agitated. If you'd like, I can give her something that will help her sleep."

"Yes, please," Mrs. Bobot said.

My thoughts raced toward the moment when Errol would arrive. I'd be waiting for him on the sidewalk. As soon as our eyes met, the voice would go away and I'd stop feeling like I was going to explode. Because then, everything would be as it should be.

*Find me. Find me. Find me.*

I drank something grape-flavored. Then the doctor sent me on my way. Reverend Ruttles sat in the waiting room, leafing through a stack of old magazines. I leaned on his arm, my legs feeling oddly wobbly as we left the hospital. Mrs. Bobot telephoned Archibald and told him about the spider. By the time I climbed into the backseat of Mrs. Bobot's car, the chanting voice had drifted away and the world had turned dull. My eyelids fluttered as buildings whizzed past.

Archibald was waiting in the alley when Mrs. Bobot pulled

into her parking spot. He scooped me into his strong arms.
My entire body felt like Jell-O. "I vacuumed all the rooms," he
said. "And changed her sheets. Hopefully that spider is long
gone."

Mrs. Bobot helped me get into a pair of pajamas, then put
me to bed. In my drug-induced daze, I could no longer follow
the conversation. But the last thing I heard, as my face sank
into my pillow, was this:

"Realm! Get away from that desk. Those papers are none
of your business."

## THURSDAY

*FIND* me. *Find me. Find me.*

I bolted out of bed. Morning sun seeped around the edges of the drawn curtains. The yearning that had plagued me yesterday, temporarily dulled by the doctor's sleeping potion, was back in full force, burning like a swallowed torch. I threw off the sheet. I didn't care that I was dressed in pink cotton pajamas. I didn't care about the pillowcase lines embedded across my face. I didn't run a brush through my tangles. The intensity of the burning could only mean one thing—Errol was near. And if I didn't go to him I would burst into flames.

Mrs. Bobot was fast asleep on my couch, a steady snore vibrating the edges of her nostrils.

I stumbled into the foyer. Someone had propped open the building's front door with a pot of geraniums, the morning's heat filling the building. A moving van was parked out front and two sweating men lumbered up the stairs, carrying a floral sofa between them.

"You didn't tell me you had two boyfriends." Realm sat on the foyer table where the mail carrier left packages. A long gray shirt hung over her black leggings.

"What are you talking about?"

"The guy on the skateboard yesterday. The one who followed you home." She took a sip from her latte cup. "He just skated by a few minutes ago. When he asked about you, I told him you went to the hospital last night but that you were fine."

This conversation wasn't the least bit interesting. I rubbed my face. I needed to do something, but what?

"And I met your other boyfriend, Errol. Do they know about each other?"

"You met . . . *Errol*?" My heart skipped a beat.

"Yeah." She tapped her fingers on the side of her cup. "He's so not your type. He's way too tortured. He looks more like my type."

Her type? The spider bite itched like crazy as a primal reaction gripped my brain. At that moment, Realm was no longer the troubled girl who came for a month each summer to stay with her grandmother. She was a warm-blooded female. *An available female.* "He's not your type. You got that? He's *MY* type." I clenched my fists. Words burst from my mouth. "You stay away from him, you hear me? He's mine. If you try to take him away, I'll kill you. I swear, I'll kill you!"

"Jeez, you're a freak, you know that?" Realm slid off the table, then crept away, probably because I was breathing like an overheated bulldog.

"Stay. Away. From. Him."

"Whatever." Realm headed toward the safety of the front porch. "If I were you I'd be careful about threatening me. I know your secret. And if you make me mad, I might write all about it in my blog."

What was she talking about? And who cared?

*FIND ME!*

I took a deep breath. The rush of oxygen fed the fire, sending agonizing flames throughout my body. I didn't need to ask where Errol was. He pulled at me like a compass needle to due north. In a blur of pink cotton, I raced up the stairs. With each step, the chanting voice grew louder.

I reached the second floor in record time. The door to the building's fourth unit stood open. The moving men passed me on their way downstairs. As I stepped into the apartment, the chanting pounded at my temples like a kettle drum. Everything blurred until the world was a sheet of rain-splattered glass. Sweat broke across my chest. He was near. The vibration of his footsteps rippled up my legs as he walked toward me, his face and body a smudge of color. The pounding intensified. I couldn't move. Could barely breathe.

He stood real close, his warm breath on my neck. Longing drizzled over me like hot honey. I threw myself at him. Wrapped my arms around his neck and kissed him on the lips—a hungry, long kiss. The yearning didn't go away. I pushed my chest against his and kissed him harder. Why didn't I feel better? I'd found him—we were together. But the chanting was everywhere and my body burned. I tightened my arms and for a moment, he kissed me back, his mouth as eager as mine. Then he pushed me away.

"I shouldn't have done that," he said.

I threw myself at him again but he held out his arms so that a space as wide as an ocean separated us. His words floated through the chaos that filled my head.

"Do you want this to stop?"

"Yes," I pleaded. "Make it stop."

"Will you write my story?"

"Yes," I whispered.

"Do you promise?"

"Yes. I promise."

"Then drink this. It's the antidote. You'll feel like yourself again."

The cold edge of a can pressed against my lips. I tasted salt, sand, and kelp. With one swallow, the world came into focus.

And so did he.

I stood in the fourth unit's kitchen and looked at the guy I'd been obsessed with for the last twenty-four hours. Only I wasn't obsessed with him, not anymore. That feeling had washed away with the clam juice, leaving behind a painful combination of embarrassment and confusion.

I'd kissed him! I'd kissed Errol! In my pink pajamas with my hair a mess, I'd thrown myself at him. My first kiss, and it had been with Errol! I didn't even know him. I didn't even like him. What was the matter with me?

He pushed off his hood. His hair was sheared to the scalp

like Realm's. Perhaps they shared the same blind hairdresser or had grabbed the same blunt scissors during a bout of self-loathing when they'd tried to change themselves—Lily to Realm, Errol to Cupid. But while Realm's hair was dirty blond, Errol's was white. Snow white.

"Feeling better?" he asked, his voice no longer a tickling whisper.

I stepped back, my recent words regurgitating in my mind. *He's mine. If you try to take him away, I'll kill you.* Oh God, had I really said that to Realm? I'd never live that down. But when those words had spewed out, all I'd felt was the blinding need to claim Errol as my own. And now there I stood, only a short time later, feeling no urge whatsoever except to crawl into a corner and hide. Clearly I'd had an out-of-body experience. My brain had taken a brief vacation, leaving my body behind to do a bunch of stupid, embarrassing things. I couldn't blame drugs or alcohol. There'd been no beer this time, and the doctor's sleeping potion had long worn off. The blame lay entirely on that catchy little term "genetic predisposition." As I'd long feared, *crazy* had finished germinating and was ready to burst into full bloom.

The ragged breath I released sounded as if it had been locked deep inside for a lifetime. Is this how my mother felt at the end of one of her episodes? Relief tainted by foreboding—wondering how much time she had before it happened again.

"You're wondering if you're going insane," Errol said, setting the can of clam juice on the counter. "You're not. It was my doing. The voice saying 'Find me.' I made that happen."

"What? How did you . . . ?"

His serious gaze swept up and down my face, then side to side, studying me. "If it makes you feel better, only sane people worry about losing their sanity."

I took another step back. "I don't know what you're talking about. I'm not worried about going insane."

The furrow between his eyes deepened and he leaned against the counter. "I'm the one who put the voice into your head. It was my doing. What I want to know is, can you still hear it? If you can, you need to drink more." He grabbed the can and shoved it at me. *Craig's Clam Juice. Processed from 100 percent organic clams and organic brine. Sixteen ounces of mouthwatering goodness. Best served over ice.* I gagged and covered my mouth as the taste of muddy bay made a repeat appearance. Then I pushed the can away.

"Get that away from me."

"Is the voice gone?"

"Yes."

"Good." He tossed the can into the sink. "You may think it's disgusting, but it's the only known antidote. The only time it doesn't work is if you have shellfish allergies. Well, even then, it stops the voice, but then it kills you." He rubbed the back of his neck. "Crap. I forgot to ask you if you had allergies."

Two moving men stomped in. "Where do you want the television?"

"I don't care," Errol said over his shoulder. "I don't need any of that stuff. It's not mine."

"Yeah, well, we've been paid to deliver it, so where do you want it?"

"I said I don't care!"

As the moving men set the television in the living room, everything I'd done during my unfortunate lapse into crazy shot right to the surface. "You moved here on purpose," I said to Errol. "That girl with the red hair thinks we planned this. Mrs. Bobot thinks I wanted you to move here. How did you know I lived here? Have you been watching me or something?"

He looked away. "We need to talk about my story. You promised to write it."

"Your story?" Oh right, his story. That envelope filled with notes. The reason I'd met him in the first place. And that's when the absurdity of the situation hit me. I needed a story and he had one. Except he was some kind of stalking lunatic.

"How much will you pay me to write it?" It was a bluff. I wasn't going to write it, no matter how much he offered.

"I don't have any money."

"Oh gee, what a surprise. Well, sorry, but I can't work unless I get paid."

"Let's go back to my room," he said.

"Your room? No way." Only a few minutes ago I would have married the guy. Now I was seriously questioning whether either one of us was sane. How could one person put a voice into another person's head? Not possible. He was delusional and so was I. I needed to forget the last twenty-four hours—forget that I'd heard a voice, that I'd made a fool of myself. But I could still feel that kiss, warm and hungry.

"I don't want to write your book. Okay? Are you listening? I don't want to write it." I hurried into the living room. "Stop what you're doing," I told the moving men. "This is a huge mistake. He's not moving in. Take all this stuff back to the van."

"What do you mean, this is a mistake?" one of the men asked. "We ain't lugging all this stuff back downstairs. That girl at the beauty parlor paid a move-in fee, not a move-out fee."

"I'll pay the move-out fee," I offered desperately.

The guy scratched his beard. "That ain't right. I can't do that without her signature. I could get sued." He pushed his empty cart toward the door.

Crud!

I stood as stiff as a tree as Errol's gaze brushed across my back. It would be a nightmare having him in the building, bugging me every day to write his story. I looked out the fourth unit's living room window, onto the building next door. Oscar the cat was perched on its fire escape, cleaning his front paw. He glanced up and looked at me. *What are you going to do*? his green eyes asked.

I didn't want to think about the fact that Errol had invaded my life. I wanted to shut myself away and work on *Untitled Work in Progress*, not simply because I needed to, but because it would take me away from the past twenty-four hours and all the embarrassing things I'd done and said. Is that why my mother wrote? To distract herself from the reality of her life? "I've got to go."

"What about your promise?" Errol asked.

"I've got to go." I headed toward the door.

With a groan, he kicked a cupboard door. Then he kicked it again. I'd almost made my escape when he cried, "Go ahead! Run back to your apartment, hide from the truth!" He grabbed the can of clam juice from the sink, crumpled it, then threw it across the room. It bounced off a wall. My legs tensed. Was he going to attack me?

But he drew a long breath then ran a hand over his white hair. "Look, Alice," he said, forcing calm into his voice. "You can go back to your apartment and never truly know what happened. You can live with the fear that everything you felt was some kind of prelude to madness. Or you can let me explain."

Curiosity held me in that doorway, a threshhold between realities. Waiting downstairs was my unraveled but familiar life. I knew how to hide in that world. But Errol wanted to pull me into his world. His words threatened to suck me in like a black hole.

"I'm sorry I shot you," he said quietly.

Surely I hadn't heard correctly. "What did you say?"

"I said I'm sorry I shot you. Maybe I shouldn't have done it. But I needed to get your attention."

"You . . . *shot* me?"

"I don't usually knock people off their feet but I've been shaky lately." He shoved his hands into his pockets. "Your wound should be gone. It goes away as soon as the spell wears off."

My hand reached under my pajama top and I slid a finger under the Band-Aid. The spider bite was gone. No welt, no itch, just smooth skin. "Huh?" My mouth fell open. There'd been no spider. No lightning. "What did you . . . ? How did you . . . ?" I blabbered. "Why would you . . . ?" His words from the bagel shop came back to me.

*I* am *Cupid. The original, one and only Cupid.*

I clenched my hands into fists. "YOU SHOT ME WITH AN ARROW?"

I pressed against the door frame as the moving men squeezed by. Errol had ignored my question and was walking to the back bedroom.

Fine. Go away. Leave me alone. I have things to do.

Who was I kidding? If I went downstairs and tried to write *Untitled Work in Progress*, I wouldn't get an ounce of work done. Call it lovesickness, call it insanity, but I'd lost control of my emotions and thoughts, and nothing terrified me more than that. If there was a chance that something other than the mutated gene of mental illness had brought on the voice and those *feelings*, then I wanted to know.

I followed Errol across the newly polished floor. Mrs. Bobot and I had worked hard last week, getting the apartment ready so people could come and look at it without sucking in a lungful of dust. My mother had never rented the fourth unit. Her mania was impossible to hide from anyone living in the building and she didn't want to share her secret with any more people. So for as long as we'd lived there, only dust balls and mice had traveled across that floor. But since her hospitalization, she needed money. So Mrs. Bobot and I had cleaned the unit without Mom's approval. It had to be done.

I stood in the doorway to the back bedroom. A striped mattress sat on the floor. The manila envelope lay on a rolltop desk. Errol motioned to a stool.

"I'll stand," I said, thinking it best to stay in the doorway, in case I needed to escape.

Errol sat on the mattress's edge. "Excuse me for not standing," he said, wiping his forehead with his sleeve. "I'm . . . *tired*." He rested his arms on his knees and cast his gaze at the floor, where his pale bare feet looked dead against the dark wood. "Life's been crappy lately."

That was the first thing he'd said that I could relate to.

I tucked my uncombed hair behind my ears. "I want to know if you shot an arrow at me."

"I did."

"But the doctor said a spider bit me."

"Doctors see what they want to see. You can tell them the truth again and again but they never listen." The sentence was spiked with bitterness. My gaze darted to the windowsill where three brown pill bottles sat, the white labels too far away to read. Errol took a long breath. "I'm sorry I knocked you off your feet. You fell pretty hard. That's not supposed to happen but, like I said, I've been shaky so my aim's been off."

I pointed an angry finger. "If you shot me with an arrow

then that's assault. I could call the police. You could be arrested. Do you realize that? You can't go around shooting people with arrows. You could have killed me!"

"My arrows don't kill."

"Wait a minute." I dropped my arm. "If you shot me with an arrow, how come we didn't find it? Tony and I looked all over the sidewalk."

"Is that his name? Tony?" He still looked at the floor.

I hesitated. He'd sounded . . . I'm not sure . . . jealous? "Yeah, his name's Tony. And we didn't see an arrow."

"They're invisible," he said.

"Right. Invisible."

"Yes. Invisible. The arrow infused you with lovesickness so you'd do whatever I wanted. You forced me, Alice."

"You *infused* me? What's that supposed to mean?"

He slowly rose to his feet and our eyes locked. I could still feel the pressure of his lips against mine. "Look, if you'd accept what I'm saying, then we can bypass all this useless small talk and get to the real issue."

"Useless small talk?" I almost laughed. "I'm trying to figure out why I acted like a total freak, and you call that useless small talk? You had no right to shoot me."

"Excellent." He folded his hands behind his back. "At last you believe me."

"I didn't say that. I . . ." My thoughts collided like bumper cars. What was going on? "Cupid's not real. He's a mythological god."

"Don't I look real?" he asked, holding out his arms. "I'm as real as you, but I'm no god. I've never been a god. I was a regular sixteen-year-old until I signed that damn contract. And I've been sixteen ever since."

I immediately felt bad for anyone who'd signed a contract. The word "contract" was one of my least favorite words, right behind "genetic" and "predisposition." "What contract?"

"Their contract. The gods. In exchange for one life of pure bliss I agreed to be their servant. There's nothing like pure bliss. It's indescribable."

"I wouldn't know."

He winced, as if in pain. Then he walked to the window and opened one of the pill bottles, popped a pill into his mouth, and swallowed. "You know, even if I'd read the contract's fine print, I wouldn't have understood. Eternal life sounds great at first. But once you've lost all the people you love, eternal life is a total nightmare." He closed the pill bottle and leaned against the sill. "As it turns out, I didn't fully understand the contract. I wasn't given eternal life. The gods simply extended my life. The fine print stated that the contract would end when the gods saw fit. So you see, I'm not a god. I'm a mortal. The end of my contract means the end of my life."

I really wanted to read the labels on those pill bottles. Velvet had said Errol was sick. What kind of illness? If it was mental illness I'd probably recognize the names of the drugs. But I was starting to think there might be something more going on besides his delusions.

"Look, I don't go around telling people I'm Cupid, because

it usually gets me into trouble. You tell someone you're a mythological being and they'll try to burn you at the stake. Or shove you into an ice bath or fry your brains with electricity." He clenched his teeth and made a sizzling sound.

In an odd way I suddenly felt better, because of the two of us standing in that bedroom, Errol was clearly the crazier. He thought he was the Roman god Cupid. Sure, I might have heard a voice in my head; sure, I might have gone a bit wacko for a few hours, but I had no delusions about my identity. I wasn't Isis, or Supergirl, or Bella Swan. I was Alice Amorous, daughter of a semifamous, mentally ill romance writer, who would soon be getting food stamps if her mother didn't turn in another book. Which I was supposed to be writing. "I gotta go."

"Wait." Errol sank onto the stool. "Look, here's the deal. What's done is done. You promised to write my story—the story of Cupid and Psyche. One of the greatest love stories of all time. I've included all the details in my notes. I'll tell you anything else you need to know about the story so you can write it, then get it published. You promised."

I was about to take back my promise, about to point out that it had been made under duress. "It's a love story?"

"Yes."

I took a long breath. "Would you say it's a . . . *romance*?"

"Definitely."

Across the room, in a manila envelope, a story waited to be written. I'd seen the notes, the work he'd put into it, the details. All I'd have to do is piece it together. It sounded so tempting, but it wouldn't solve my problem because in the end it would be his story, not my mother's.

Errol tapped his foot. "I know you're trying to come up with another excuse but there's no time for excuses. My story must be written soon. In the next few days."

"The next few days? Are you crazy?" I cringed at my choice of words. "I mean, I'm really busy and—"

"Busy with what?"

"It's . . . private."

Odd shadows fell across Errol's face as morning sunlight seeped into the room. He suddenly looked very old, as if an ancient face had been projected over his young face, giving me a glimpse of eternity. "If my story isn't written, then it will be lost. Do you understand? If the story about my only love is lost, then what is the value of my life?" His voice was hushed but fiery, his eyelids trembling. Then he grabbed the manila envelope off the desk. "You must write the story before time runs out. *You promised.*"

How many promises does a person make over the course of a lifetime? How many of those are kept, how many forgotten or outright broken? With all the ranting about time running out and arrows being shot, I knew that Errol wouldn't care about my own predicament—that I didn't have one second to waste on his book or on Realm's book, or anyone's book unless it was called *Untitled Work in Progress.* "I'm sorry but I—"

"Why are you so stubborn? You're just like her!" he cried.

Her?

He pressed a finger to his temple and closed his eyes. Silence filled the room, interrupted only by the sounds of the moving men. When Errol opened his eyes, he spoke with focused control. "I'm sorry. It's just that you remind me of someone. Look, I know a few days is not much time. I would have come here sooner but I was . . . *overseas*."

I said nothing. We stared at one another.

"Why are you fighting the truth?" he asked.

The conversation was going nowhere. I folded my pink pajama–clad arms. "Here's the truth. You threw something at me because you were mad at me or maybe you just wanted to get my attention and it knocked me off my feet. And maybe you're sorry for doing that, but maybe you're not. And then a brown recluse spider bit me, just like the doctor said, which is why I couldn't think straight. But now I'm all better and I don't have time to write your story. I've got my own life and it's very stressful. You have no idea. NO idea."

"You kissed me. I suppose you're going to blame that on the spider."

The longing might have disappeared, but I remembered the tingle in my stomach when we'd kissed, the warmth of his lips, the strength in his arms around my waist. "It didn't mean anything," I said. "I made a huge mistake. It didn't mean anything."

Errol's shoulders fell and he looked away. There he sat in his dingy hoodie, the manila envelope on his lap. At first I couldn't read his expression, his eyes unmoving, his mouth downturned. But then I recognized the look. It was the same look my mother had worn so many times when I'd visited her at Harmony Hospital.

It was defeat.

In the end, I didn't want to torment him. Why question his delusions? He was sick. He just wanted someone to pay attention to his story. What difference would it make in my life to pretend to keep my promise?

So I walked into the room and gently took the envelope from his lap.

"Thank you," he said quietly.

As I headed toward the open doorway that would lead me out of the fourth unit and back into my real life, Errol called after me.

"I need to get some rest. Then we'll start on chapter one."

THAT wasn't going to happen.

OUTSIDE unit four, I bumped into Mrs. Bobot, who had come upstairs to see what was going on. Having spent the night on my couch, she still wore her bedazzled shirt from yesterday. Her long gray braid had come undone. "Alice, what are you doing up here? Were you in that boy's bedroom?" she asked, her eyes widening with each word. "In your pajamas?"

"We were just talking."

"Uh-huh." She looked me up and down. "How are you feeling?"

"Fine. I feel fine. The spider bite is gone."

"Really? I'm so happy to hear that. You do seem better." Then she pointed to my hand. "What's that?"

I hid the envelope behind my back. "It's just some stuff. Errol wants to be a writer. He was hoping Mom would look at his work."

"Oh dear. You didn't tell him, did you? About your mother?"

"Of course not," I said, my stomach growling. Had I eaten

anything since yesterday's chow mein lunch? "I'd never tell anyone. Never."

"Of course you wouldn't." Mrs. Bobot tucked a lock of hair
behind my ear. "I just wanted to make sure. Sometimes we
tell our boyfriends things."

"Errol is *not* my boyfriend."

"He's not your boyfriend?"

"No." I gripped the envelope. "God, no. I don't even know
him. Not really. I didn't want him to move here. That Velvet
person has it all wrong."

Mrs. Bobot clasped her hands together and smiled. "What
a relief! I'm so glad to hear that. There's nothing wrong with
having a boyfriend, but . . ." She looked over her shoulder,
then stepped closer to me. "But he doesn't sound like the
right boy for you. Velvet said he's had lots of girlfriends. And
I started to worry that you were sneaking around. Do you
want him to leave? I think we can get the rental contract
nullified."

"Yes," I whispered. "That would be great." Really great.
Because when he woke up from his nap, he'd start bugging
me about the first chapter. And I had my own first chapter to
deal with. First chapter? I still hadn't come up with the story.
*Untitled Work in Progress* was not a catchy title for a book.

"Then I'll take care of it. I'll call Archibald over at the law
office and ask him what we should do. If one of the lawyers he
works for can deal with this, then we can avoid an uncomfortable confrontation."

Like getting knocked off your feet? Should I tell her about

that? She'd call the police and then there'd be a huge scene. And what evidence did I have? "Thanks," I told her.

There was no shortage of hugs in my world, because Mrs. Bobot tended to deliver them throughout the day at regular intervals. As she hugged me then and there, I felt so much better. She'd make things right, I knew, as she hurried to her apartment, her steps determined, her gray hair swinging. Mrs. Bobot would make the whole Errol thing go away.

I started down the stairs. The front entry to the apartment building was still propped open, sunshine streaming in. Tony Lee had skated past earlier. According to Realm, he'd asked about me. After my fall at the library, he'd felt the back of my head and had looked into my eyes. He'd make a great doctor one day. Tony was probably the nicest, cutest boy in the world. He was a stroke of normal in the surrealist painting that was my life.

"Watch it," one of the moving guys said as the pair headed up the stairs, carrying a grandfather clock. I flattened myself against the railing as they squeezed past.

That's when I noticed it—a reddish haze that floated around the second man's head. It wasn't a shadow from the stained glass window because it clung to the man, moving where he moved. As he passed by, I reached out to touch the haze, then changed my mind. Squeezing my eyes closed, I told the haze to go away. When I opened my eyes, the man had reached the top step and the haze had disappeared. An illusion. Nothing more.

I tossed the melted flip-flops into the garbage. Archibald

had scrubbed the lipstick love notes from the bathroom walls. Most had come clean, except for a few stubborn pink stains. He'd left a bottle of cleaner with a note, "Wash that man right off of your walls." I showered, then brushed my teeth and gargled, chasing away the lingering aftertaste of the lovesickness antidote. What would Craig, the clam juice manufacturer, think about this unique use of his product?

Dressed in a clean pair of shorts and purple tank top, and having eaten a couple of bowls of Archibald's leftover chow mein, I cleared the papers from my mother's desk, including *Death Cat,* which Realm had once again removed from the junk mailbox. She'd also left a note: "Read this! You promised!"

I never promised. Never. I'd lied, but that's different from a promise. I sneered at Realm's name, written on the title page of her manuscript. Who would want to read a book about a cat that murders people? But what really bugged me was the fact that Realm had written a book. An entire book from beginning to end. Well, if she could do it, then so could I.

The editorial assistant from Heartstrings Publishers had left a phone message. Everyone at the publishing house was very excited about the new book. Was there a title? They'd love to know the title as soon as possible.

I collected the writing guidebooks and propped them on the desk. I got out my pen and notebook, then sat in the swivel chair. I sat very still, trying to clear my mind of everything that had happened that morning. What, what, what would the story be about? Love, of course. True love. I tapped the pen on the desk. But who is the hero? What's her name? What does she do? Where does she live? I chewed on the pen. Who is her true love? What's his name? What does he do? I tore little pieces off the edge of the paper, creating a pile of snow.

I looked over at my mother's books. She always started her stories with the heroine and hero meeting. In *Love's Like a Bit of Heaven*, Trixie Everlast was eating a pomegranate and she choked and Van Diamond saved her. In *Love Is a Mountain*, Felicity Fairweather was skiing in the Alps and she tumbled into a ravine and Baron Hans Helmeister rescued her. And in *Love on the Savannah*, Phillipa Willowsby was almost crushed by a rampaging black rhino when Maximus Steele, big game hunter, shot the rhino with a tranquilizer dart.

What should my girl be doing? Should she be standing at her window, watching her fantasy boyfriend skate by—too scared to talk to him? Should she go to the library because she's got this crazy idea that she can be a writer and then she runs into her fantasy boyfriend at the library? And just when he's about to ask her out, should some freak shoot her with an arrow?

Yeah. Right. What kind of story was that? Not a romance novel, that's for sure.

The paper snow pile grew. Sweat broke out on the back of my neck. I turned on the air conditioner.

It made perfect sense that Realm had written a horror novel, because she had the personality of a vicious troll. But who was I kidding? It was one thing to know the rules of romance, another thing entirely to understand romance. I didn't have a clue. Me, the girl who spent most every night watching TV or hanging out with old people. What did I know about love? What did I know about writing? I couldn't even write the first line, for God's sake. *Anyone Can Write a Romance Novel* was a big fat lie. Somebody should sue that publisher.

As I tapped my pen on the desk, my thoughts drifted, and I soon found myself not thinking about *Untitled Work in Progress* but about the undeniably freaky stuff that I'd just been through. I'd kissed Errol. What was wrong with me? Sure, he was handsome, but the creepiness factor outweighed the handsome factor. My behavior had been totally irrational— as irrational as anything my mother had ever done. And I couldn't deny that I'd heard Errol's voice in my head. Hearing voices wasn't normally listed as a symptom of bipolar disorder, but extreme forms of mania and depression, which my mother suffered from, could bring about hallucinations, both visual and vocal.

Had my mother ever heard voices? I could ask but she wouldn't answer. She hadn't spoken a word to me in weeks. But there was one other person who might know. And I hadn't yet made my morning call to the hospital.

"Hello, can I speak to Dr. Diesel?"

Dr. Diesel was on rounds and not available to come to the phone. I rested my head on the desk, which was cold against my cheek. My disappointed sigh scattered the snow pile. "It's really important. Would you tell him I called?"

The receptionist then forwarded my call to the cafeteria where my mother was having a late breakfast. "She's got some orange juice and a banana muffin," the nurse told me, setting the scene as she probably did for other families. "And she's wearing her periwinkle bathrobe and her hair is pulled back into that lovely new hair clip that Mrs. Bobot gave her. She's looking at me right now. She knows you're on the phone. Here she is."

I didn't know if my mother was actually holding the phone or if the assistant was pressing it to her ear. "Hi, Mom," I said, trying to keep my voice calm. I wouldn't mention Velvet or Errol, or the spider bite, or the publisher's deadline. Or the possibility that I would soon be admitted to the hospital and we could sit side by side, staring into oblivion together. "I just wanted to say hi," I said.

"Alice."

I bolted upright. The voice had been barely audible, but it was her voice, no doubt about it. "Mom? Oh, Mom, hi. Hi." My lower lids filled with tears. This was a good sign. A very good sign. "How are you feeling?"

She said nothing, but it didn't matter. That one word, with its two consonants and three vowels had meant everything to me.

I didn't want to put any pressure on her, so I filled the rest of the call with small talk. "It's another hot day. We're having a heat wave. Archibald made chow mein yesterday. The reverend's been busy with his church meetings. Realm came for her visit. Mrs. Bobot's taking good care of me. There's a new antique store called Lee's Antiquities. I think you'll like it. It's different." I pushed aside the questions I desperately wanted to ask. *Mom, did you ever hear voices? Did you ever see colors floating around people's heads?* Instead I said, "I love you. I miss you. Hope you can come home soon."

*Please come home soon.*

"This is wonderful," the nurse told me. "She nodded and listened to everything you said. I think it was your voice, Alice. Your voice managed to break through to her."

I closed the phone and grabbed my backpack purse. Mom had spoken. She'd listened. My voice had cut through the darkness. If she saw me in person, she might wake up even more.

Thursday was grocery shopping day for Mrs. Bobot. Archibald was at work and Reverend Ruttles would soon be off to one of his meetings. They couldn't get angry at me for not asking for a ride. My voice had broken through! I wanted to see my mother, alone. Just the two of us. I needed to hear her voice again. And I'd get through to her again. I knew I would.

So I slipped a note into Mrs. Bobot's mailbox and left the building.

THE bus dropped me off at the Mukilteo ferry terminal. "Bye," I said to the little boy who'd been sitting across the aisle from me. He smelled like peanut butter and fabric softener, which was kind of nice. He'd spent the entire ride killing robots on a tiny screen while his mom had read a magazine. I'd spent the entire ride staring at a blank notebook page and chewing on my pen.

It was too hot for clam chowder at Ivar's fish and chip stand. Besides, I'd lost my taste for clams, so I grabbed lemonade instead. Sunlight glistened on calm water as I sat on the ferry's upper deck. When the boat picked up speed, a nice breeze blew through my hair. The other passengers were putting on sunblock, taking photos, sipping from water bottles. How many of them had scrawled things on their bathroom walls yesterday? How many had thrown themselves at a guy they didn't even know? How many had to write an entire novel by the end of the summer?

At one o'clock on that Thursday afternoon, after getting off the ferry, I caught the Whidbey Island shuttle bus. During the ride, the driver pointed out the island's tallest tree and a honey farm. Then he dropped me at the end of Harmony Hospital's driveway. After the bus's exhaust cleared, I took a long breath. My mother had said my name. She'd listened to my voice. The new medication was doing its job and was changing her brain's chemistry. I'd come to help wake her up—to rescue her. But I'd also come to rescue myself.

Up the winding, single-lane road I walked. I imagined the lumber baron stumbling around, desperate with grief, trying to replant the trees. He'd done a good job, because the sun was having trouble breaking through the dense, leafy canopy. Trunks stood at silent attention as deep as the eye could see. Not a car passed by. The birds fell silent as my tennis shoes beat an anxious rhythm. The eagerness of the forest was palpable, its undergrowth pressing against the sides of the road. If people disappeared, how long would it take nature to reclaim the pavement, roots crumbling the cement like dried clay?

"I'm here to visit my mother, Belinda Amorous," I told the receptionist, a woman I didn't know, since Thursday wasn't my normal visiting day. I had to show her my old Welmer Girls Academy ID.

"She's probably at the concert. Over in the conservatory."

I pinned the plastic visitor tag to my tank top. What if I lost it? *Young lady, we've been looking for you. It's time for your medication.* I made sure the word "visitor" faced the right direction.

A local quartet had come to perform a selection of Baroque music that afternoon for the patients. Music soothes the savage beast, so they say. It soothes other beasts as well—stress, fear, self-doubt, you name it. Which is why much of the staff had gathered, too, to close their eyes and absorb the clear notes as they soared from the instruments like welcome raindrops on that searing day.

My mother wasn't in the conservatory. "She's taking a nap," a nursing aide told me. I started down the hallway. "No, not that way. She's been moved to a different room."

"What? Why?"

The aide shrugged. "All I know is that they moved her from a private room to a shared room."

I tucked my sunglasses into my purse. Everything always came down to money. You had it or you didn't have it. Didn't matter that my mother had written thirty novels, that she'd entertained countless readers on airplanes, in waiting rooms, and alongside resort pools—a private room in a private mental health facility was reserved for those who could pay the monthly bill. End of story.

"I sure liked her book *Love on the Savannah*," the aide told me as she led the way. "That Maximus Steele was a total jerk, but he ended up being such a nice guy."

A security guard sat outside a private room. Some big celebrity had just been admitted and had come with his own entourage. The curtains were drawn in my mother's new room. Her roommate was apparently enjoying the concert. Family photos of a bald husband and five well-fed kids sat on the dresser. My mother was asleep in the bed by the window. I wanted to shake her awake. *I'm here. Talk to me. You're getting better, right? Tell me you're getting better.*

"Alice?" Dr. Diesel stepped into the room. "I'm surprised to see you today," he whispered.

"I want to see my mom," I whispered back.

"Well . . ." He tucked the chart under his arm and thought for a moment. "Her sleep schedule is a bit messed up. Drowsiness is one of the new medication's side effects. I understand she was a bit agitated last night. I think it's best we let her sleep. Do you want to get something to eat in the dining room and then come back?"

"She said my name this morning," I told him.

"Yes, that's what I heard. Such good news." Then he frowned. "I spoke to the hospital's director. I'm afraid I wasn't able to convince him to give your mother more time to pay her bill. But I had her moved to this room to help lower your costs. She didn't seem to mind."

"Oh." I fiddled with my visitor tag. "Dr. Diesel? Can we talk?"

"Yes, of course."

A pair of nurses stood within earshot. "Could we go somewhere . . . private?"

"Certainly. Let's go to my office."

I'd never paid much attention to the framed diplomas in Dr. Diesel's office. I'd always been too freaked out to notice much of anything in there. But I was glad to see they weren't just paper rectangles with fancy gold seals—they were proof that he'd gone to school for a very long time, proof that he knew stuff I didn't know. Hope had propelled me to Harmony Hospital on that Thursday afternoon, but fear led me to the doctor's leather couch, which squeaked when I sat.

Dr. Diesel settled into a high-backed chair and folded his hands on his desk. A bust of Sigmund Freud watched from the corner. "What's on your mind?"

I crossed my legs, then crossed them the other way. *Just ask the question. Ask it!* "Dr. Diesel, did my mother ever hear voices?"

He raised his graying eyebrows. "Why do you want to know this?"

"Because I just want to know."

He tapped his index finger on the desk. Once. Twice. "Well, I don't think it would breech doctor-patient confidentiality to tell you that vocal hallucinations are not part of your mother's illness." He leaned forward and stared at me with such intensity that I wouldn't have been surprised if he could actually see past my skull and into my brain. "Are *you* hearing voices?"

I shifted my legs again. Why couldn't I get comfortable? "No. Why would I be hearing voices?"

He widened his eyes.

"I'm not," I said. "I'm just wondering." Then I looked away, focusing on the smoothness of Sigmund Freud's plaster head. The two shrinks stared at me, willing me to spill my deepest, darkest fear. What was worse—not knowing or knowing? Hiding from the truth or facing it? "Maybe I heard *something.*"

Dr. Diesel picked up a pen. "Tell me about this voice."

Fully aware that I was going to sound like a lunatic, and more than a bit worried that the visitor badge might be replaced by a patient badge, I took the plunge. "It's this weird guy who moved into my building. His name is Errol and he wants me to help him write a book. He thinks he's Cupid. Isn't that idiotic?"

Dr. Diesel said nothing.

"Anyway, it was his voice I heard, saying 'Find me' over and over."

"When was this?"

"Yesterday."

"Had anything unusual happened yesterday?"

"Yeah. A brown recluse spider bit me and the poison made me act weird. That's what my doctor said. But Errol says that he shot me with an invisible arrow and that's why I heard his voice. He expects me to believe that."

"Errol sounds confused."

"Totally." I paused. "Why do you think I heard the voice?"

"The question is, why do *you* think you heard the voice?"

"Because . . ." I took a long breath. "I think I've inherited my mother's illness." My eyes welled with tears and before I could fight them, they streamed down my cheeks and my shoulders started to shake. I was a complete wreck. Dr. Diesel pulled a tissue from a box, then walked around the desk and handed it to me. As I wiped my eyes, he sat in the couch's matching armchair.

"Do you hear his voice now?"

"No. It's gone."

"And this was the first time you'd heard a voice in your head?"

"Yes." I crumpled the tissue and waited for the diagnosis as one waits for a guillotine's blade to fall—the result being equally permanent. The life I'd known would abruptly end. Alice Amorous, daughter of Belinda Amorous, you are doomed.

Dr. Diesel tucked the pen back into his pocket and propped his elbows on the chair's armrests. Then he smiled gently. "Alice, I've been diagnosing and treating mental illness for most of my adult life and there's one thing I know with absolute certainty. Families of severely ill patients go through as much stress, sometimes more stress, than the patients themselves. One of the common offshoots of this stress is to focus on the various symptoms of the illness, then to convince oneself to be suffering the same affliction. First-year medical students do the exact same thing. They read about a horrific disease and they worry that they have the exact same disease."

I unclenched my fingers. Surely he wasn't telling me that I'd imagined the entire thing? "But what about genetic predisposition?"

"Sometimes bipolar disorder runs in families, that's true, but the odds are small. Besides, your mother suffers from a very extreme form of the illness. Her condition has been so difficult to treat, I'm not even sure we should call it bipolar disorder. It's one of those situations where the illness doesn't quite fit into a category." He pressed his fingertips together.

"Clearly, Alice, you are under a great deal of stress worrying about your mother, and I know there are financial issues. But I can see from the look on your face that you are not convinced. Let's knock this off the list of things to worry about, shall we?" He grabbed his pen and a pad of paper, then asked a series of questions. "Do you have times when you can't slow down your body or your thoughts? Times when you can't drag yourself out of bed to shower or eat? When it's so dark that you can't think any happy thoughts? When you can't stop doing a task, even if you're sleepy?"

On and on the questions went, and to each one I answered, "No."

Dr. Diesel returned the pen and tablet to his desk. "I have just described your mother's illness."

"But the voice. That's not normal."

He walked over to the watercooler and filled a cup, then handed it to me. "Where does normal begin and where does it end?"

"You're asking me? Aren't you supposed to know the answer?"

He filled a cup for himself and took a long drink. "Where does imagination begin and end? What are its boundaries? One person is deemed creative, another is mad. Perfectly sane, perfectly healthy people see and hear things that can't always be explained. I myself saw a ghost when I was about your age. I don't believe in ghosts, but my mind conjured it one night and as sure as I see you sitting on that couch, I saw that ghost." He threw the cup into the wastebasket. "Truth is, we've

barely begun to understand the brain. It's still mostly a guess-
ing game."

A clock ticked. A distant phone rang. I wiped my eyes
again. "I don't understand," I mumbled. "I don't understand
why she's like this . . . now. She was never this bad. She always
managed to take care of things. Do you still think she's going
to get better? Do you think it will happen before they make
her leave? Do you think she'll be able to write again?"

"We must have realistic expectations. While I think this
medication will bring her out of her depression and stabilize
her mood swings, it may be some time before she feels
like going back to work."

"But she needs to write her next book," I said.

Dr. Diesel smoothed his comb-over, then returned to the
armchair. "This is not something she can control, Alice. You
understand that, don't you?"

I looked at my shoes.

"You understand that this has nothing to do with you. That
she still loves you very much. You know that, don't you? You
know that she loves you?"

The room felt very small. I didn't want to sit there anymore.
Every sound, the clicking of someone's heels in the hall, the
whir of the overhead fan, the bubbling of a corner fish tank,
became amplified. "I gotta go," I said, heading for the door.

"Alice," Dr. Diesel gently called. "Sometimes it helps to
talk to people who know exactly what you're going through.
There's a group that meets here on Monday nights—a support
group for family members. Would you like to come?"

"I'll think about it," I lied. Not in a million years would I sit with a bunch of strangers and tell them what my life was really like. Talking wouldn't erase the bad memories. An understanding nod wouldn't soothe the loneliness. I couldn't bring back the lost friends, or collect the hours of sleep I'd worried away, or gather the longed-for hugs into a bouquet.

"Yes, please think about it," Dr. Diesel said. "You would be most welcome. And I'm here anytime you wish to talk."

The lumber baron's eyes followed me as I hurried across the lobby. Mary, the woman I'd met on Tuesday, sat hunched over her desk, working a calculator. I managed to slip past without being noticed. I checked my mother's room but she was still napping. It was good to know that she hadn't been tormented by voices. And that Dr. Diesel thought it was no big deal that I'd heard a voice. He was right about one thing—I was totally stressed out. I whispered good-bye to my mother, then called Mrs. Bobot to let her know that I was heading for the ferryboat and would be back in time for dinner.

When I got back to Seattle I stopped at the post office. The monthly newsletter from the International Romance Writers' Guild had arrived. I stared at its pink cover. Then I crumpled it into a ball. Not a gentle sort of crumpling as one might do with a gum wrapper or a grocery receipt. My face turned crimson. I threw my entire body into that crumpling as if my life depended upon rearranging the pink paper's molecular structure. Then I threw the wad of paper on top of the garbage can. As I stomped out of the post office, the newsletter began to uncrinkle until its headline could be read by any curious soul who might pass by.

"Make Way, Belinda Amorous. A New Queen of Romance Has Been Crowned."

CAL Anderson Park was crowded with people searching for ways to escape the heat. I headed straight for the nearest cart and bought an orange Popsicle. An oak tree offered its shade so I sat on a bench beneath the green canopy. Because I hadn't read past the International Romance Writers' Guild's headline, I didn't know who had taken my mother's place as the Queen of Romance. Even though it wasn't the new queen's fault, I despised her. They'd throw her a huge party with champagne and a bubbling chocolate fountain and everyone would congratulate her. "Whatever happened to Belinda Amorous?" they'd ask.

"She hasn't published a thing in three years."

"She didn't come to the last two conferences."

"She's overseas."

"Well, we can't have that kind of person as our queen. Off with her head."

Orange syrup dripped down my wrist, the Popsicle's life span cut short by the heat wave.

"Where've you been?" Errol sat next to me, his hood drawn over his head. "I've been looking for you. We don't have a lot of time and chapter one's not going to write itself." His bossy tone was like sandpaper grating across my nerves.

I turned away. "Leave me alone, Errol."

"What's your problem?" he asked.

My jaw clenched. "I think the question should be, what's *your* problem?" The rest of my Popsicle fell onto the ground where a pigeon started pecking at it. "That's just great." I held up the empty stick as if it were some sort of symbol for my life.

Errol reached into his hoodie pocket and pulled out a pill bottle, which he opened, then popped a pill into his mouth. I watched from the corner of my eye, hoping to read the label. After returning the bottle to his pocket, he slumped against the back of the bench. "Are you going to tell me what your problem is?" he asked.

"Why would I?"

"Because I care. I care about you." He sounded serious and for a moment I believed him. But then I remembered Velvet's comment about girls falling in love with Errol all the time. He'd probably told every one of them that "he cared."

"Right. You don't even know me."

"How can you say I don't even know you? We kissed, didn't we?"

Even in the shade, my face got all hot. A kid ran by, chased by another kid with a squirt gun. A trio of pigeons competed for the last drops of my Popsicle. "You want to know what my problem is?" I threw the stick on the grass and looked right into Errol's dark eyes. "I'll tell you what my problem is. My problem is that, according to a guy with a whole mess of diplomas, I've got an overactive imagination and I worry too much. I need to join a support group for people like me who imagine and worry too much. And then we can all sit around and talk about how worried and imaginative we are."

He narrowed his eyes. "Is that it? You call that a problem?"

Was this some sort of challenge? Oh, it was on. I narrowed my eyes. "My problem is that my mom used to be the Queen of Romance but she hasn't written anything in a really long time so she's been dethroned and I don't know when she's coming home. And because she's gone, I had to leave school to take care of all her stuff, and the apartment building, which means I have no life." I took a quick breath. "My problem is that if my mother doesn't write a book by the end of summer, she'll have to return one hundred thousand dollars to her publisher. She doesn't have one hundred thousand dollars. We can barely pay the bills. She'd have to sell the building and then where would we live?" As I kicked a pebble, the pigeons flew off. "My problem is that because I'm the daughter of a writer, people like you and Realm want me to help you get your books published, but I don't have time to deal with your books. Don't you get that? I'm trying to write my own book. I'm trying to write it so my life won't totally fall apart, and I can't even come up with a stupid title!"

I hadn't planned on sharing all that information with Errol, but the confession, like a burp, had brought some relief. "I'm sorry," I said, though it seemed weird apologizing to the guy who'd thrown something at me. "My problem is that it's really, really hot and I'm having a really, really bad day."

Errol pulled a pair of sunglasses from his pocket and slid them on. Then he pulled the hood farther over his forehead. He looked like he was about to rob a gas station. "I'm sorry you're having a bad day," he said. "Really, I am. But are you always so dense?"

"Huh?"

"You need a love story and I've got a love story. The greatest love story ever."

*Here we go again.* "Well, good for you," I said. "But your story isn't going to help me. The publishing contract doesn't have your name on it. They want a Belinda Amorous story."

"Look, I'm giving you my story. You can write it and put your mother's name on it and then you've got your book. I told you it was your destiny to write my story, remember?"

Mist from a nearby squirt gun war drifted over my shoulders. I sat up straight. "What do you mean you're *giving* me the story?"

"I don't need my name on the cover. And I don't care about making money. All I want is for the real story to be told. As long as you stick to my notes and write it the way it happened, you can have it."

"What do you mean you don't care about money? That girl who came by, Velvet, she said she's paying for the apartment because you're broke."

"Yeah, I'm broke. So what? I used to have money. Lots of

it. But I don't need it anymore." He eyed my lemonade. I handed it over and he took a long drink. "The only thing I care about is that my story gets told."

I sat even straighter. "It's a love story?" He nodded. "And you know the entire story? From beginning to end? And all the other parts?"

"Know it? I lived it. Haven't you been listening to me?" He tipped some ice into his mouth.

"And it's never been published? You're not plagiarizing or something like that?"

"It's *my* story."

So there I sat, the backs of my legs sticky, my brow furrowed, considering making a deal with the devil. Okay, so maybe he wasn't the devil but let's look at the facts. He thought he was Cupid. He'd been stalking me. He'd moved into my apartment building so he could continue to stalk me. And he'd thrown something at me.

"What do you really want?" I asked. "Because I'm not going to have sex with you, if that's what you're thinking."

He crunched the ice, then smiled. "If I'd wanted to have sex with you, we would have had it by now. You were pretty lovesick, remember?"

*No comment.*

He stretched an arm along the top of the bench, confidence settling around him. He had what I needed. He knew that. And I was listening. "You don't have to worry, Alice. The only thing I want is for the world to know my story. Nothing is more important to me than that."

I didn't even know if his story was any good. What if it was about a killer cat?

People covered every square foot of the park, sunbathing, listening to music, reading, walking, wading in the rectangular pools, but not a single person, other than Errol, was offering to give me a story. I pulled my notebook and pen from my backpack purse. "Okay, tell me what you've got and then I'll decide whether or not it's right for me."

"Of course it's right for you. It's why we've been brought together."

I tapped the pen on the bench seat. "Just tell me the story."

"My pleasure." He folded his hands in his lap. "The year was 535 and I was—"

"Uh, 535?" I interrupted.

"Yes. BC. They call it something else now, don't they? BCE?"

My shoulders fell. "Five hundred and thirty-five years before Christ. Are you kidding? No one wants to read about 535 BC. That's way too long ago. No one's going to care about a story like that."

He slid his sunglasses to the end of his nose and focused his dark eyes on me. "Are you saying that no one cares about Helen and Paris of Troy, the second greatest love story ever told? Because their story is even older."

He had a point. "Fine. Go on."

"Thank you." He slid his glasses back in place, then continued. "The year was 535 BC and I was waiting for my next orders. That's the way it worked in those days, all because of that little contract with the gods that I'd signed. One life of pure bliss in exchange for servitude. In 535 BC, the gods were very busy complicating and manipulating people's lives. It's how they amused themselves. So I didn't get much rest."

A few tiny beads of sweat appeared on his upper lip. Though the oak tree still offered its shade, the air was hot and heavy. My tank top clung to my lower back. I was about to suggest we go into Neighborhood Bagels, where the air was sure to be chilled, but he continued.

"Each year during harvest season, you couldn't walk very far without finding a festival to Bacchus, the god of wine. One of the highlights of these festivals was the crowning of the Wine Princess. Think of it as a Miss America beauty pageant but without the talent and swimsuit competition. The cities had the biggest festivals, of course, but even small towns crowned their own Wine Princesses. Anyway, I was on a hillside trying to get some sleep, having spent the night shooting arrows at a bunch of virgin priestesses that Jupiter had his eye on, when the order came in. A rumor had reached the gods' ears that one of the new Wine Princesses was more beautiful than Venus, the goddess of love." He curled his upper lip. "That didn't go over well."

I was intrigued. A beauty pageant was a great place to start a romance novel. "Go on," I said.

"Shouldn't you be taking notes?" he asked.

"Not yet. Just go on."

He swirled the lemonade cup and drank the last drops. Then he crumpled the cup and tossed it into a garbage can.

"The gods didn't like to walk among people. They could, but they preferred not to. That's why they needed servants like me. They told me to go and check out the Wine Princess, to see if she was as beautiful as people said. So I stole a horse and set out." He suddenly winced, the way he'd done in his bedroom. Then he took a long breath and his face relaxed. "Where was I?"

"You went to find the Wine Princess."

"Right. By the time I reached the town, night had fallen and most of the festivalgoers were lying around in drunken stupors. No one knew the Wine Princess's name or where she'd gone. I'd be in big trouble if I didn't find her. A few families were camping just outside the town's gates and an old man invited me to join him by the fire. He gave me some bread. I asked him if he'd enjoyed the festival and he smiled. 'My daughter was crowned today. Who would have thought that the daughter of a lowly farmer could become the Wine Princess?'

"What luck. 'I hear she's very beautiful,' I said. 'More beautiful than Venus, but I don't believe it.'

" 'It's true,' he said, and he led me to a little tent. Holding a candle, he pulled back the tent's flap and I saw her for the first time. She was asleep, the candlelight dancing across her face.

" 'What's her name?' I asked.

" 'Psyche,' the father replied."

Errol stopped talking.

I waited, but he didn't continue the story. Even though the sunglass lenses hid his eyes, I could feel his gaze on me, searching every inch of my face. "So?" I asked. "Was it true? Was she prettier than Venus?"

He kept staring.

"Errol? Was it true?"

He sat up straight, then turned away. "Yes, it was true. So there's your first chapter."

It was the perfect first chapter. It couldn't have been more perfect. The most beautiful girl in the world meets a servant boy who falls in love with her. Except . . .

"What's the catch?" I asked. "There has to be a catch. The chapter should end with a cliff-hanger so the reader will want to go on to the next chapter."

"The catch was that I was ordered to tell the gods the truth, but if I told them the truth, they would surely kill her. And if I lied to them, they would surely kill me."

"Oh, that's good," I said, scribbling as fast as I could. "Truth meant the gods would kill her, a lie meant the gods would kill you. That's very good." Excitement bubbled inside of me. Despite the heat, I felt practically effervescent.

"All the details you need are in the envelope. What the horse looked like, what the weather was like, everything I can remember about the night we met." Then he looked past me, his eyebrows raised in a silent question. I turned to see what had caught his attention.

"Hi," Tony said, walking up to the bench, a bouquet of flowers in his hand. "I heard you were in the hospital. You're okay?"

"I'm fine," I said, smiling guiltily, as if I'd been caught

doing something wrong. Which was ridiculous. Errol was giving me the story.

I got off the bench and stood next to Tony. He and Errol looked at each other. Why did this feel so awkward?

"Tony, this is Errol," I said. Did I need to say more than that? We'd kissed, for reasons I had yet to understand, but he wasn't my boyfriend. He wasn't even my friend. But Tony wasn't my boyfriend either. Or my friend. Really, I didn't know either of them very well. Yet I'd kissed one and I'd dreamed about kissing the other. "Errol lives in my building."

"Hey," Tony said with a nod.

Errol said nothing.

"These are for you," Tony told me, holding out the bouquet.

"Thanks." I took it. Little yellow roses snuggled between sprays of baby's breath and feathery ferns. No guy had ever given me flowers except for Archibald. This proved it. Tony liked me. Even though he knew I'd been watching him from my window, he liked me. Even though I'd turned him down and had fallen like a total klutz on the sidewalk, he still liked me. I wanted to cherish the moment, press it in a keepsake box, but Errol's story was racing through my head.

Errol slid his sunglasses down his nose again and he and Tony locked eyes. The tension was as thick as the heat. "Am I interrupting something?" Tony asked, leaning on his skateboard.

"As a matter of fact, you are," Errol said coldly.

"We're working on a project," I told Tony. And as much as

I wanted to walk away with him that moment, into some kind of happy ending where we'd be totally into each other, I couldn't. I had a story to write. "These flowers are really pretty," I told him. Then I led him away from the bench and spoke quietly. "I'm helping Errol with some writing stuff."

"Oh. Okay." Tony shrugged. "Well, I'm glad you're feeling better." And with that, he jumped on the dragon's back and glided off down the path.

Why was our timing always off?

"You were rude," I told Errol, who was still sitting on the bench.

"I'm just looking out for you. You need to focus," he said. "That guy would only be a distraction." Then he stood, slowly, and started to walk away, but in the opposite direction of our apartment building.

"Errol, where are you going?" I asked, following.

"I've got things to do. Go write chapter one." And that's when he doubled over. As I grabbed his arm, a few people turned and looked at us. "Errol? What's that matter? Are you sick?"

"We're all sick," he said, yanking his arm away. Then he straightened, shoved his hands into his jean pockets, and walked away.

FRIDAY

LATE last night I finished chapter one. Sitting at the key-board, I wrote the scene as Errol had told it to me, filling it in with his details—like how the horse's hooves kicked up dirt in the road, and how the fields of lavender rustled in the breeze, and how the farmer's bread had a thick crust but was soft inside. I loved the first chapter and couldn't wait to hear more of the story. This was it—my mother's next book. I still needed to figure out a title but I knew, without a doubt, that Heartstrings would love the story too. I'd need to get some sort of legal document because it would be a nightmare if Errol showed up at Heartstrings six months from now, claiming his story had been stolen. That could happen. He'd told me he didn't need money, but everyone needs money. What if his friend Velvet stopped paying the rent?

Archibald would help me. His being a legal secretary sure came in handy. And he wouldn't tell anyone that I was writing my mom's book. I could trust him with yet another secret.

After hitting the print button, I did a happy dance. *Untitled Work in Progress* by Belinda Amorous had a first chapter!

Friday was a new day. I showered and dressed, even sang out loud. Errol was upstairs reading the chapter, and when he finished reading he'd tell me how good it was, and then he'd tell me what happened next so I could write chapter two. Then chapter three, chapter four, and soon I'd have the entire story to send to Heartstrings Publishers. Now this was the way to write a romance novel—let someone else figure out the plot. At this rate I'd easily get the book done in a few weeks. Then the publisher would send us a big fat check for one hundred thousand dollars and I'd pay the hospital and have plenty left over. And Mom's medication would start working, and she'd come home and be so grateful that I'd saved the day. Finally there'd be lots of time for me to do other things like . . . dating.

Dazed with happiness, I traipsed upstairs to see Errol. "Alice," Mrs. Bobot called from her doorway. "Come on in. I've just made breakfast."

"Okay." There was time for breakfast, and my stomach was empty after I'd written most of the night. Creativity burns a ton of calories.

Realm sat in the living room watching the morning news. The weatherman was talking about Seattle reaching 104 degrees and warning people about heatstroke. "Did you read *Death Cat?*" she asked.

"No."

"Why?"

"I haven't had time." I offered no other explanation. Her dirty looks ricocheted right off my shield of happiness.

Toast, eggs, and juice were on the menu, along with Mrs. Bobot's homemade marmalade—a bit chunky but edible. She'd added something that was bright green. "I made a few jars for William," she said. A few jars turned out to be ten jars and they sat on the counter, a pretty ribbon tied around each one. "He doesn't eat enough fruit." Counting marmalade as a fruit serving was a bit of a stretch but Mrs. Bobot just wanted an excuse to cook for the reverend. "What are your plans for the day?"

I smiled innocently. "I need to sort through the mail. And do some laundry." I was wearing my last clean tank top. "Stuff like that."

"I wish you'd waited for me yesterday. I could have taken you up to see your mother. You shouldn't go through those visits alone." She rubbed my shoulder. I nodded, but didn't say anything. Then we both sat at the kitchen table. Mrs. Bobot added sugar to her coffee and stirred. "I spoke to one of the lawyers at Archibald's office. She's going to draw up a thirty-day notice to terminate the rental agreement. That should give Velvet plenty of time to find a new place for that boy. I'll even help them look." She pointed to the newspaper, where she'd already highlighted apartment rentals in the classifieds.

We couldn't kick Errol out. Not now. At least not until I'd finished writing the book. "I think we should let him stay."

"What?" Mrs. Bobot set her spoon on the table. "Why?"

"Mom really needs the rent money. Maybe we should just see how things go."

Mrs. Bobot folded her hands, her brown eyes staring into my very soul. "You and that boy aren't—"

"No. We're not." I quickly buttered my toast. "It's only about the money."

"I hope that's what it's about because that boy strikes me as very odd. What's the matter with him? Why does he need a place to get better? And why does he have so many girl-friends? I saw two of them yesterday, bringing him food. They were wearing uniforms from Velvet's beauty parlor." She fiddled with the red and white rosettes that she'd glued to the collar of her apron. "A boy with so many girlfriends can't be trusted. You need to meet a nice boy."

Realm barged into the kitchen. Her baggy sweatshirt hung to her knees. "How come you didn't read it?"

"Read what?" Mrs. Bobot asked.

"My book. Alice said she'd read it."

"Oh?" Mrs. Bobot smiled. "That's so nice of you, Alice."

"Yeah, real nice," Realm said. "So when are you going to read it?"

"I don't know. I've got a lot of . . . fan letters to answer for my mom. But I'll read it when I can." It wasn't a total lie. I'd look it over. Skim it, probably. Just not today.

A flash of anger widened Realm's eyes. Then she marched back to the living room. "Realm," Mrs. Bobot called. "Come back and eat your breakfast."

"I'm not hungry."

Mrs. Bobot looked at the plate she'd prepared for her

granddaughter. The toast, cut into triangles, the pile of eggs, the dollop of marmalade. "It's not right," she told me quietly. "She barely eats enough to keep a bird alive. I don't know what to do."

I'd read all about eating disorders in the health class at Welmer Girls Academy. I knew what anorexia looked like because I'd seen it on Oprah. And there was this one anorexic woman who walked in Cal Anderson Park every day, whose legs were like chicken bones. Realm wasn't that skinny, but even though she hid her body beneath layers of clothing, her weight loss showed in her thin neck and sunken cheeks.

"It's so nice of you to help her with her book," Mrs. Bobot said. "She needs something like that—something to help her feel better about herself." A tear sparkled at the corner of Mrs. Bobot's eye.

I felt about as slimy as a peeled grape. "No problem," I said. Okay, I'd help Realm. I'd read her book, and I'd even show her how to submit it to my mother's publisher. But not today. Today was all about chapter two.

I ate my toast. Then I ate all the scrambled eggs, even though they were speckled with burned bits and way too much pepper. "Thanks," I said, rinsing my plate in the sink.

"Don't forget that we're all going to the lake tomorrow for a picnic and a swim," Mrs. Bobot said. "That includes you, too, Realm."

"No friggin' way," Realm said from her grandfather's chair. "I don't do bathing suits." While they argued about the lake and the benefits of fresh air, I slipped out.

Muffled television sounds drifted from Errol's apartment.

If Mrs. Bobot heard me knocking on Errol's door she'd get all
worried. Fortunately I didn't have to knock because the door
opened and two girls walked out, both dressed in pink aprons
that read "Velvet's Temple of Beauty." One of them held a laundry basket filled with jeans and black hoodies. They smiled
at me, then hurried down the stairs.

*Weird*, I thought, then shrugged. It was his business, not
mine. If he wanted to have a million girlfriends, who was I to
say anything? We were working together, that was it.

Furniture and packing boxes, unarranged and unpacked,
were crammed into the corners of Errol's apartment. Nothing
had been organized. But a feast was laid out on the kitchen
counter—lattes from Tully's, bagels and cream cheese from
Neighborhood Bagels, a bowl of fruit, and a platter of cold
cuts. *Gifts from the girlfriends*, I thought.

I found Errol in the living room with the lights off and the
curtains closed. He sat on the carpet, real close to the television the way a kid sits, its eerie glow dancing across his
face. A tear-streaked sweet sixteen filled the screen as she
sobbed about life not being fair. "She wants to tattoo her boyfriend's name on her ass," Errol told me. "But her parents
won't let her." He wore the usual black hoodie, its hood nes-
tled around the back of his neck. It looked like he'd plugged
his white hair into a socket, like each strand was a filament of
light. Chapter one lay on the carpet next to him.

"Did you read it?" I asked.

"Yeah."

"Well, what do you think?"

He pressed a button on the remote. The sobbing girl disappeared and the bluish glow faded. "I'm disappointed," he said matter-of-factly, his face expressionless.

"Disappointed?" Surely I hadn't heard him correctly. Surely he was joking around. "That's not funny. I worked all night on it." I waited for him to break into a grin, then say, "Just kidding, it's great!" But he said nothing. "But I wrote exactly what you told me to write."

"Yes, that's what you did. You wrote exactly what I told you." He sighed. "I could have done that. Anyone could have done that."

"What?"

He grabbed the pages. "It's dry. It reads like a textbook. He saw this, he saw that. He moved here, he moved there. She did this, she did that. It's like a newspaper article, informative, but it's . . ." He paused, closing his eyes as he searched for the right word. His eyes popped open. "*Boring.*"

"Boring?" The word cut like a paper's edge, sharp and stinging. "BORING?" My bare toes gripped the floor. "What do you mean it's boring? It's *your* story."

"Yes, but you're supposed to make it readable," he said, waving the pages. "You're supposed to infuse it with . . . I don't know . . . with . . . *feelings.* Emotion. Stuff like that."

I folded my arms. "You didn't tell me your feelings."

"That's why I need a writer. I can tell you what Psyche looked like. I can tell you about the weather and about the landscape, but I can't put into words the way I felt. It's too difficult. I'm not good with feelings. I imbue people with love, Alice, but I have no idea how to describe love. I'm not a poet."

Something brushed against my leg. I reached down and picked up Oscar the cat, who must have followed me inside.

Errol slowly got to his feet. The hems of his jeans swished against the floor as he walked across the kitchen. With Oscar tucked in my arms, I followed. Errol set chapter one on the counter—the chapter I'd worked on all night, the chapter that had put me into such a good mood, the chapter that was NOT boring. Errol grabbed a can of Craig's Clam Juice from the refrigerator, then popped open the lid. Oscar wiggled madly as the scent escaped its aluminum prison. After pouring the juice into a bowl, Errol set the bowl on the floor. Oscar hurled himself from my arms, then settled in front of the bowl, lapping blissfully. "Cats love the stuff," Errol said.

Sunlight poured through the kitchen window and Errol's white hair practically glowed. Did he bleach it at Velvet's salon? With hair like that he'd fit in with any rock band. At that moment he didn't look sixteen. There was a sculpted strength to his chin and nose, a maturity to his features that most teenage boys have to grow into.

I laid my hand protectively over the chapter. "I don't think it's boring."

"Well, it's not exciting." He tossed the can into the sink.

Chapter one stared up at me, a bunch of neatly typed words on crisp white paper. Could Errol be right? Sure, there were sweeping descriptions of the Roman landscape, and a whole mess of details, but had I written a step-by-step rehash

of the event itself—Boy Meets Girl—without the most important part? Writers call that "inner dialogue" and without it, a
story is as flat as a slice of Wonder Bread. I grabbed a pencil.
"I can fix it. Just tell me how you felt."

"I told you, I don't know how I felt. It's too hard to describe.
How do you feel when you see someone for the first time and
you know you'll love her forever? How do you feel when you
talk to her for the first time? When she looks at you for the
first time?"

Suddenly I was standing in front of our living room window, watching Skateboard Guy glide past, my heart racing,
my legs turning to cement. Waiting, waiting, waiting for his
face to come into focus, and then there it was—like when
you've been sitting in the dark during a storm and suddenly
the power turns on and everything jumps out, brilliant and
on fire.

But then I took a deep breath. The living room window
disappeared and Errol stood directly in front of me, so close
that his breath tickled my forehead. As I tilted my neck, his
eyes locked with mine. "What does it feel like?" he asked as
he slid his hand around my waist. A tingle spread down
my legs and I forgot how to breathe. "That moment just
before . . ." His hand moved up my back and he pressed closer.

This was crazy. One second I was drooling over Tony and
the next second I was tingling over Errol. Maybe it wasn't
Errol, exactly. Maybe it was simply the way he was touching
me. Yes, that was it. It was his hand on my back and his breath
on my neck. Because there was no way I was going to have

"feelings" for this guy. He was too confusing. Too unstable. Too dangerous.

"Do you remember how it was?" he whispered. "When we were together? When you were my wife?" Just as his lips touched mine, I snapped out of it.

"Your wife?"

His arms dropped to his sides and surprise swept across his face. "I . . ." He blinked quickly, as if waking up from a dream. "I'm sorry. I keep drifting. This is difficult." He stepped away. "I don't think we should work together."

"Wait a minute." Whether or not he was delusional, I needed Errol. I needed his story and there was no way I was going to let him take it away. Not now. Not when I'd gotten my hopes up and everything was going right. "You said it was my destiny to write your story, remember?"

"Well, I lied," he said.

"What?"

"I lied." He slid his hands into his jeans pockets. "I tried to write the story but I was a total failure. So when I saw the sign in the bookstore's window that the Queen of Romance would be visiting, I thought I'd found my solution. But the next day, when I came back for the event, there was this note on the window that the queen wouldn't be there. So I thought I'd get one of the other romance writers to help me. But then I saw you and . . ." He grimaced, the pain staying longer this time. He hunched his shoulders and held his breath.

"Errol?" I asked. "Do you need your pills?"

He shook his head. "I saw you . . ." He grimaced again. "I

saw you . . ." He leaned against the counter as if his legs might suddenly give out. "I saw you and everything changed."

"Me? Why?"

As the pain passed, his face relaxed, and he sighed. Then he pulled himself to his full height and looked at me with the same serious expression he'd worn when he'd told me he was Cupid.

"Because you look just like Psyche."

I'M not that gullible. Flattery is one thing, and who doesn't appreciate a little flattery now and then, but if he expected me to believe that I looked like Psyche, a girl who was prettier than Venus, then he was under the impression that I was as delusional as he.

I fought the urge to roll my eyes because truly, I felt sorry for Errol. His physical pain looked totally overwhelming. His mental pain seemed equally real. Maybe the Cupid persona had begun as a game, a way to deal with the stress of being ill. I knew what it was like to spin so many lies that they start to take over your life. Or maybe Errol was one of those people Dr. Diesel had referred to—someone who walks a tightrope between creativity and madness.

"Errol, can we just talk about the story?"

"I'm trying to explain why I chose you," he said, smacking the counter with his palm. Startled by the sound, Oscar the cat scurried away. My entire body tensed. This was the side of him that I hated—the quick temper, the parental tone.

"It's true," he said. "Except for your hair color, you look like Psyche. Just like her. I couldn't believe it when I saw you walk into that bookstore. That's why I didn't give my notes to one of the other romance writers. I thought you were evidence that the gods hadn't abandoned me. A girl who looks just like Psyche, a girl who's the daughter of a famous romance writer—that couldn't be a coincidence. I stupidly thought that the gods had sent you to me. So I told you it was your destiny to write my story because I wanted it to be true." As he looked out the kitchen window, his tone softened. "But the gods did abandon me. People stopped believing in them, so they went away and left me behind, forgotten—to live on and on and on without them. But now it's coming to an end and I've wasted precious time with you just because you look like her. I'm a fool. I should have given my notes to one of the other writers."

The world was trying to collapse again. Everything had fallen into place but now it was spinning. Whether or not I looked like Errol's imaginary wife didn't matter. The fact that he was delusional didn't matter. The story mattered. I needed that story. "We can fix the chapter, Errol. I'll go work on it. My mom always has to revise a couple of times before she gets things right." I knew what I'd do. I'd load the chapter with emotion. I'd steal some phrases from my mom's books and weave them between the lines of dialogue. *Temptation filled my soul. Yearning ate at my brain. Titillation made me quiver.* Stuff like that.

"I don't know." He walked back to the living room and sat on the carpet. I threw myself next to him.

"Give me a second chance. I can make it work. I know I can. Tell me the next chapter." Like a kid waiting to open a birthday present, I waited for the story that would fix everything. "Come on, Errol. Tell me."

He ran a hand across his face, as if wiping away his doubts. "Okay." Then, elbows on knees, hands clasped, he continued his story.

"While Psyche slept that night, I took a long walk, trying to get her out of my head. She hadn't said a word to me, hadn't even looked into my eyes, but I couldn't stop thinking about her. The gods were waiting for my report. If I told them the truth, Venus would inflict a horrid punishment. Her jealousy was uncontrollable. Look at what she did to Medusa."

"Medusa?"

"The girl whose hair was made of snakes. Her only crime had been beauty and she was changed into a creature so hideous that she could kill with a single glance. I couldn't let them maim Psyche. I couldn't bear it. So I lied to the gods. I told them that Psyche was nothing. That those who'd claimed she was more beautiful than Venus had simply had too much to drink at the festival."

"Had you ever lied to them before?"

"Never. Oh, I'd been lazy many times. Late with my tasks, forgetful, that kind of thing. But I'd never outright lied. This is where the mythology books get it wrong. Most claim that I shot myself with my own arrow and that's why I wasn't thinking clearly. That makes me look like an idiot. Of course I didn't shoot myself with my own arrow. I lied to the gods because I was in love. Real love. Not something induced by a spell."

He paused, stretched out his long legs, then continued.

"Morning came and I didn't dare introduce myself to Psyche. I followed her and her father home, to make sure that they arrived safely, but mostly because I couldn't tear myself away. I kept my distance, watching from the hilltop behind their farm. I couldn't bring myself to speak to her. It was like I'd lost all my courage. I felt . . . I felt . . ."

"Afraid she'd reject you."

"Yes." He nodded. "Yes. I couldn't bear her rejection. But it made no sense. I'm Cupid. I wield the power of love. All I had to do was shoot her with an arrow and she'd be mine forever. But I didn't want to use magic. I'd used magic on plenty of girls, just to spend a night with them. But I wanted Psyche to love me for real. Nothing I did from the moment I looked at her sleeping face made any sense. I couldn't stop thinking about her. I closed my eyes and saw her face. I heard her voice."

"Lovesickness," I whispered.

He nodded. "I had it bad. And clam juice wouldn't cure it because it wasn't caused by my arrow. It was real love."

"Go on," I urged.

"Her father owned a small farm—some goats, a vineyard, nothing much. This is another place where the mythology books get it wrong. They will tell you that Psyche was the daughter of a king and queen and that men traveled from all over the world to gaze upon her. Because they were so busy lusting after her, Venus's temples went ignored. Sure, Psyche got a lot of attention from the village men, but Venus's temples were as busy as ever. The truth was, Venus grew jealous of a simple peasant girl just because she'd been born beautiful."

"How did Venus find out the truth?" I asked.

"It was simply a matter of time. I stayed on that hillside for days, neglecting my duties, sleeping in the grass. The gods hadn't come looking for me yet, but they would. As soon as they needed to make a queen fall in love with a bull or an artist fall in love with his sculpture, they'd find me. They'd find us. And they'd punish Psyche for her beauty and they'd punish me for my disobedience. How could we be together without the gods knowing? How could we hide from them? That was the question I asked myself over and over as I sat on that hill."

"What did you do?"

"I disguised myself."

"How?"

"Psyche couldn't know my true identity. She'd tell her sisters—women tell each other everything. The mythology books claim I visited Psyche only at night, to keep her from seeing my face. The stories say we were lovers in the dark, and just before sunrise I'd disappear. That's ridiculous because even in the dark she'd still notice my white hair. It was a lot brighter in those days. When the gods were in full power, it actually glowed." He swept his hand over his head.

It did glow. Velvet had probably given him some hair gel that absorbed light.

"No one else had hair like mine. I wore a hat whenever I wanted to blend in, and when I wanted to be noticed I let it hang loose. But I intended to make her my wife and I couldn't wear a hat every moment I was with her. So I went to the nearest market and bought some henna to color my hair. Then I knocked on her farmhouse door."

The grandfather clocked ticked while I waited for the next sentence. But Errol closed his eyes. "Errol?"

"That's the end of chapter two," he said quietly. "I wrote the description of the farm in my notes, and the old woman who showed me how to use the henna, along with all the other stuff you'll need."

"But what made you change your mind? I mean, how did you work up the courage to go talk to her?"

He opened his eyes. "It comes down to this—you either go out and get what you want or you don't."

Oscar the cat rubbed against me. I ran my hand along his back. "Don't worry," I told Errol as I took back chapter one. "I'll put lots of feelings into it. I can do it. It's a really good story."

"Chapter three is about our first date," Errol said. He struggled to his feet, then led me to the door. "I suggest you go out and get some experience."

"Huh?"

"You understand the craft of writing but you have very little experience when it comes to love. I saw the way you looked at that guy when you were standing outside the library. Your aura was on fire."

"My aura?"

"Go ask him out and be sure to take notes. Take lots of notes about how he makes you *feel*."

"But—" I frowned. "I thought you said he was a distraction."

"Look, Alice. I could imbue you with all sorts of feelings, but I'm not going to do that. Even if it meant that I might relive a few cherished moments, I still won't do it. You are not Psyche. You are a girl living in the twenty-first century who merely looks like Psyche. And even if I wanted to have a relationship with you, you are clearly attracted to this other guy. And that's what you need to feel—something that's real."

I didn't know what to say.

"We're running out of time." He gently pushed me into the hallway. Oscar the cat followed. "Remember, we've only got a few days to finish this. Go out there and get some experience." He shut the door.

"What do you mean we only have a few days?" I called.

No answer came. I glanced over at Mrs. Bobot's door, hoping she hadn't heard. Then I put my mouth close to Errol's door and said, "If I do this, if I get some experience, then you'll tell me the rest of the story?"

The door cracked open and Errol's eye stared out at me. "Yes."

ONE of the top places to avoid during a heat wave is a city bus, because those things have no air-conditioning and the windows only open an inch and everyone stinks. But I didn't have the money for a cab ride all the way to Pioneer Square. So I sank onto a black vinyl seat.

I'd called Harmony Hospital before catching the bus. The nurse told me that my mother had asked for coffee. The nurse called it amazing progress, but to me it felt like an inchworm crossing a football field.

The backs of my thighs stuck to the seat. I could blame my sweaty underarms on the heat wave, but I started sweating the moment I realized I was going to ask Tony on a date. I tried to think of it as an assignment, like a journalist being sent to cover a political rally or a traffic accident. This was research.

In *Anyone Can Write a Romance Novel*, the author stresses the importance of doing research before writing the book. A writer will get into big trouble if she describes orange trees growing in the Scottish Highlands or narwhals swimming in Puget Sound. My mother got into trouble once. In *On the Road to Love*, Babette Spangles drives her Volkswagen into a ditch. As fate would have it, a mechanic comes along, this guy named Rod Marshal. After a long, steamy description of his rippling muscles, my mother wrote that Rod Marshal opened the hood in the front of the car to check the engine. Mom got hundreds of letters about that one because the original Volkswagen engines were not in the front.

My research goal was to collect some feelings and write them down, then apply them to Errol's story—thus proving to Errol that I could make his story sing. But why was I so nervous? Tony had asked me out twice already. He'd given me yellow roses. As I looked at my reflection in the bus window, at my plain brown hair and round face, I wondered if his interest fell into the "friendship" category. He'd just moved to Seattle and didn't know many people. I'm the kind of girl a guy might want to be friends with—*just* friends.

That's when I saw it—a sandwich board with big pink letters: VELVET'S TEMPLE OF BEAUTY. Without a moment's hesitation, I reached up and grabbed the red cord. A buzzer sounded up by the driver's seat. He stopped at the next stop and I jumped off. My plan was to pull the oldest trick in the book. "A little hair spray, a little lipstick," my mother often said, "and you can turn a frog into a princess." Maybe I wasn't a frog, exactly, but I couldn't remember the last time I'd used a blow-dryer and round brush, or had my eyebrows waxed.

I turned down an alley that ran between a coffeehouse and a pharmacy. Velvet's pink neon sign beckoned from the alley's end. I opened the salon's door and stepped into an air-conditioned land of pink—pink product bottles on pink shelves, a pink couch with fuzzy pink pillows, pink curtains, pale pink walls, a checkered pink floor. A catchy hip-hop song played overhead, its rhythm echoed in the tapping feet and swinging hips of Velvet's salon girls. Dressed in pink aprons, they formed a line along the back wall, their hands flying this way and that as they worked their magic. Their clients read celebrity magazines, their feet also tapping to the music. The pink intensified when I took off my sunglasses, like seeing the world from the inside of a cotton candy machine.

"Alice." Velvet hurried up to me, her red curls bouncing. "It's so nice to see you. Girls, this is Alice. She's Errol's new girlfriend."

The salon girls turned and waved at me. They were young and beautiful, with perfectly made-up faces and trendy hair-cuts. I recognized the two who had brought Errol breakfast and had collected his laundry. "I'm not Errol's . . . ," I started to explain but Velvet took my hand and pulled me to an empty chair.

"I bet you came for your free makeover. This will be so much fun. I just love doing makeovers." She grabbed a pink smock and tied it behind my neck. Then she pushed me into the chair. A mirror spread across the entire wall. "So," she said, folding her arms. "What should we do with you?"

I had no answer. We stared at my boring reflection.

"There's some reason you want a makeover," Velvet said. "You obviously haven't had your hair cut in ages, so why today of all days?"

"There's this guy," I said quietly.

"Errol?"

"Uh, no, it's not Errol."

Velvet smiled wickedly. "That's all I need to know." She swiveled my chair around and ran her fingers through my hair. "There are a few universal truths about beauty. While some guys like short hair and some like straight and some like curly, they all like long hair. It's always been that way. So let's keep your hair long, but how about we add some nice layers to make it bouncy and fresh?"

That sounded good.

An assistant washed, conditioned, and combed my hair. A different assistant served me sparkling cider in a champagne glass with a pink paper umbrella. Then Velvet started cutting my hair, her hands flying to the beat of the music. Small strands flew here and there, falling to the floor. Hair doesn't lie. That's what we learned in eighth-grade biology. Each strand of hair records a person's life—the diet, the chemicals, emotional stress, all sorts of things. If you analyzed one of my fallen strands you'd find that it was mostly made of unhappiness. Good riddance.

Even though my hair was still wet, it already felt lighter and bouncier. The last time I'd gone to the beauty parlor was the day my mother was crowned Queen of Romance. I'd sat by her side as they prepared her for the photo shoot, a treat from her publisher. She'd been so happy that day, floating between the extremes. And I'd been so happy sitting next to her. The hairdresser had woven a ribbon in my hair to match my mother's gown. I even got to try on the tiara.

"How long have you known Errol?" Velvet asked.

"Just a few days," I said. "I know you think I'm his girlfriend, but I'm not."

"But you have a mad crush. Go on, you can admit it. We've all had a mad crush on Errol, haven't we, girls?"

"He's so gorgeous," one of the salon girls said.

"Totally gorgeous," said another.

Velvet snipped some layers around my face. Her cleavage sparkled with glitter and she'd swapped her grape perfume for vanilla. "Do you remember how ragged he was when he stumbled in here?" she asked her girls. They nodded. "He'd run out of money and had no place to go. We felt so sorry for him. We all wanted to take care of him." Then she turned on the dryer and worked my hair into impossible waves. The assistant grabbed a pink can and sprayed. A thick cloud, like nuclear fallout, filled the air above my head.

When the cloud cleared, the assistant wheeled a little cart and set it next to my chair. Velvet dipped a brush in hot wax, then applied it to my eyebrows. "The second universal beauty truth is that guys like big eyes," she said. "Women have known that forever. The bigger, the better. Eyes may be the windows to the soul but windows are boring without the right trim and curtains." I winced as little strands of hair were ripped from my brow.

"Where did Errol come from?" I asked. "I mean, why didn't he have any place to stay?"

"He's very mysterious about his past," Velvet said. "He won't tell me anything about his family. It was so weird but even though I didn't know him when he first came in here, I felt like I had to help him." She shrugged. "It was this overwhelming feeling. I don't know how to explain it."

Nor did I.

"But we're not sleeping together, so you don't have to worry. It's not like that. Now hold very still and don't speak so I can do your face." She grabbed a palette of eye shadows and lipsticks and began dabbing and brushing as if my face were a piece of canvas.

Fifteen minutes later, she stepped back. The salon girls gathered round and smiled at me. "I've worked a small miracle," she said. They nodded. I tried to turn around to look in the mirror but she held the swivel chair in place. "One more little touch before you look." She held out a tiny heart, like the one she wore at the corner of her eye. She peeled off its sticky backing.

"Velvet?" I asked, as she pressed the heart onto my upper cheek. "What's wrong with Errol? Why does he take so much medicine?"

"Because he's dying," she said.

# DYING.

She'd said that word very matter-of-factly. Then she said, "Ta-da!" and turned me around to face the mirror. I gasped. A girl with huge eyes and bouncy hair looked back at me.

"Dying?" I asked.

"Three rounds of chemo couldn't beat the cancer," Velvet said, removing my smock. "That's where all his money went. And now the doctor says there's nothing more to be done. It's just a matter of time."

*We only have a few days*, Errol had told me.

*Errol has cancer*, I thought as Velvet fluffed my hair. Time was, once again, squeezing my world with its impatient fingers. And Errol's world too. As Velvet reached for a can of hair spray, I slipped out of the chair.

"Thank you so much for the makeover," I said, hurrying toward the door.

"Wait. Don't you want to know the third universal beauty truth?" Velvet called. I stopped, mostly just to be polite.

"Okay."

"The third truth is that no guy's going to think you're beautiful if you don't believe it yourself."

"Thanks again," I said, panic rising in my throat. Only a few days.

"Good luck!" she called as I stepped back into the humid July air.

Soon after, I stood on the cobblestones of Pioneer Square, staring across the street at the red door with the golden pillars. My pits were sweaty again. Errol wanted me to do this. This was for him. For his story. For *our* story. This was research. So why was my heart pounding? Why was I feeling like a total chicken?

An OPEN sign beckoned from the window of Lee's Antiquities. I imagined myself turning the knob, opening the door, and stepping inside. Tony would be sitting at the counter just like before and he'd smile at me. I took a step. I took another step. It felt like a moth was trapped in my stomach.

Still summoning courage, I darted into the candy shop next door to Lee's and bought some chocolates. *Get over yourself. Tony likes you, you know that. So march right in there and ask him on a date. And if you're still too nervous, then remember that this is a mission to save your mother's career, and, as it turns out, to help a dying guy with his final request.*

Poor Errol. Three rounds of chemotherapy. No wonder he thought he was a Roman god. Chemicals had fried his brain.

Back on the sidewalk, little paper bag in hand, I lifted my foot to take that big step, when a girl darted in front of me.

She peered through Lee's picture window and waved. The red door opened right away and Tony stepped out. "Hi," he said to the girl, whose long blond hair was the color of honey.

"Hi," she said back.

Tony leaned against the doorway, his arms tan against the pale blue of his T-shirt. I stood off to the side, stiff and silent. He'd opened the door so quickly. Had he been waiting for her?

She swept her hair behind her shoulders. "You said noon, right?"

"Yeah. Noon." Those two freckles danced on his cheek as he smiled at her. Then his gaze drifted over her shoulder and he saw me, standing there. Just standing there. The girl turned around and they both looked at me. Still just standing there. "Alice?" His smile dropped. "What are you doing here?"

What was I doing there?

"Alice?" Tony repeated. "You look different."

The little moth went spastic in my stomach. "I'm doing some errands."

Tony looked from me to the blond girl, then back to me. The girl glanced at her watch. Tony shifted his weight. No one said anything. No introductions were made, and you'd think Tony would introduce us because he always seemed so polite. *Blond Girl, this is Alice. I gave her a bouquet of yellow roses. Alice, this is Blond Girl. I'm going to marry her.*

"Okay," I said. "Bye."

"Alice?" he called as I walked away, fighting the urge to break into a run.

The sun beat down on my shoulders as I waited at an

intersection. A Turkish rug seller tried to convince me to come into his shop but I ignored him. Honestly, why would a sixteen-year-old want to buy a rug? And why wouldn't Tony want to go out with that cute girl? I'd had plenty of opportunities. I could have accepted his offer to go to the movies when we first met. I could have called him after he'd given me the flowers. I could have said something to him all those times he'd skated past.

I picked the little heart off my cheek and flicked it away. Then I reached into the paper bag and grabbed a chocolate that might have once been round, or might have once been square, but was now just a wad of melted goo.

That's what happens when you wait too long.

TONY Lee was a distraction. I didn't need him.

And I didn't need to do any research. Errol was totally wrong about that. I'd read a million romance novels. I knew exactly what Heartstrings Publishers liked. I didn't need experience with first dates or second dates or even with sex to write about it. Writers constantly write about things they've never experienced. What fantasy writer has actually slain a dragon or melted a witch? Do mystery writers actually commit murder? Do most romance writers have steamy affairs with ripped, long-haired hunks? I highly doubt it.

Five blocks from home I ran into Archibald. On lunch break, he sat at a kosher delicatessen's sidewalk table, safely tucked beneath the shade of a pin-striped awning. "Alice," he called with a graceful wave. "Your haircut is adorable."

We hugged. Archibald's hugs didn't come with soft rolls of belly fat like Mrs. Bobot's hugs or with the vast six-foot-six expanse of the reverend's hugs. Archibald was lean and just a little taller than I was—the perfect size to be my dance partner, if I ever needed one.

"I don't think I've ever seen you in so much makeup."

"I got a makeover," I told him.

"Well, you look very beautiful. Have you had lunch?"

"No. But I've got some stuff to do." I looked anxiously in the direction of our building.

"Sit down and eat something and then you can go do whatever it is you're going to do. It's important to eat in hot weather."

Why hadn't Errol told me he was dying? Now I understood his pushiness and impatience. He wanted this story written before he died. He hadn't been able to do it himself and time was running out, so he'd come up with all these lies to convince me to help him—that he was Cupid, that it was my destiny, that I looked like Psyche. I plopped into the chair next to Archibald. "What kind of a document do I need if I want to write a book based on someone else's story?"

Archibald set half of his pastrami sandwich and a fat pickle slice onto a napkin, then pushed it toward me. "I'm not sure. That sounds a bit complicated. There's an attorney at our office who specializes in copyright law. Do you want me to ask him?"

"Yeah, that would be great." I took a bite of the sandwich.

"So, how are you? What's new besides your hair?"

"Well . . ." I mentally sorted through all the newness in my life. "Mom said my name. Her doctor thinks it's a really good sign that the medication is kicking in."

"That's fabulous." Archibald beamed his one-dimpled, lopsided smile. Then he went to the counter and got some salt and vinegar chips and lemonade for me. That day's Hawaiian shirt was blue with white orchids and it brought out the sea in his gentle eyes. "I'm so happy to hear about your mother."

"Well, there's some bad news too. I haven't told her yet. Actually, I just found out yesterday."

"What?"

"She's not the Queen of Romance anymore. They crowned someone else." I ripped open the bag of chips. "How can you give someone a title, then take it away?"

"It doesn't sound fair." He sipped his iced tea. "I suppose they've replaced her with someone younger. That's always the case."

"Probably. I hope no one tells her. That's the last thing she needs to hear right now."

"The secret's safe with me." Archibald patted my hand. Then he opened a packet of Splenda and dumped it into his tea. "I met the new tenant yesterday. I assume he's the same Errol that all the fuss was about." Archibald didn't ask why I'd written Errol's name all over my bathroom walls, but the question hovered like an annoying insect. "Obviously I don't know him as well as you know him, but my first impression wasn't . . . good. There were two girls coming out of his apartment late last night."

"Oh, yeah, they're his friends. They bring him food."

"Uh-huh." Archibald raised his eyebrows. "I was reading that a girl who doesn't have a father often looks for affection from the wrong sort of boy. You know you can talk to me about anything, Alice. I'll never judge you."

*What about a girl who doesn't have a father or a mother?* I wondered.

I ate a chip. The vinegar made me wince. "He's sick from cancer. That's why those girls are taking care of him. That's why he's so pale."

"Oh. I'm very sorry to hear that."

I ate as quickly as I could, the calories converting to confidence. Errol wanted more emotion. I'd fill the story with so much emotion you'd need a box of tissues to get through it. I'd fill it with so many feelings it would be like reading a thirteen-year-old's diary. It would be the best romance novel ever. I'd show that stupid International Romance Writers' Guild that Belinda Amorous was still their queen.

While I shoveled in the last bites of lunch, Archibald picked an ice cube from his glass and ran it along the back of his neck. "I've ordered a nice roast for Sunday's dinner. I'll slow cook it while you're at church."

On the third Sunday of every month, Mrs. Bobot, my mother, and I attended the eleven a.m. service at the reverend's church. On the third Sunday, Reverend Ruttles was the guest speaker and for ten minutes he returned to the pulpit to pontificate on a subject of his choosing. This weekend was the third Sunday. "Archibald, how come you never go to church with us?"

"I've never been invited."

"But Mrs. Bobot's always asking you to go." I'd wiped all

my lipstick onto the paper napkin. "You think the reverend doesn't want you there. You think he's ashamed."

Archibald fiddled with the potato chip bag. "Perhaps ashamed is too strong a word. More like embarrassed. William's worried about what the congregation will say if they find out their retired reverend has chosen a gay man for a roommate. Some people will jump to the wrong conclusion. But I can't do anything about that and I can't pretend to be someone I'm not. I lived a lie for a very long time." Archibald looked into my eyes and I knew, at that moment, that I could ask him anything and he would give me nothing less than total honesty. "When we place more value on what other people think of us than on what we think of ourselves, it's a formula for misery."

I dropped my hands to my lap. Then I looked away. "You mean like my mother. Because she doesn't want anyone to know that she's sick."

Archibald didn't reply. Instead, he looked down the sidewalk. A man approached, a panting corgi at his side. Archibald poured ice water onto his bread plate, then set it on the sidewalk for the dog, who lapped it up appreciatively. The man exchanged a nice smile with Archibald, then he and the dog continued on their way. Archibald rested his chin in his hand. "I sure miss Ben." Then he looked at his watch. "Well, I'd better get back to the office." Before leaving he pulled me into another hug.

"Never be ashamed of who you are," he whispered in my ear. "Who you *really* are."

A bunch of messages were waiting for me from Heartstrings Publishers. Two from a worried publicist who wanted to spin the whole "dethroning" incident. She needed a new photo of my mother, without the tiara, and she wanted her to make a statement congratulating the new queen. She wanted to set up some interviews so my mother could tell the world that she'd enjoyed her reign and that her next book was going to be the best ever. There was another message from a frantic marketing assistant who needed the book's title and synopsis that very moment. Another message from the editor asking how things were going and a final message from Mrs. Bobot that she'd be at a craft fair all afternoon but would expect me for dinner.

And so it came to be that I skillfully ignored the messages and sat at my mother's desk and wrote chapter two, sifting through Errol's notes. An hour passed, then two, then three, and to my astonishment, I hit print and twelve beautiful pages shot out of the printer. I smiled at the pages, proud of all those sentences, some Errol's, some mine. He'd love this chapter. It was crammed with feelings! I'd show him right away.

But a chill suddenly swept across the back of my neck. Realm was standing right behind me. Why was I always forgetting to lock the door? "It's rude to sneak up on a person," I snapped.

"Yeah, well, it's rude to make promises and not keep them." She clutched a latte cup. Its plastic lid sparkled with lip gloss. "What are you doing? Are you writing something?" She snatched a piece of paper from the printer. "Chapter two? *You're* writing a book?"

I grabbed the paper from her hand. "It's none of your business."

"What did you do to your hair?"

"Realm, I don't have time for this."

"Oh, really?" She planted herself on the living room couch. "Well, I think you'd better make time for this because I know your secret."

The last time I'd seen Realm smile, and I mean *really* smile, she'd been her former self, the rosy-cheeked Lily. But there, on the couch, smug satisfaction pulled a smile across her face, exposing perfectly straight teeth.

"I don't have a secret," I said.

"Everyone has a secret." She propped her tiny feet on the coffee table, her black leggings hanging loose around her ankles. "I know your mom isn't overseas. I know she's at a hospital up on Whidbey Island. A *mental* hospital."

I gripped the top of the desk chair. My mind raced, conjuring lies like a witch conjures spells. I lined them up in my head, preparing to fire them as needed.

"You're wondering how I found out." She took a sip from her cup. "Maybe it's not nice to snoop through other people's stuff, but who cares? You were passed out from that spider bite and everyone was running around, worried about perfect little Alice. I was bored. I found the hospital bills."

I pushed away the panic. This was an easy situation to manipulate. "She went up there for a break. So what? It's like a spa for famous people when they get tired. They've got a great masseuse and a yoga instructor."

"I don't think so," Realm said. "She's been there for months. I read the doctor's letter. You're trying to hide it from the world, aren't you? Her publisher doesn't even know. I read through all the papers on the desk. They think she's writing."

"You're wrong," I said, making sure not a muscle in my face twitched, making sure to look her right in the eye.

But Realm laid a great steaming pile of blackmail at my feet. "So here's what I'm thinking. You don't need to read *Death Cat* after all. You don't need to recommend it to your mom. All you need to do is write a letter and sign her name. You've been doing that a lot lately."

"What kind of letter?"

"Your mom's publisher has an imprint called Firestorm. They do horror novels. I want you to write a letter to Firestorm's editor in chief saying that *Death Cat* is brilliant, and then sign your mother's name." She pulled a piece of paper from her denim shirt's pocket. "Here's the editor's name and address."

"And if I don't?"

"Have you ever seen my blog, Alice? I've got quite a few followers. And I'm sure one of those tabloid papers would be very interested to know that Belinda Amorous is crazy."

I wanted to slap Realm. I wanted to walk right over to the couch and smack her hard. We locked eyes. The breath coming from my nostrils was hot against my upper lip. "So I write this letter and then what? What else will you want, Realm?"

"I want to get *Death Cat* published. That's it."

"That's it?"

"That's it."

"Fine!" I cried.

While Realm dictated from the couch, I wrote a letter on my mother's stationery. Realm made me write idiotic things like "earthmoving debut" and "raw undiscovered talent." When I finished, I dropped the letter onto her lap.

She held it like a trophy. "This is great. My dad doesn't think I can be a writer. He says I don't have the focus. He said I couldn't lose weight, either. He was going to send me to fat camp, but I showed him." She slunk away, down the hall, back to her cave. "And I'll show him again."

If *Death Cat* was the worst piece of crap ever written, and it probably was, then the Firestorm editor would simply think my mother knew nothing about the horror genre and Realm would get a polite rejection letter. So in the end, the forged letter was no big deal—except it was a matter of principle. And dignity. No one likes to be cornered by blackmail. Realm had power over me. And she'd wield it again—this I knew for sure.

It was almost dinnertime. I grabbed chapter two and raced upstairs. In Errol's kitchen, the morning's buffet had been replaced by a jug of orange juice, a loaf of French bread, and some sliced cheeses. The living room furniture had been arranged and adorned with Velvet's signature pink pillows. But neither Velvet nor her salon girls were there. I found Errol in his room, lying on his mattress. "Errol? Are you okay?" I asked.

The curtains were drawn but enough light crept in to see clearly. Even though a basket of fresh sheets and blankets sat in the corner, Errol lay on the bare mattress, a pillow wadded beneath his head. Sweat glistened on his forehead. He'd changed, just since that morning. I could see it now, the cancer—not the tumors or anything like that, but how it was eating away at him. The dark circles under his eyes. The sunken cheeks. The slow movements. He rubbed his face. "What's up?"

"Why didn't you tell me that you had cancer?"

He didn't sit up. "Why didn't you tell me your mother was at Harmony Hospital?"

"How did you . . . ? Realm!"

"She came in earlier," Errol said. "She's lonely. She just wanted someone to talk to."

I pushed the image of me strangling Realm from my mind. "I finished chapter two." I set it on his desk. "I'm ready for chapter three."

He lay still.

"Errol?" I sat at the end of the mattress. His feet reached over the edge. "We need a title. Do you have a title?"

"Why not call it *The Last Story of Cupid*?"

That didn't sound romantic. "How about *The True Love Story of Cupid and Psyche*?"

"Whatever."

"Errol?" I had a sudden urge to comfort him, to reach out and rub his leg. Or bring him a cold washcloth, or something. "I need a short summary of the story, for the publisher. Just the main plot points."

"You want the main plot points?" He pushed his pillow up against the wall and sat up with a groan. "Well, we fell in love. We got married. Venus got pissed and killed Psyche."

My mouth fell open. "What?"

"We fell in love. We got married. Venus got pissed and killed Psyche."

You could have hit me over the head with a rolling pin right then and I wouldn't have noticed. "WHAT? She killed Psyche? Psyche *dies*?"

He cocked his head and managed a weak smile. "You changed your hair."

"Okay, we've got a problem," I said, scrambling to my feet. Now that I look back at it, I shouldn't have been so surprised. When a stranger offers to give you something that you desperately need, with no strings attached, there are always strings attached. When things sound too good to be true, well, you know the rest. "My mother writes romance novels. Romance novels have happy endings."

"Why?" He reached for a bottle of water, then took a drink.

"Because it's one of the rules. In every guidebook ever written it's one of the rules. It's *the* rule."

"Why?"

"Because that's what the readers want. They want happiness. They want happily ever after."

"Why?"

"Why? Because happiness is better than misery, that's why." There had to be a way to fix this. "Okay, so I'll end at the part where Cupid and Psyche get married. That will work. That's what I'll do."

Errol took another long drink. Then he screwed the cap onto the water bottle and said, "No. That won't do. You can't end the story like that."

"What?" I could feel the ugliness in my face as it tightened with desperation. "Why?"

"Because that's not what happened." He slammed the water bottle onto the floor, angry determination flashing across his face. "The reason I'm giving you this story, Alice, the reason I want it written, is so the true story will be told. That's the purpose. That's why I'm hanging on. The myths claim that Psyche and I got married and lived together forever. But the gods killed her. Then they convinced this writer named Apuleius to write the happy ending. Psyche's death was cruel and merciless and it was my fault. My fault. And I can't die until I've made certain her story is told. There is no happy ending. That's the way it is. Life is not like a romance novel. People should stop reading romance novels and read real stories. You write it the way it happened or I'll find someone else."

He looked away and silence followed. Dreadful silence. There I was, worried about my future, when Errol didn't even have a future. "You don't have time to find someone else," I said softly.

Talking to someone about dying was bad enough, but talking to the person who was doing the dying, well, I could barely look at him. This felt so intimate and we still barely knew each other. "I'm sorry," I said.

Even though the world outside baked beneath a blistering sun, a chill clung to Errol's room. A few goose bumps sprouted on my bare arms. He was dying. Shouldn't he have family visiting, flowers, sympathy cards, something? If I were dying, I'd have Mrs. Bobot and Archibald and the reverend at my side. And maybe my mother, though maybe not. But aside from me and the salon girls, Errol seemed very much alone.

"Errol, where's your family?"

"Long dead."

"What about Velvet? Is she your girlfriend?"

"No."

"What about the other girls?"

"They help me." He sighed. "Look, I'm not proud of it, but sometimes I have to use my charms to survive. I've run out of money and I need inconvenient things like food and shelter."

"Don't you have anyone?"

"Stop looking at me like that," he snarled, pulling his hood over his head. "Stop pitying me."

"I'm not," I lied. "Errol, I want to keep writing. I like writing your story."

"You can't change the ending."

"But . . ."

"No changes. That's it. Enough." He rolled onto his side. "I'm tired, Alice. Go away."

I left Errol's room, feeling as if the world was made of walls, and no matter which way I turned, I'd smack into another one.

## SATURDAY

ON the sixth day of the heat wave the *Seattle Times* asked its readers: "Is This the End of the World?"

"If it *is* the end of the world," Mrs. Bobot said, "then what better way to spend our final day than at the lake?"

I hadn't slept much last night. Earlier that morning I'd gone upstairs but Errol had refused to tell me any more of his story. And his mood hadn't improved. Even with the fresh supply of croissants and poppy-seed muffins he'd been as grumpy as ever. "No happy ending," he'd growled.

But there was no way to get around it. My mother, the dethroned Queen of Romance, had never written a book that didn't end happily. Neither Heartstrings Publishers nor my mother's readers would accept such a dramatic change. It was risky enough that the story was set in ancient Rome, but to kill the heroine was unthinkable. Especially if the death was cruel and merciless.

"Go away," he'd told me. "Come back when you're serious about writing a real story. Not some stupid romance."

I tried to watch the *Sweet Sixteen* show, but as soon as the girl started whining, I turned it off.

So, instead of coming up with an excuse not to go to the lake, I figured I might as well go jump in it.

I settled into the backseat of Mrs. Bobot's car. Reverend Ruttles settled in the front seat. He wore a button-up white shirt, as usual, but his long legs stuck out of a pair of Bermuda shorts. Mrs. Bobot, in a batik sundress, slid into the driver's seat. "Hello, William," she said, smiling sweetly at the reverend.

"Hello, Wanda."

"I made some raisin cookies, especially for you."

"Well, you know how much I like your raisin cookies."

"Where's Archibald?" I asked.

"He's working some overtime today," Reverend Ruttles said. Then he looked over his shoulder. "How's your mother this morning?"

"The same," I said. No more words, the nurse had told me. But she'd eaten a heaping plate of waffles.

Just as Mrs. Bobot turned on the engine, Realm decided to join us. "I'm totally bored," she said as she climbed into the backseat. After smirking at me, she set her journal on the space between us and clicked her seat belt into place.

"I'm so glad you changed your mind," Mrs. Bobot said, reaching back to pat Realm's knee. "The sunshine will be good for you." No sun, not even the angry one that had parked itself over Seattle that week, could break through Realm's layers of clothing.

The reverend's seat was pushed all the way back for the comfort of his aching knees. "You have enough room?" he asked Realm.

"Yeah," she said. She pressed into the corner, staring out the window. I remembered past car trips with Lily bouncing around the backseat like a caffeinated frog, excited about whatever outing had been planned. Realm, however, was as exuberant as a sloth. I tried not to feel sorry for her as I stared at one of her fragile wrists, poking out from her long-sleeved shirt. She'd trespassed into my private life. Any chance of us ever becoming friends had been smothered by her blackmail.

"Praise the Lord," Reverend Ruttles said as the car pulled into the street. "What a glorious day."

"What's so glorious about it?" Realm asked. "It's too hot to breathe."

The drive would only take forty-five minutes in light traffic, but time moves agonizingly slowly when sitting next to someone you despise. Time's so cruel. I turned my back to Realm and rested my forehead on the window, staring into passing cars. Because Mrs. Bobot always drove ten miles below the speed limit, there were lots of passing cars.

What was Tony doing? Did he have to work on Saturday, or did he have the day off to spend with the blond girl? Maybe they were skateboarding together or sitting in an air-conditioned movie theater, kissing. Maybe Tony was like Errol. Maybe he had lots of girlfriends and he sent yellow roses to all of them. Maybe Errol was right, maybe romance novels were stupid and we should stop reading them.

"Do you think a great love story should end happily?" I asked, as if everyone had been listening to my thoughts and should therefore be on the exact same wavelength. Realm opened her mouth but I held out my palm. "I know what you're going to say. I'm asking your grandmother and the reverend."

"Well," Mrs. Bobot said, gripping the steering wheel as the cars flew past, "I'm not so sure about that. There are a lot of great love stories that don't end happily. Now that I think of it, most of the great love stories are tragic."

I leaned forward. "Like what?"

Reverend Ruttles adjusted his canvas hat. "Well, the greatest love story of all is Adam and Eve. It's the original, of course."

"That's not a love story," Realm said. She'd grabbed her journal because I'd been partially sitting on it. "That's a relationship story. There's a difference."

I hated the fact that I actually wanted to hear what Realm had to say. "What do you mean?" I asked.

"Love stories are the things your mother writes," Realm said, setting her journal on her lap. "People meet, they fall in love, they live happily ever after. A relationship story can go in any direction. Adam and Eve didn't end happily ever after. Adam let Eve take the blame for everything that's wrong with the world. What kind of sick relationship is that?"

Reverend Ruttles cleared his throat. "Well, that's not quite—"

"You know what love story is my favorite?" Mrs. Bobot interrupted. "*Gone with the Wind*. Now that's a love story."

"But that doesn't have a happy ending either," I said. "Rhett Butler leaves Scarlett O'Hara."

"She was better off without him," Realm said. "He was a jerk."

"No, he wasn't," Mrs. Bobot said. "Scarlett was too blind to see that Rhett was perfect for her."

"Bella and Edward have a happy ending," I said.

The reverend frowned. "I'm not familiar with that story."

"Bella ends up an undead, married teenage mom. If that sounds like a happy ending to you then you've got issues," Realm said.

"I think it's the tragic love stories that stand the test of time. Like Romeo and Juliet, King Arthur and Guinevere, Cathy and Heathcliff," Mrs. Bobot said.

"Helen and Paris, Antony and Cleopatra, Samson and Delilah," the reverend added.

"Why would anyone want a happy ending? Happy endings ruin stories," Realm said. "You don't have to be a rocket scientist to figure that out."

Why do we always use rocket science as the model of genius? We should say, "You don't have to be a romance writer to figure that out."

Maybe tragic love stories did stand the test of time, but the new Queen of Romance wouldn't mess around with the perfect, bestselling formula. And my mother couldn't afford to, either.

"I know. What about *Beauty and the Beast*? That ends happily," Mrs. Bobot said. "She kisses him and he turns into a prince. And everything in the castle that was dark and ugly becomes beautiful again."

"Maybe Errol will be Alice's beast," Realm said, making a kissing sound at me.

"I don't like that kind of talk," Mrs. Bobot said. "Alice has assured me that she is not dating this Errol boy. Isn't that right, Alice?"

"We're not dating."

"Then why'd you say you'd kill me if I got near him?" Realm asked, another smirk tugging at the corners of her mouth.

"I never said that."

"You did! The other morning. You told me to stay away from him."

"Shut. Up," I said between clenched teeth.

"Girls!" Mrs. Bobot smacked her palm on the steering wheel. "Please don't argue. I can't focus on my driving."

Reverend Ruttles looked over his shoulder. "Is there any particular reason you're asking about love stories, Alice?"

"Alice is writing a book," Realm said. "I saw it in the printer."

"You're writing a book?" Mrs. Bobot's smiling face filled the rearview mirror. "Oh, Alice, that's a wonderful idea. You could become a writer just like your mother. I'm sure you've inherited her talent." But before we could launch into a conversation about what I may or may not have inherited from my mother, we arrived at the lake.

Mrs. Bobot had crammed an absurd amount of stuff into

the trunk—blankets and towels, folding chairs, a beach ball, air mattresses, hats, umbrellas, five types of sunblock, magazines, and a picnic hamper. We had to make two trips just to get it all to the picnic site.

Willow trees graced the park, creating huge pools of shade. Truckloads of families had invaded with their smoky barbecues, noisy kids, and goofy golden retrievers. Most of the kids charged along the half-moon, white-sand beach, or played in the roped-off swimming area. Beach balls flew here and there and shouts of "Marco Polo" resounded in an endless loop. The park's lifeguard blew his whistle whenever the roughhousing got out of hand.

Reverend Ruttles and Mrs. Bobot chose a quiet spot at the edge of the picnic area, not far from the parking lot but far from the crowd. There they set up the lounge chairs. After blowing up two air mattresses, Reverend Ruttles lay on one of the chairs, placed his canvas hat over his face, and fell asleep. Mrs. Bobot pulled out a knitting project. Realm tucked herself under an umbrella. "Those kids are gonna make me insane with the Marco Polo." She slipped on her headphones and started writing in her journal.

I took off my shorts and shirt. My bathing suit still fit even though I'd bought it over a year ago. Looked like my boobs weren't going to get any bigger. The gene pool had decided not to supply me with my mother's curves.

I grabbed an orange air mattress and walked to the lake's edge. Tall groves of cattails crowded the shallows looking like hot dogs on spears. First my big toe, then my entire foot, then both feet made their acquaintance with the chilly water. As I waded to my knees, a tennis ball landed nearby and a golden retriever plunged in after it. With a deep breath, I lay on the mattress, then took shallow breaths as my belly got used to the water temperature.

"Don't go too far," Mrs. Bobot called. "I want to be able to see you." She was treating me like a kid, but she was doing her duty. "Don't go too far" is one of the required statements of parenthood.

Slowly, I paddled away from the roped-off beach, to a quieter world. Soon I reached a carpet of round, shiny leaves. A few of the water lilies had blossomed and looked like white teacups sitting on green saucers. I rested my chin on my hands as the mattress floated along the carpet's perimeter. Black-and-white dragonflies flitted past, occasionally landing on my arms. The red dragonflies were less abundant, but equally beautiful.

Back on shore, Reverend Ruttles still slept beneath his hat and Mrs. Bobot still sat beside Realm, knitting and talking nonstop even though Realm couldn't hear a word with her headphones on.

There's nothing like a good float to ease away the worries—trusting the water to bear the weight of whatever troubles you carry. There, in the dappled shade, I felt normal, like a regular girl on a regular air mattress. There was nothing more to my life than a gentle tickling of water on my toes, a red dragonfly's dance, and the song of a bullfrog. Where did my body end and where did the water begin?

Reaching out, I ran my finger over a leaf, accidentally disturbing a small frog. Had it been watching me, wondering why I chose to be alone rather than playing on the beach with the others? Pumping its legs gracefully, the frog swam, then disappeared beneath another lily. Must be a quiet life down there.

I closed my eyes. Time drifted by. The distant cry of "Marco Polo" kept me grounded in that place, but my thoughts drifted elsewhere. Down a cobblestoned street and to a red door. To a boy with two freckles on his cheek who had carried my books. A boy who made me feel jittery every time I saw him. Every time I thought about him. A boy I'd missed the chance to get to know. It would never be a love story. It would never even be a relationship story. The story had ended before it had even begun.

"Hello."

The orange plastic squeaked as I turned my head. Tony Lee floated next to me on a blue air mattress.

I nearly lost my balance as I pushed myself up onto my elbows. "What are you doing here?" The question came out more accusatory than a matter of curiosity.

He also pushed up onto his elbows. "I stopped by your building. I wanted to explain about yesterday, at my dad's store. You didn't answer your buzzer so I buzzed the other units. A girl with red hair came out of the building and told me that you'd come here, to the lake."

I was scowling at him. I didn't mean to scowl but I was so surprised.

"Look, maybe I should go," Tony said.

"No. Don't go." Our air mattresses collided.

"You sure?"

"Yeah. I'm sure." I wished I had a cuter bathing suit. "Thanks again for the flowers. That was really nice of you."

"You're welcome." He dipped his hand in the water, then ran it through his hair, pushing it off his forehead. "So, how are you?"

"I'm fine." I sat up and wrapped my legs around the mattress. It formed a *V* around my body.

He sat on his mattress. Water droplets rolled down his smooth chest. The edge of his checkered swim trunks floated above his thigh. I picked a stray lily pad off my leg.

"So," we both said.

"You first," Tony said.

What did I know about this guy? He liked to skateboard. He worked for his dad to save money for college. He liked to read. He used to like me.

"You're not wearing your glasses."

"I left them in my bag. I don't usually swim with them."

Now I knew something else. But I wanted to know more. A million questions lined up in my head, but then I'd sound as if I were interviewing him for the position of boyfriend. But there was one nagging question.

"That girl I saw you with . . . Is she your girlfriend?"

"I knew that's what you thought. That's what I wanted to tell you." He shook his head. "She's not my girlfriend. She's a student at the university where my dad teaches. She came to interview him for a school project. I couldn't remember her name. That's why I didn't introduce you."

I pressed my teeth together so I wouldn't grin like an idiot.

Then we looked into each other's eyes and I knew, in that long moment, that Tony Lee had come to the lake because he wanted to see me. And I knew that if he tried to kiss me, I'd let him.

I wanted Tony to kiss me, but not the way I'd wanted Errol to kiss me. That thing with Errol had made no sense. Girls like bad boys, I know that. The whole dark and dangerous thing is tempting, and Errol definitely had that going on. But I didn't long for dark and dangerous. I longed for someone I felt safe with, someone I could trust and be myself with. If Tony and I got to know each other better, I'd be able to tell him the truth. And it would be okay. That's what I wanted.

I pushed all the negative energy away. The worries about Mom. The worries about Errol. I cleared my head and lived in the moment as Tony and I floated, suspended by water and by one incredible, amazing stare.

Then he took a big breath and rolled off his mattress. His checkered shorts faded into the murky depths. I looked from side to side, waiting for streaks of skin to dart past. Was he going to grab my feet and make me scream? He shot up a moment later and shook his hair from his eyes. The spray fell across my shoulders. "Can you swim?" he asked, playfully tugging on my mattress.

"Yes, but don't you dare."

With a devilish smile, he disappeared again. And then I was in the lake, my mattress overturned. We treaded water, slowly moving around one another. I wanted to slide close to him and wrap my arms around his shoulders. But then he was right in front of me, his arms around my waist, and he kissed me. I closed my eyes as his lips pressed a bit harder. The kiss tasted like lake water and sunblock, which under normal circumstances is a really terrible taste but under those circumstances, well, it was great.

It's really hard to kiss while treading water so it was a

short kiss, no longer than the time it takes to fill a bowl with cereal or to forge a name in a book. But it was a moment I would relive a million times. A moment I could drag out forever and never get tired of.

I climbed back onto the air mattress, my skin pink and goose bumpy. He climbed onto his. Lying on our stomachs, we paddled from the shady lily jungle back into the sunshine to warm up. He held the edge of my mattress, keeping us so close that I could see water droplets on his nose and eyelashes. My entire body buzzed, liquid happiness running through my veins. I felt good. Real good.

"Do you miss Los Angeles?"

"Kind of. It's hard leaving all your friends, you know?"

I knew. "Does your mom work at the antiquities store?"

"Mom died when I was two. It's just been me and Dad for as long as I can remember. How about you?"

"It's just been me and Mom for as long as I can remember."

"What happened to your dad?"

I didn't tell him that my mother couldn't remember the man's name. That he'd been some hookup one night while she'd been spinning out of control. "I never knew him."

He nodded understandingly. "It's weird not knowing a parent. I've got a photo of my mom, but I don't remember her. She was a neurologist. Dad says that's why I get good grades in science, because I inherited her brain. And why I suck at drawing." He smiled. "What about you? Are you like your mom?"

I smiled weakly. "I'm not sure."

Then my mood suddenly soured as a red air mattress approached. The theme song from *Jaws* played in my head. Realm had rolled up her leggings and had stripped down to a T-shirt. Streaks of sunblock ran across her skinny white arms.

"Hey," she said, bumping into Tony's mattress. "You're the guy on the skateboard."

"I'm Tony."

"I'm Realm." She adjusted her salad plate–sized sunglasses. "My grandma's driving me insane. She keeps trying to get me to eat her crappy lunch."

"You live in the same building as Alice, right? You two go to school together?"

"Alice doesn't go to school," Realm said before I could stop her. "She does Internet school."

Tony brushed a fly off his arm. "I thought you said you went to Roosevelt?"

Once again, I wanted to strangle Realm. But it wasn't her fault that I'd lied to Tony—a stupid, unnecessary lie. He looked at me, waiting for an explanation. "Oh, you thought that I'd gone to Roosevelt? Sorry about that. Simple mistake. I'd *like* to go there."

"Internet school sounds boring," Tony said. Then he pointed at the water. "Hey, I just saw a fish. Maybe we can catch it for your cat."

"Alice doesn't have a cat," Realm said, in her Boy Scout–like determination to expose me for what I truly was.

"Didn't you say you have a cat?" He raised an eyebrow. "Didn't you buy fish for it, from the market?"

"Well . . ."

Nearby, a kid started crying as his beach ball floated beyond the swimming ropes. "Be right back," Tony said. He rolled off his mattress and swam toward the ball.

"I saw you kissing him. Errol's going to get jealous," Realm said.

"Errol is not my boyfriend. How many times do I have to tell you that?"

"Well, excuse me. I'm not the one who wrote his name all over my bathroom walls."

With a groan, I started paddling away. Realm followed. "Stop following me," I snarled, paddling faster. But even with those bony arms she managed to catch up and grab the edge of my mattress.

"I think we should write some more letters," she said. "Why waste time with just one publisher? I'll have a much better chance if your mom sends a letter of recommendation to all the publishing houses."

"All the houses?" I sat up and yanked my mattress from Realm's hand. "I'm *not* writing any more letters."

"Oh yes you are."

"Oh no I'm not. That wasn't the deal. The deal was one letter. One fake letter from my mother so you'd leave us alone."

"Don't forget my blog."

Cornered again. I hate being cornered! "My mom wants to

keep her life private. Don't you get that? She has a right to keep it private. It's *her* life. What did she ever do to you? She's always been nice to you."

Realm fell silent and looked away. Over on the beach, Tony waded into the shallows and handed the ball to the kid. For a moment, Realm's expression softened. "How long is she going to be in there, anyway?"

"I don't know. She's sick. She's very, very sick." I waited, angry tears threatening an escape. Maybe, just maybe, Realm would remember all those times my mother had included her in our adventures to the zoo, or to the aquarium or the Seattle Center. Maybe she'd stop this cruel game.

But when Realm looked up, determination filled her eyes. "I'm sorry your mom's sick, but this is my chance to prove my father wrong. It's just a few letters. What's the big deal?"

I could write a hundred letters and Realm would still know the truth. That was the big deal. She'd know what Mrs. Bobot and Archibald and the reverend and I had painstakingly kept hidden. But she was just the beginning, because eventually others would find out. A patient at Harmony Hospital would tell a friend, who'd tell another friend. A staff member would sell a photo to a tabloid. It was only a matter of time.

My chest tightened. The sun beat upon my face. The willow trees that hugged the lake turned blurry. Every sound, from bullfrog to my labored breathing, got real loud. I took a deep breath, slid off the mattress, and sank into the lake. It was quiet under there. Ribbons of sunlight filtered through the murky water like party decorations. At first my legs felt heavy, as if tangled in underwater vines—like one of those dreams where you can't escape your pursuer. If I opened my mouth and took a breath, everything would stop.

It would be so easy. Just to stop.

It would also be beyond stupid.

I couldn't fix all my mother's problems. I'd tried, but I couldn't. And we couldn't keep this secret any longer. Archibald was right, you should never be ashamed of who you are. My mother hadn't chosen her illness, and we'd never be entirely free of it, but we could choose to be free of the lies.

I reached out and took a long stroke, then another. The rhythmic movement worked its magic. I swam until I could no longer hold my breath. A purple bikini came into view, then a pair of white swim trunks. Setting my feet in the mud, I stuck my head out of the water.

"Marco Polo! Marco Polo!" a red-haired boy in goggles cried.

I'd reached the kiddie beach. Tony was swimming toward me, having returned the ball to its owner. "Tony, I need to get back to the apartment. Will you drive me?"

"Sure," he said. "What's up?" He followed me out of the water.

As he stood in the sand, his checkered shorts clinging to his legs, water dripping from his black hair, he was adorable, and possibly my future boyfriend if we could ever spend more than a few minutes together. But I'd started something and I was going to finish it. Truth was, I'd loved writing Errol's story. During those hours, I'd felt more peaceful than I'd ever felt. And I could be good at it. I knew that in my heart. I was meant to do it. I'd just needed some guidance to get started. Now I'd found the confidence to keep going.

So if Heartstrings Publishers didn't want to publish *The True Love Story of Cupid and Psyche* with its unhappy ending, well, someone else would!

"You know those books I checked out at the library? I told you I was doing some research and the truth is, I'm writing a novel. Errol and I are writing a novel together and it's really important that I get home. We only have a few days to finish it."

"Okay," he said with a slight shrug. "I'll take you home."

"Thanks. I need to get my stuff."

As Realm dragged our three air mattresses from the lake, Tony and I started toward the picnic table where Mrs. Bobot had laid a homemade tablecloth and platters of food. And that's when I noticed Errol up the hill, at the edge of the parking lot, his face hidden behind the shadows of his hood.

"ALICE!" he yelled.

"Who's that yelling?" Tony asked. "I can't see that far without my glasses."

"It's Errol," I said. "I'll go see what he wants." I hurried up the hill, barefoot, stepping around a pile of golden retriever poop. "Hey," I said when I reached him. His eyes were bloodshot. "How'd you get here?"

"The bus." Errol's gaze traveled down my body, then flew to the top of my head. "You've changed," he said, his voice raspy, his expression serious. "Your aura has changed."

"What are you talking about?" Why was he staring at the top of my head? I brushed my hand over it, in case a dragonfly or piece of lily pad was stuck to it. "I was swimming," I said, suddenly wishing I'd put on my shorts or had wrapped a towel around my waist.

"That's not what I'm talking about." He kept staring at my head, so I brushed it again. Nothing was there. Then he looked down the hill at Tony, who was next to the picnic table, gathering his things. "He's the reason you've changed."

Why did he sound so sad?

"Errol, you're right. I have changed. I don't care about happy endings. I want to write the real ending. Let's go back to the apartment and we can work on the next chapter."

He kept staring at Tony.

"Errol? Didn't you hear me? I don't care about the ending. It doesn't need to be happy. We can write it the way you want."

He swung around. "What do you mean you don't care? She died. They killed her." His hands clenched into fists. "You should care. You must care."

"I do care." I stepped back.

He grabbed my arm, his eyes wild. "Why don't you believe me? If you believed me, then you'd care about the ending. I'm Cupid. Why don't you believe that? I'm Cupid and you're—"

"I'm Alice," I said, yanking my arm free.

"Hey, Alice," Tony called from the picnic table. He'd pulled on a T-shirt and his bag was slung over his shoulder. He pointed to my beach bag. "This one?"

"Yes," I yelled. Then I turned back to Errol. "Let's go home and we'll start chapter three. I'm ready."

"You're not ready," Errol said in an angry whisper. "You don't believe me. I want you to believe me so you'll believe in the story. So you'll care about what happened to the only girl I've ever loved." Then his hands began to move, as if sculpting something out of air. His face contorted like a madman conjuring a mad spell. Even though I knew he was sick, knew his brain was messed up by pain and chemicals, I was fascinated—like a driver slowing to look at a car wreck. Errol extended his left arm straight out, held it rigid. Then he pulled his right hand to his right shoulder. He closed one eye, as if taking aim.

Foreboding washed over me, just as it had outside the library the moment before I'd landed flat on my back. And though I didn't believe for one moment that Errol owned an invisible bow and arrow, I did believe that something was going to happen.

"Stop it, Errol. I hate this game. Just stop it."

"This will make you believe." The fingers on his right hand sprung open. I gasped as the memory surged through me—the impact to my chest, the tingling in my arms and legs, the brightness of the sky as I lay on the sidewalk. But the memory shattered, like a sheet of ice, and I was still standing on the hill at the edge of the parking lot. Nothing had happened. No impact. No tingling. Nothing.

Of course nothing had happened. This was a day at the lake, in the middle of the worst heat wave to ever hit the Seattle area. Of course nothing had happened. He wasn't Cupid. This wasn't a Disney movie.

"Do you believe me now?" A smile spread slowly across Errol's pale face—a satisfied smile, a conqueror's smile, a "you don't have a clue" smile. But he wasn't smiling at me.

I slowly turned around.

Tony Lee lay sprawled next to the picnic table like a rag doll.

**NO** *way, no way, no way.* There is no such thing as an invisible arrow. And no one, even if that no one has delusions of grandeur and believes that he's Cupid, can conjure an invisible arrow from plain old parking lot air, or from any air for that matter, then load it into an invisible bow and shoot it. No one.

Tony squinted against the sunlight. "What happened?"

I crouched next to him, my shadow falling across his dazed expression. Realm, Mrs. Bobot, and the reverend had also rushed to his side.

"Did he trip?" Mrs. Bobot asked.

"I think he fainted," the reverend said. "He needs water. Realm, get some water."

"Why do I have to get the water?"

The sun beat upon my shoulders and back as I tried to conjure my own magic—an explanation. Maybe he'd tripped. Maybe he'd fainted.

Or maybe he'd been hit by an invisible arrow.

*No way, no way, no way.* I grabbed his shoulder. "Do you think something hit you? Did you feel something hit you?"

"Yeah. In the chest. Something hit me in the chest." He sat up, then scratched his chest. My heartbeat rose into my throat. "What are you doing?" he asked as I grabbed the front of his T-shirt, my fingers flying across the fabric. There it was, a tiny hole.

"Alice, what are you doing?" Mrs. Bobot cried as I pulled Tony's shirt up to his face, exposing his smooth chest. He didn't say anything as I leaned real close, almost touching his nipple with my nose.

"Here's the water," Realm said. "Jeez, what is Alice doing?"

Oh God, there it was. A welt. A WELT! Right over the place where his heart beat.

I let go of the shirt and scrambled to my feet. Then I spun around and glared at Errol, who still stood at the top of the hill. "Errol!" I yelled, running toward him. "What did you do? Errol! I want the truth!"

But halfway up the hill, Tony ran up behind me and grabbed my arm. His irises swept back and forth, taking in every inch of my face. His hair stood up like it was full of static. *"Alice,"* he said, releasing the word as if he had held it inside for an eternity. *"Alice,"* he repeated, taking my hand.

Instead of holding my hand in a normal way, he caressed it, running his fingers along my fingers, squeezing and massaging as if my hand were a lump of clay and he had an art project due. I pulled away. "What are you doing?"

For a moment he furrowed his brow, puzzled by his own behavior. "I don't know." Then a glassy sheen fell over his eyes and he grabbed my hand again. "I've never felt like this before. I don't know why but it's like I can't see anything but you." He put my hand to his mouth and kissed it—not a "how do you do" kiss or a "thank you for inviting me to your picnic" kiss. He held his lips against the back of my hand, and held them there, and held them there. Then he closed his eyes and sighed. And still, he held his lips to my hand. A blush came full on, burning from the tips of my ears to my toes.

"Uh, maybe you should go sit down," I said, slipping from his sweaty grip.

"*Alice*," he said, reaching his hand under his T-shirt to scratch the welt. "I know this sounds crazy but I think I'm in love with you."

"What?"

"Yes, I'm definitely in love with you. I can't live without you. Do you love me? Tell me you love me," he pleaded. Not an ounce of joy rang in his words. Instead, they were frantic and pained. When one declares love for another, shouldn't there be an ounce of joy? A teaspoon of joy? A sliver of joy? "I want you to love me. Tell me you love me."

Desperation clung to Tony's declarations of love. I remembered feeling that way, when I'd needed to see Errol. When I'd felt as if I'd shrivel up and die if I didn't get close to him.

I shook my head. "You don't know what you're saying."

"I know exactly what I'm saying." He grabbed me around

the waist and pressed his lips to my ears. *"Alice,"* he whispered. "We were meant to be together. We must be together."

The whisper sent a shiver down my arms. I might have enjoyed the attention except that he was seriously freaking me out. This transformation wasn't natural. He'd been instantly changed. He took my hand and pressed it against his chest. "Can you feel my heart beating, Alice? It's beating only for you. I love you. I love you with all my heart."

When he paused to scratch his chest again, I twisted out of his grip. He grimaced, fighting against the onslaught of emotion, the way one fights against nausea as it builds. Tony Lee was sick—lovesick—and he needed help. "Errol!" I hollered.

A whizzing sound broke through my panic. I reached out my left hand and caught the can as it soared overhead. *Craig's Clam Juice. Processed from 100 percent organic clams and organic brine. Sixteen ounces of mouthwatering goodness. Best served over ice.*

"Alice." Tony clutched my arm. "Don't leave me. Please don't leave me. I don't know why this is happening but I can't breathe without you. Tell me you love me or I'll die." He squeezed my arm harder. I popped open the clam juice.

"Drink this," I said. "Don't ask me why. Just do it."

I held the can to his lips. His gaze never leaving my face, he took a drink. He swallowed. His face relaxed. He took a long, deep breath. Then he looked around, as disoriented as a sleepwalker waking in the middle of an outing.

"How do you feel?"

He didn't need to answer because I knew exactly how

he felt. He would remember every embarrassing thing he'd said and done, just as I remembered. "I don't know why I said those things," he muttered.

"Don't worry about it." Perhaps if I started laughing I could pretend that it had all been a funny joke. And then he could pretend it had been a joke. I tried to force a laugh but it came out more like a grunt—because when it came right down to it, there wasn't anything funny about the situation. I couldn't close my eyes and make this go away. "I know you didn't mean any of those things," I said gently.

"I feel so confused." He ran a hand over his hair, which was once again static free.

Errol didn't offer an apology or explanation. He leaned against a willow tree.

A long, agonizing silence swirled around Tony and me. What does someone say after confessing passionate, all-consuming love? A bright blush broke out on Tony's cheeks and traveled down his neck. He'd stopped scratching his chest, a very good sign—until his upper lip began to swell.

"Uh, Tony?" I pointed. "Your upper lip is swelling."

"Wha?" He touched it. "Wha is ma whip swebbing?" Then a welt broke out on his neck. Another on his cheek. He pointed to the can in my hand and his eyes widened with fear. "Wha dib I dwink?"

"Craig's Clam Juice," I replied. "It's organic." As if that mattered in the least. "Oh my God, Tony, you're turning purple."

And that wasn't the worst of it. The swelling had branched

out to his cheeks and ears. Right before my eyes, he was turning into some sort of Asian version of the Elephant Man.
"Tony?"

And then I remembered what Errol had asked, right after
curing me of my own lovesickness. I grabbed Tony by the
shoulders. "You're not allergic to shellfish, are you?"

So that's how I ended up at Swedish Hospital for the second time in as many days. After an ambulance took Tony, I threw some clothes over my bathing suit and climbed into Tony's car, an old Jeep. Reverend Ruttles drove, Errol sat in the backseat. Mrs. Bobot and Realm stayed behind to clean up the picnic.

We were mostly quiet during the drive. I chewed on my lower lip until I tasted blood. To my left sat Reverend Ruttles, who said we should have faith that God would look after Tony, but in the next breath he told us we should pray, just in case. Behind me sat Errol. He said nothing. No apology. Nothing. Gripped in my hand was the deadly weapon—Craig's friggin' Clam Juice. And with every mile covered I imagined that I'd killed Tony, or worse—that I'd permanently mangled his handsome face and he'd be doomed to a life hiding in the back room at the antiquities store or working for a freak show.

Errol refused to enter the hospital. He said he'd never step foot inside one again. He said he'd wait across the street, on a bus bench. The hospital lobby was quiet and gleaming. We had to wait for an hour. I replayed the lake scene a million times in my head, trying desperately to come up with an explanation that didn't involve an invisible arrow.

Finally a nurse said we could visit. I tiptoed past a mosaic wall mural and into a white room. Tony, dressed in a cotton hospital gown, lay on an examination table. An IV hung on a metal stand, steadily dripping clear liquid into his right arm. His eyes were closed. A man sat next to the bed, Coke-bottle glasses perched on his nose, which was stuck in a *Woman's Day* magazine, the only choice in the room. A slight man with long black hair, he was an older version of Tony in his jeans and short-sleeved shirt.

I wrung my hands nervously. "Mr. Lee?" I whispered. "I'm Alice. Is Tony okay?"

Startled, Mr. Lee bolted to his feet. Tony opened his eyes and sat up.

"Hello, Mr. Lee." Reverend Ruttles hobbled into the room, his voice filling the sterile space with its rich baritone notes. "We've come to check on your son."

Tony's facial swelling had lessened somewhat, though his still over-plumped lips looked like bad plastic surgery. "Dad, this is Alice. And this is her neighbor . . ."

"Reverend William Ruttles," the reverend said, enthusiastically shaking Mr. Lee's hand. Then he handed over the car keys. "Tony's Jeep is parked in the hospital lot, section A. His beach bag and towel are on the backseat."

"Thank you very much," Mr. Lee said.

"And here are your glasses," I said to Tony, handing them over.

"You gave us all quite a scare, young man. How are you?" the reverend asked, looming over Tony's table.

"Fine." Tony scratched his neck. "They said the hives and the swelling should be gone by morning, but they want me to spend the night for observation."

"I'm so sorry," I told him. "I didn't know. I shouldn't have given you that clam juice." I'd tossed the can into one of the hospital's garbage bins on my way in.

"*You* gave him the clam juice?" Mr. Lee's eyes flashed behind the thick lenses of his glasses. But his scorn was not directed at me. "You know better than to drink clam juice. Why didn't you read the label?"

Tony hung his head. Neither of us wanted to talk about the events that had led to the drinking of the clam juice. So I did what I did best. "He choked on something from lunch. He was coughing like crazy so I grabbed the first thing I could find," I explained. "He didn't have time to read the label."

Reverend Ruttles cleared his throat. "Well, it's all worked out, hasn't it? Alice saved Tony and almost killed him at the same time. God certainly works in mysterious ways." He glanced at his watch. "And speaking of God, I've got to write my sermon for tomorrow. Alice, do you mind if we get going?"

Tony had barely looked at me. Whether it was anger, or embarrassment, or both, I didn't know, but I wanted to make things right. "I think I'll stay for a little bit, if that's okay?"

Reverend Ruttles cleared his throat. "Oh, of course if you want to stay and visit with your friend that's fine with me." He made sure I had enough money for the bus ride home, then he shook Mr. Lee's hand again. "Good-bye." As his cane echoed down the hall, his final baritone note popped like a bubble, leaving the shiny hospital room silent once again.

Mr. Lee removed his glasses and cleaned them on his shirt. I went back to chewing on my lower lip. "So, Alice, how do you know my son?" he asked stiffly.

Tony lay back on the table. "She came into the shop, Dad. She's the one who found our package on the sidewalk with the little Cupid figurine. Her mom's that famous romance writer, Belinda Amorous."

My mouth fell open. "How did you know that?"

"I figured it out. I mean, how many people have Amorous as a last name?"

The nurse came in. She asked us to leave so she could do some stuff. Mr. Lee and I stepped into the hallway. "Mr. Lee? Tony said you teach mythology at the university. Do you know very much about Cupid? I'm . . . helping my mom with some research."

This question softened Mr. Lee's expression and he relaxed his rigid posture. "Well, he's the Roman god of love. More precisely, of passionate love. The earlier Greek version is Eros. Translated, eros is the irresistible attraction between two people."

"Did you say *passionate* love?"

"Yes, as opposed to other forms of love such as romantic

or familial or platonic. In the classic stories, being struck by Cupid's arrow meant that you were suddenly overcome with desire. Uncontrollable desire."

"Suddenly overcome," I murmured. "Mr. Lee? What does Cupid look like? I mean, on all the valentine cards he's a fat baby."

Mr. Lee returned his glasses to his face. "That has much to do with his antics. He was playful and endlessly mischievous, destroying marriages, ruining reputations left and right. He ignored social restraint and often lacked empathy for his victims, that's why artists began to depict him as a child. Is Cupid a character in your mother's story?"

"Yes."

"Then I'm sure your mother has familiarized herself with the story of his true love, Psyche."

"What happens in that story?" I asked eagerly.

"Well, Psyche was a princess and so beautiful that men traveled from all over the world to gaze upon her and lay offerings at her feet. Venus, the goddess of love, became overwrought with jealousy because no one was paying any attention to her or to her temples. She was not about to share the spotlight with a mere mortal. So she ordered Cupid to shoot his arrow and make Psyche fall in love with the most hideous, most vile creature that lived. But instead of shooting Psyche, Cupid accidentally shot himself. Consumed with passion, Cupid then shot Psyche so she'd love him in return, then he moved her to a secret palace so he could marry her without Venus knowing." Mr. Lee folded his hands behind his back.

"He visited her each night but only in darkness because Cupid knew that if Psyche recognized him, it would put them in great danger. He forbade her to light any lamps. But when Psyche became pregnant, she began to worry that maybe her husband, whose face she had never seen, might be some hideous monster and thus her child would also be a monster. So, encouraged by her sisters, she waited for Cupid to fall asleep, then held a lamp over his face and gazed upon his beauty. But a drop of oil fell from the lamp and woke him. He was furious at her disobedience and left her."

Errol hadn't gotten to that part of the story yet. I leaned closer as Mr. Lee continued.

"Psyche was heartbroken and she set out to find Cupid. She took this very long journey and finally ended up at Venus's temple where she begged the goddess to tell her where Cupid was hiding. Venus agreed, but only if Psyche could complete three tasks. Psyche failed the last task so Venus cursed her and put her into an eternal slumber."

The nurse came out into the hallway. "His vital signs are fine. But he's hungry. It'll take a while to get a meal up here. We're short of staff today. There's a cafeteria downstairs if you'd like to get something right away."

"I'll go get him something," Mr. Lee said.

He was about to walk away when I asked, "Mr. Lee? Is that how it ends?"

"No. Cupid came to the rescue. He woke Psyche from her slumber and they lived together forever. Happily ever after." He adjusted his glasses, then pressed the elevator button.

But that was the wrong version, according to Errol.

"Your dad probably hates me," I told Tony when I'd gone back into his room. "He should. I almost killed you."

Tony was sitting up again. He rubbed his reddened eyes. "He doesn't hate you. This just freaked him out. I haven't had an allergic reaction since I was eight. If that lifeguard hadn't had an EpiPen in his kit . . ."

I sank into the plastic chair. "I'm so sorry." I was, with all my heart. But I was also confused. There I sat, after nearly killing a guy I'd met just a few days before. A nice guy. A guy who'd done nothing wrong but step into Errol's and my craziness.

"Do you believe me now?" Errol had asked. He'd knocked both me and Tony off our feet and had turned us into lovesick idiots. How could I deny that?

Tony scratched his neck and turned his eyes to the floor. "I don't know why I said all those things. It was like I couldn't stop talking."

"You don't have to explain," I told him.

"But I want to explain. That's never happened to me. I don't mean the falling part. I fall all the time. I'm a skateboarder."

"Tony, don't worry."

He groaned. "You must think I'm a freak, saying those things. I like you, Alice, I really do. And I liked kissing you."

"I liked kissing you too."

He finally looked at me. And as we looked into each other's eyes, the embarrassment faded away and we held the gaze until the last drops of embarrassment evaporated. I climbed onto the examination table and sat next to him. He took my hand and despite the room's coldness, I felt warm all over. "I'm so glad you're going to be okay," I said, laying my head on his shoulder.

"I can't believe you gave me clam juice," he said with a little laugh. "Of all the things to give me."

"I know. Weird, huh?"

"Where'd you get it?"

My thoughts flew back to Errol. I slid off the bed and walked over to the window. A few floors down, a glass catwalk connected one building with another, and across the street Errol still sat on the bus bench. He pushed his hood from his head and looked up at me, his white hair radiant with sunlight.

*Do you believe me now?*

My focus moved to my own reflection, staring back from the hospital window. My hair hadn't been combed since the swim in the lake and I still had a patch of sunblock on my nose. But just above my head was an orange glow. I moved. The glow moved with me. I ran my hand through it.

*You've changed, Alice. I can see that you've changed.*

And I could see it too.

I almost knocked Mr. Lee off his feet as I ran down the hall.

"**WHAT** is this?" I asked, pointing to the top of my head.

Errol's upper lip glistened with sweat. An awning covered the bus bench but the shade added little relief in the heat. "What's what?"

"This glow. I know you can see it. You were looking at it when we were at the lake."

"Sure, I can see it. But I didn't know you could."

Frustrated tears filled my eyes. It was official. Errol and I shared the same hallucinations. We were destined to while away the years in a mental hospital, comrades in crazy. Mornings would be spent playing bingo with some guy who wore underpants on his head or with a serial killer wrapped in a straitjacket. Errol and I would take turns telling stories to the other patients during utensil-free dinners—stories of how he'd shot me with an invisible arrow and how I glowed with a light no one else could see.

I stood at the edge of the sidewalk in a patch that had once been grass, but thanks to the heat wave had turned brown and then disintegrated. I looked into the eyes of the guy who'd been in my life since the book signing at Elliott Bay Books, only five days ago. Like Tony's postallergic eyes, Errol's eyes were laced with red lines. But there was nothing puffy or swollen about his face. Quite the opposite—the hollows of his cheeks had deepened dramatically, as if he'd lost a substantial amount of weight during the drive from the lake to the hospital.

"Why am I glowing?"

"That's a very good question," he said as a bus pulled up. "Get in and I'll explain."

In a Belinda Amorous novel, one of the main characters always surrenders to the other. It might be an emotional surrender as in *Love's Desperate Days*, a physical surrender as in *Kidnapped by Love*, or an intellectual surrender as in *I'm in Love with My Professor*. So I followed Errol onto that bus. We found two seats near the back.

ONE HUNDRED AND FIVE DEGREES, a bank's sign announced. THE HOTTEST DAY EVER IN SEATTLE!

"Why didn't you tell me you could see love?" Errol asked.

I gripped the seat in front of me. "See love?"

"That glow around your head. It's love. Love is more than a feeling, it's a form of energy. It can manifest itself in an aura. You know what an aura is, don't you?"

"Not really."

"It reflects a person's emotional state. Everyone has an aura. It's the atmosphere around each person. Love is the emotion that colors an aura."

I'd seen that red haze around the moving man's head. Had that been his aura?

"Lots of people have clear auras because they shut themselves off from love. That girl in your building . . . what's her name?"

"Realm?" I asked.

"Yeah, Realm. Her aura's clear. Yours was clear too, except for the time outside the library, and today at the lake."

I'd shut myself off?

Errol pointed out the window. "Do you see that man?" A businessman stood on the corner, his shirt collar unbuttoned, his tie hanging from his pocket. "He has a contented aura, a nice blue glow. He's probably happily married, well fed. Can you see it?"

"No," I answered honestly.

Errol frowned. "That's because you don't want to see it. You're holding back."

"I'm not holding back. I don't see it."

"Let's try another one," Errol said, pointing. "See that woman over there, coming out of the store, pushing the stroller? She has a mother's aura. That's the most beautiful aura of all. It sparkles like fairy dust. Can you see it?"

"Fairy dust?"

"Can you see it?"

I shook my head, then looked away.

"Your mother may be the Queen of Romance, but you, Alice Amorous, are the Queen of Denial."

The bus stopped on our block. I hurried down the aisle

and out the door. Errol didn't call after me as I ran up the front steps. Oscar the cat meowed from one of the geranium pots. *Fairy dust*, I thought. *Sparkles like fairy dust.*

Once inside my apartment, I bolted the door. Then I grabbed the photo box from my mother's room and poured its contents onto the carpet. Searching frantically through the pile, I found a photo taken three years ago when I was thirteen and home for spring break. It was a book signing at an annual romance convention near the airport. My mother sat at a table, pen in hand. I stood next to her, a tight smile stuck on my face. I'd had to wake Mom that morning and help her get dressed. I'd been the one to make the coffee and to call the taxi. We'd arrived late but the readers hadn't cared. My mother had forced herself to focus during the signing, as she always did. She'd put on a great show as the beautiful, confident, successful writer. No one had suspected that just the night before, she'd stumbled in after disappearing for three days.

I searched the pile again until I found what I was looking for. The event was a gardening club luncheon. My mother sat with a group of ladies, each adorned with a sherbet-colored floppy hat and white gloves. Three-year-old me, in a strawberry-patterned dress, my hair in pigtails and red ribbons, sat on Mom's lap. Though many years had passed, I held a single memory from that luncheon. But it wasn't of the food I'd eaten, or the perfumes I'd smelled, or the conversations I'd heard. It was the way my mother had sparkled.

Holding the photo in both hands, I stared at my little happy

face, a plate of chocolate cake at my side, a smudge of chocolate at the corners of my mouth. My mother's smile was equally
cheery, her arm wrapped around my waist. A moment of pure
happiness caught on a piece of paper. The moment lifted off
the paper and caressed me. When I was little it always felt
that way.

And there it was, floating behind my mother's head—a
shimmering halo of fairy dust.

The apartment phone rang. The answering machine bleeped
and Mrs. Bobot's cheerful voice skipped into the bedroom.
"Alice? I called the hospital and the nurse told me that you'd
left and that your friend was doing fine. Come up as soon as
you get back. There are plenty of picnic leftovers for dinner."

"Alice." Realm's voice interrupted. "Hey, I want those letters
tomorrow. You know what I mean. I want to mail them on
Monday morning."

Then Mrs. Bobot's voice returned. "Oh, I meant to tell
you, I picked up a new pack of tarot cards on the way home
and you'll never guess what happened. Brand new, sealed and
everything. It was even a different manufacturer and guess
what? I opened them when we got back and they're all Cupids.
Cupids! Isn't that odd?" The machine beeped and stopped
recording.

I stumbled to the bathroom mirror. The same green eyes
and narrow nose and pierced ears greeted me. And there it
was, the orange glow all around my head.

What does a person do when confronted with a situation
that is either madness or magic? Madness was what I most
feared and magic was what I'd never considered.

For to consider magic would be, well, madness.

Both photos clutched in my hand, I tore up the stairs.

Errol's apartment was filled with pink flowers, bursting from vases of all shapes and sizes. A tablecloth had been laid, with candles in silver holders and china plates. A bowl of olives, another bowl of figs, and a bottle of red wine sat on the counter. His bedroom door was open, the curtains drawn. He sat hunched over his desk, writing. "Errol?" I pleaded.

He said nothing.

I inched into the room. "Errol? Would you look at this photo and tell me what you see?" I placed the photo on the edge of his desk, the one of my thirteen-year-old self and my mother at the romance convention.

Errol stopped writing. "I see you and a woman and a bunch of books."

"Do you see anything else?"

"A table, a wall, an electrical socket, a bottle of water." He started writing again.

I set a second photo on the desk, the one of my three-year-old self at the garden party. "What do you see in this photo?"

"Do you really want me to answer that question? Because you're not going to like the answer."

I swallowed. "Answer it. Tell me the truth."

"There is no truth, Alice. There is only perception."

"Please. Tell me exactly what you see."

The pen slipped from his fingers and he picked up the photo. "I see a group of women at some sort of party. They're dressed up with hats and gloves. There's a little girl and she's smiling."

"Do you see anything . . . *else*?"

"Of course I see something *else*, but you don't believe in something else, do you, Alice?"

I tried to stop my lower lip from trembling. "Please, Errol, please tell me what you see."

He slid a finger over the photo, pointing with a ragged nail. "I see a mother's aura behind this woman's head. Some of the sparkles have fallen here." He pointed to my mother's napkin. "And here." He pointed to my mother's bare arms. "But most have fallen here." He pointed to my little head. "There's an aura around the girl too. Silver and white. Very pure. There are rays jutting out from her aura."

My shoulders began to tremble.

Errol's finger moved along one of the rays. "Each of the girl's rays wraps around the woman. Like a hug."

I sank onto the bare mattress and curled my arms around my legs.

"I take it you see the exact same thing?"

I nodded.

"Well, now we're getting somewhere." Errol pushed his stool away from the desk. Then he leaned over me, his fore-arms resting on his knees. "It's a rare gift, seeing auras. I was able to do it even before I signed my contract of servitude. That's why the gods chose me." He paused, then sat up straight. "Do you know what this means, Alice?"

I had absolutely no idea what anything meant anymore.

"It means that the gods have remembered me." He rose to his feet. "You're the proof. I didn't choose you after all. *They* chose you." His voice grew loud with excitement. "I was worried that I'd made a mistake, that I'd wasted time with you, Alice. That I was only thinking about how much you looked like Psyche, and how much I loved just looking at you. But it wasn't a mistake. The gods led me to you because they knew you were the perfect person to write my story. They heard me when I prayed to them, when I told them I wanted only one thing before I died—to tell my true story. After all this time, they're letting me tell it."

"Why would they do that?"

"Maybe they feel some sense of guilt for leaving me behind. Who knows? They're totally unpredictable and most everything they do baffles me." Then he nearly blinded me with a joyful smile. "But they found you, a girl who can see auras, a girl who can see love. You are their gift to me before I die." For a moment he didn't look sick. Happiness filled his eyes and masked the dark shadows in his face.

"But Cupid can't die," I said.

"Why not?"

"Because that would be like having Santa Claus die."

"That's ridiculous. Santa Claus isn't real." He walked over to the wall and leaned against it. As his smile faded the sickness crept back, silent as a spider, taking its place beneath his eyes and in the hollows of his cheeks. "I'm useless here. I served the gods, not mortals. Mortals fall in love on their own. They screw up their marriages on their own and make fools of themselves on their own. But now my contract has expired. It's all over. I'm almost done."

Still sitting on the mattress, I hugged my knees. "Oh my God, Errol. I don't understand any of this."

"The only thing you need to understand is that you've come face-to-face with your destiny. You can see love. You're destined to be the greatest romance writer ever."

"But I don't see love. I've only seen it a few times."

"You're not going to see it if you don't want to. You have to be in the right frame of mind, which means you can't be ruled by fear." He held out the photo of three-year-old me. "Look. This little girl used to have a brilliant aura." He held out the photo of older me. "But then it disappeared. At some point she cut love out of her life."

"That's not true." Anger surged through my entire body but I didn't move. "People stopped loving me. I never stopped loving them."

"People? What people?" He pointed to my mother. "This person?"

His question invaded me. It pierced a deep, private place. No one had a right to go there. No one. It was MY place and only my place. My breathing grew shallow as I glared up at him, furious that he dared to question my feelings. His eyes widened. "Alice?"

I started to cry. A good cry, the kind where your mind just shuts off and the rhythm of it takes over, and everything gets salty and blurry. Errol sank onto the mattress. He wrapped his arms around me and held me to his chest. A bitter scent of medicine clung to his breath. "Alice," he said softly, "here is something most people never understand. If you believe that you are unlovable, then all the Valentine's Day cards and boxes of chocolates in the world won't do a damn bit of good. But if you believe that you are lovable, then your aura is only limited to every conceivable color in the universe." Then he sighed. "It really disgusts me how much I sound like a Hallmark card right now."

"I'm tired of being worried all the time," I said. "I'm tired of feeling sad."

"Me too." His words sank to the floor, heavy with truth. Then we pulled out of the hug. He wiped my eyes with his sleeve. The crevasses around his own eyes had deepened. Some people call themselves old souls. Looking into Errol's eyes, right at that moment, I knew I was in the presence of one.

"You're Cupid," I said. It was a moment of pure awe and it filled me like a long drink of cool water on a scorched day. "You're Cupid," I whispered, a little shiver running across my shoulders. "Cupid."

He wove his fingers through mine. "You look so much like Psyche, it breaks my heart."

"Would you please tell me the rest of the story?"

His fingers slipped from mine. Then he groaned, wrapped his arms around his stomach, and fell back onto the mattress.

"Errol!" I cried. Grimacing, he pointed to the brown pill container on his desk. Grabbing the bottle, I tore off the cap and shook a pill into his hand. He swallowed it. I grabbed the water bottle and he took a long drink. "Errol? Should I call 911?"

"No," he whispered. "Don't worry, it's not time yet. But it's getting closer."

"Closer?" I grabbed his arm. "How close?"

He squeezed his eyes shut. "I can't tell you the end of the story, not yet. I need to rest. Use the notes. The notes will guide you. Everything's there. Go."

I pushed a pillow under his head. "Are you sure? Shouldn't I call the doctor?"

"I don't want a doctor. I don't want any more doctors. Go. Write as much as you can. Use my notes."

This time I didn't care that he was giving me orders. I believed. I knew who he was and I knew what I had to do.

I ran back to my apartment. As I skidded to a stop at my kitchen table, I reached for the manila envelope—the envelope stuffed with notes, the envelope given to me at Elliott Bay Books, before I knew Errol, before I believed in Roman gods or auras or even in myself.

But the envelope was not there.

SUNDAY

THE air whispered.

During the night, a writhing mass of storm clouds gathered over the Pacific and headed our way. In Cal Anderson Park, no suffocating heat greeted the morning dog walkers. No brightness blinded the joggers. The ice cream vendors slept in. "Relief on the Way," the *Seattle Times* announced.

Noting the shift in the weather, Archibald Wattles ended his Hawaiian shirt spree. He stood in the foyer in a crisp linen shirt and a pair of jeans, a whisk in his hands. He always made his gravy ahead of time, then reheated it with drippings from the roast just before serving Sunday dinner. "Wanda, you look gorgeous," he said as Mrs. Bobot twirled two times, the ruffle at her dress's hem rippling. She'd matched the royal blue dress with a pair of royal blue shoes.

"I made it," she said.

"I don't suppose you know that blue is William's favorite color?" Archibald asked slyly. Mrs. Bobot blushed.

I listened to the conversation while crouched behind my apartment door, peering through a crack barely big enough to notice.

"What's that?" Archibald pointed to a china plate that Mrs. Bobot held.

"It's a chocolate cake. To eat after the sermon." She'd covered the cake with black-and-white chocolate curls. "I used a recipe this time."

"An actual recipe?" Archibald chuckled. "I don't suppose you know that chocolate cake is William's favorite?"

"Is it?" Her feigned astonishment wouldn't have fooled anyone.

"We're going to be late!" the reverend announced as he limped into the foyer. His reverend's collar sat stiffly in place. One hand gripped his cane, the other clutched some papers.

"Break a leg," Archibald said.

"That's a ridiculous saying," Reverend Ruttles complained. He always stayed up late when writing a sermon, which made him grumpy. "Come on, come on," he insisted, shuffling toward the back door, his cane tapping an anxious rhythm.

"William? Did you see Wanda's new dress?" Archibald asked.

"I don't have time for dresses. Let's go or I'll be late."

Though she was sixty-two years old, Mrs. Bobot suddenly looked like a little girl as disappointment spread across her face.

"What about the nice cake she baked? Did you see—?"

"No time for cakes!"

"Wanda?" Archibald reached out to touch her arm but she shook her head. Then she handed him the cake.

"No matter," she said, composing herself. "You sure you won't join us?"

Archibald smiled sadly. "Maybe someday."

Then the person I was waiting for tramped down the stairs, her headphones protecting her from any cheerful morning conversation that might drift her way. I narrowed my eyes like a cat, wanting to hiss at her. "The weather guy said there's a huge storm coming. Isn't that freaky?" Realm said. "First a heat wave, now a storm."

"A storm in July," Mrs. Bobot said. "What a strange summer."

I waited until Realm had followed her grandmother out the back door. When I heard the car engine start, I ran into the foyer.

"Alice?" Archibald said. "You'd better hurry. They're in the car already."

"Mrs. Bobot knows I'm not going." I peered out the back door to make sure Mrs. Bobot's car was pulling away, with Realm in it. "Archibald, you still haven't found that manila envelope, have you?"

"Not since the last time you asked. Which, in case you don't remember, was two a.m."

I'd been up most of the night, desperately searching. I'd asked Errol if he had the notes. "Of course I don't," he said. "Now please, Alice. Let me get some rest."

"But, Errol, I can't find them."

"You have to find them," he mumbled from the darkness of his room. "You must find them."

I'd told Archibald, Mrs. Bobot, and Realm about the envelope. I'd explained that the notes belonged to Errol and that they were for a book we were writing together. I'd pleaded for help because Errol was dying of cancer and there were no copies of his notes. Mrs. Bobot promised to look for the notes, as did Archibald. Realm made a snippy comment about how everyone else's book was more important than her book. Reverend Ruttles told everyone to be quiet because he still had a sermon to write. At some point, after searching and searching, I collapsed on the couch and fell into a deep sleep.

"I'm sorry to hear that the envelope is still missing," Archibald said. Then he sniffed. "Uh-oh. Something's burning." Brandishing the whisk, he raced into his apartment.

I tightened my fingers around the key I'd been holding. Up the stairs I flew, two steps at a time. Because my mother was the landlord, a key to each apartment was kept in a bowl in our kitchen. Throughout the night, I'd gone over every possibility. I hadn't taken the envelope out of the apartment. I hadn't given it to anyone. The last time I'd seen it, it had been sitting on the kitchen table. And now all that sat there were blank pieces of my mother's stationery. Someone had taken the envelope and put the stationery in its place.

Someone.

I grabbed Mrs. Bobot's doorknob and slid the key into the lock. The apartment smelled like pipe tobacco, which meant that Mrs. Bobot had been missing her husband lately. I headed straight to Realm's room. DO NOT ENTER THE REALM OF REALM, the sign warned.

It didn't take long to search the room. The place reminded me of a motel, sparse and tidy. Just a few belongings—clothes in the closet, a couple of books by the bed, some products on the dresser. None of Mrs. Bobot's homespun items had made their way into the Realm of Realm.

When I reached under the bed, my pulse quickened. I pulled out a book, which turned out to be Realm's journal. Revenge danced through my head. Realm had taken Errol's notes, I knew that. What better way to get them back? She'd come into *my* home and had read *my* private papers. What comes around goes around—wasn't that the saying?

I opened the journal to its first page and found a glued photo of Realm's predecessor, Lily. Smiling like the Cheshire cat, Lily sat next to a smiling man and woman, an ice cream cone in her hands. It would have been a nice photo, one that you'd see in most family albums, except that someone had drawn a mustache on Lily's chunky face and had scratched x's all over her body. The words *I'M SO UGLY* were scrawled at her feet. I could sense the sadness contained in each little *x*. The self-loathing.

That's when I realized what Realm had done. For so many summers, Lily had come to visit in her sundresses and ribbons. And then one summer, she was gone. She couldn't be the perfect little girl that her father wanted. By starving herself, covering herself in layers and shearing her hair, Realm had destroyed Lily, sending her into the abyss, just like the day when she'd burned her name.

What Realm didn't know, but what I knew, was that a sparkling silver cloud floated around the man's and woman's heads in the photo, just like the cloud I'd seen so many times around my mother. And around Lily's head was a soft green cloud.

*Her aura's clear,* Errol had said. *Some people have clear auras because they shut themselves off to love.*

Realm used to have an aura, a soft green one.

I closed the journal, then shoved it back under the bed. A queasy feeling spread over me. Maybe I should have been nicer to Realm. Would it have killed me to read a few pages of *Death Cat* rather than throw it on the recycling pile?

But then I saw it. Not Errol's manila envelope, but a piece of paper—a single lined sheet that had fallen behind Realm's door. The scrawled handwriting described a temple that had been built for Venus. "I knew it!" I said, grabbing the paper. "I knew it!" All the pity I'd felt for Realm instantly disintegrated. "She took it!" I searched the bedroom again, then started to search Mrs. Bobot's living room. But craft supplies cluttered every corner. It would take forever to search.

Errol didn't have forever.

Evidence in hand, I flew downstairs and grabbed my backpack purse. Archibald was busy mashing hard-boiled yolks for deviled eggs. "Can I borrow twenty dollars?" I pleaded. "I need to get a cab."

"Of course. You're going to try to make the sermon?" He handed me a crisp bill. "Go wait out front. I'll call Yellow Cab for you."

"Magnolia," I told the driver when he arrived five minutes

later. "The Magnolia Community Episcopalian Church. Go as fast as you can."

Impeded by stoplights and pedestrians, the flow of traffic along Broadway was so slow I thought I'd explode. "Can't you go any faster?" I squirmed, a giant clock ticking in my head. Errol was dying. Every minute that passed brought him closer to the end. I'd promised to write his story. What if he never got the chance to finish?

"Why are you stopping?" I cried when the taxi slowed.

"You want me to hit a bike rider?" the driver asked. "What could be so important?"

*What could be so important?*

Over the course of that week, three stories had defined my every waking minute. All were love stories. One had been lived, very long ago. One was still being lived, though a ferry ride and an illness separated us. One had yet to be lived.

"What could be so important?" the cab driver repeated.

"My destiny," I said. "Hurry!"

The dark clouds were on the move. I flung myself from the cab and ran up a walkway that was bathed in filtered, gray light. A gust of humid wind swept across the path, pushing me sideways and blowing into my eyes. Spitting a strand of hair from my mouth, I stumbled toward the church.

The Magnolia Community Episcopalian Church sat on a bluff overlooking Puget Sound. The old wooden building used to be an Elks lodge. My mother and I had listened to many of the reverend's sermons over the years. I always suspected that what my mother liked most about going to this church was the horde of church ladies who would surround her afterward, admiring readers each and every one.

The kid who'd been handing out programs was just closing the door as I pushed my way in. "The service already started," he told me. I hurried past the coatroom, past a table covered in pamphlets about various community projects and services.

Rows of worn pews faced a stage, where a man named Reverend Miles stood at a podium, addressing the congregation. I stopped at the end of each pew, searching for a head of sheared blond hair. "Beloved in the Lord," Reverend Miles said.

"Amen," the congregation chanted.

"Please stand and sing hymn number seventeen, 'Thou Only Light, Thou Only Life and Joy.'"

Everyone stood. Hymnals were lifted, pages turned, and a cacophony of voices filled the room. I listened for Mrs. Bobot's soprano, but didn't find it among the voices. Finally, it was a radiant blue dress that drew me to the third aisle. Mrs. Bobot stared out the window, a distant expression frozen on her face. Realm stood next to her, still plugged into headphones, chewing on her black-polished fingernails.

"Please be seated," Reverend Miles said. Everyone sat.

"Excuse me," I whispered, stepping over knees and thighs as I made my way down the row.

"Alice?" Mrs. Bobot looked up. "Whatever are you doing?"

I pushed between Mrs. Bobot and Realm, forcing everyone on the bench to wedge uncomfortably close. Mrs. Bobot frowned at me, but didn't lecture me about wearing shorts and a T-shirt to church. She simply sighed, and looked back out the window.

I pulled Realm's headphones off her head, releasing a blast of angry rap music.

"May I remind everyone to please turn off all electronic devices," the reverend said snippily. Realm turned off her music.

"Where is it?" I demanded.

"Gross," Realm said, wiping a fleck of my spit off her cheek.

"Let us now offer prayers," Reverend Miles said. Then he read from a list. "Let us pray for Edwina Hortmeyer, who will be having knee surgery on Wednesday. And let us pray for Charlie Miller's son Carl, who will be facing the parole board this week." More names were read as Realm and I glared at each other.

"Let us pray," Reverend Miles said and everyone bowed their heads—except for Mrs. Bobot, who still stared out the window. And except for Realm and me because we were locked in a tug-of-war over the headphones.

"Give those back," Realm snarled.

"Not until you tell me where Errol's notes are."

"Shhh," Mrs. Hortmeyer hissed from the end of the pew.

I let go of the headphones and folded my arms angrily. I'd come for something and I was going to get it.

Reverend Miles made some announcements and then he introduced Reverend Ruttles. That's when I grabbed the piece of evidence from my purse and thrust it at Realm. "I found this in your bedroom," I said. "Where's the rest of it?"

Realm's eyes burned with fury. "You went into my bedroom?"

"You had no right taking that envelope. I want it back now."

"Shhhh!" Mrs. Hortmeyer spat.

Mrs. Bobot, who would usually be the one to do all the shushing, simply fiddled with her purse, lost in her own thoughts. She wasn't even watching Reverend Ruttles as he stepped to the podium.

"Good morning," he said, his voice rolling over the congregation like the great flood. "I always look forward to my monthly guest sermon. To look out and see so many familiar faces is a delight. Thank you, Reverend Miles, and thank you, everyone, for joining me here today." Reverend Miles nodded and took a seat near the choir.

Reverend Ruttles continued. "Earlier this week I was reminded of a glorious saying when I pulled it from a fortune cookie. 'Love thy neighbor.' I chose that saying as the theme for my sermon."

I poked Realm's scrawny arm. "Give me Errol's envelope."

"You want the envelope? You write the letters."

"Fine."

"Let's go."

"Where are you two going?" Mrs. Bobot asked as Realm and I stepped over her knees.

"SHHHHH." Foam gathered at the corners of Mrs. Hortmeyer's mouth. She was on the verge of throwing a fit.

"Hurry up," I said, pulling on Realm's arm.

Reverend Ruttles stopped talking and cleared his throat.

All eyes turned as Realm and I stumbled into the aisle. "We have to hurry," I said.

"You can find the words 'Love thy neighbor' in the Book of Mark. Love your neighbor as yourself . . ."

"Why do you care more about Errol's story than mine?" Realm wrenched her arm from my grip. "Why do you want to be friends with him? I always wanted to be your friend and you just ignored me, just like everyone else ignores me."

"GIRLS!" Reverend Ruttles's voice barreled down the aisle. Realm and I froze. The reverend looked pleadingly at Mrs. Bobot. "Wanda? Can't you do something?"

"Girls," Mrs. Bobot said with as much gusto as a person in a coma.

At this point, the entire congregation turned to watch the show that was taking place two-thirds of the way up the center aisle and was, by far, much more interesting than any of Reverend Ruttles's sermons.

"I never ignored you," I told Realm.

"Oh, really? Well, how come you've never invited me to do anything with you?"

I threw my hands up. "Because I don't *do* anything. Haven't you noticed? I have no life."

"Wanda?" Reverend Ruttles called. He motioned with the back of his hand. "Do something."

Mrs. Bobot looked toward the pulpit and narrowed her eyes. Then she started grinding her teeth.

"Maybe I care more about Errol's story because he's not blackmailing me," I told Realm, giving her shoulder a push.

"I wouldn't have blackmailed you if you hadn't ignored me." She pushed back.

Reverend Ruttles cleared his throat. "Wanda, why are you just sitting there? Girls, this is not the time or place. Go sit next to Mrs. Bobot and listen. You might learn something about neighborly love."

Mrs. Bobot bolted to her feet. "Learn something about neighborly love?" she cried. Her cheeks erupted. "Don't you talk to us about neighborly love. We do everything for you and you never appreciate it." She flung her braid over her shoulder and pushed her way down the pew and into the aisle. Reverend Ruttles's mouth fell open.

Realm and I watched, wide-eyed, as Mrs. Bobot stomped up the aisle. Just before reaching us, she spun around and shook a furious finger at the pulpit. "And why isn't Archibald here? That's what I want to know! How do you translate that into neighborly love?"

Reverend Ruttles stood, for the first time in his life, quite speechless. Never in the history of the Magnolia Community Episcopalian Church had such a spectacle taken place.

"Come on, girls," Mrs. Bobot said.

We followed her from the church, a rumble of distant thunder accompanying our exit.

OTHER than Mrs. Bobot's mutterings about the stupidity of men, and other than the honking of impatient drivers who wanted Mrs. Bobot to either go faster or get out of the way, the ride back to the apartment was silent. Neither Realm nor I said a word. We'd never seen Mrs. Bobot so upset. She clung to the steering wheel like a woman hanging off the edge of a cliff. It may have looked like we'd called a truce, but beneath the surface my blood boiled, and as soon as we got out of Mrs. Bobot's range of hearing I was going to KILL REALM!

Once the car was parked, we hurried into the apartment building. The unmistakable, succulent, salty smell of Archibald's Sunday pot roast had filled the building's every nook and cranny. Archibald, who'd been sweeping the foyer, leaned the broom against the wall. "What's everyone doing back so early?" Teary-eyed, Mrs. Bobot stormed right past him and up to her apartment. "Dinner's at five," he called. The slam of her bedroom door reverberated down the stairs.

The truce ended. "Go get the envelope!" I yelled at Realm.

"Fine! But you said that you'd write as many letters as I want. If you go back on that, I'll tell everyone what I know."

"Really, Realm?" I got right in her face. "Are you really going to blog to all your friends that my mother's insane? Is that *really* what you're going to do?"

"Alice," Archibald scolded. "Your mother's not *insane*. You should never use that word."

"What word will you use, Realm? Crazy? Mad? Nuts?" My face felt like it was on fire. "What will you blog? Belinda Amorous, the famous romance writer, is a *lunatic*?"

Realm glanced self-consciously at Archibald, then put her hands on her hips. "If you write those letters, then I won't have to blog anything. It's your decision."

"No, Realm, it's *your* decision. You're the one who sat at my mother's desk and read her personal papers. You're the one who took Errol's notes. You're the one making all the threats." I clenched my fists until they ached. "You know, maybe you deserve to be as miserable as you are."

"Alice?" Archibald stepped forward but I waved him away.

"Look at her. She's starving herself because she hates herself. And she wants us to feel sorry for her. Well, guess what, Realm? I don't feel sorry for you. I don't even care about you. Everyone has problems and some are much bigger than feeling like your parents don't love you."

That last sentence hung in front of me like a banner. I stepped away from Realm. The words had flown out, propelled by anger, so they didn't count—did they? I tried not to notice the shame in Realm's eyes. But I did notice it, and I recognized it. God, I knew exactly how she felt. Every cell in my body knew. So many years of wondering if my mother loved me. Of convincing myself that she didn't.

A sort of suffocating sound came out of Realm, then she fled up the stairs. Archibald stood silently behind me, but I didn't turn to look at him. Oscar the cat meowed and wound around my feet, but I didn't bend to pet him.

"Realm!" I called. "I'm sorry. I didn't mean that."

A few doors slammed, then Realm was back, standing at the top of the stairs. "Here. Take the stupid envelope!" With a grunt, she hurled it at my head. I lunged and caught it in both hands. A sense of relief almost brought me to tears as I hugged it to my chest. Finally, one thing would go right. I'd make one thing right.

Realm wiped tears from her eyes. Her body seemed to shrink beneath the layers of clothing that she wore like armor.

"I take it that's what you were looking for," Archibald said quietly.

I nodded, then looked up the stairs, but Realm had gone.

That's when a cab pulled up out front and Reverend William Ruttles limped up the front steps and into the foyer. "Never been so humiliated in all my life," he announced, shaking his cane in the air. "Irreparable damage to my reputation. Irreparable." Then he marched into his apartment, and his own bedroom door slammed shut.

"I don't know what's going on with everyone around here. And now we've got a storm coming." Archibald picked up

Oscar the cat. "We'd better not lose power because I've been working on that roast all day. Dinner's at five," he said again, then walked into his apartment and gently closed the door.

I stood alone in the foyer, the wind whistling through a crack in the stained glass window. Clutching the envelope to my chest, my heart pounding, shame washed over me. I'm not sure how long I stood there, trying to figure out how to apologize to Realm, when a shuffling sound made me look up. Errol was walking down the stairs, his footsteps slow, his hand gripping the railing. His white hair didn't glow. "I'm ready to tell you the rest," he said.

I needed to push everything from my mind and help Errol.

He settled on my couch. I didn't have salon girls delivering my meals and I hadn't been to the store in a while, so I tore open a bag of Cheetos and poured some lemonade. If I'd known that Cupid himself would be visiting my apartment, I would have cleaned up a little, bought some cookies or something. I turned on the computer. My plan was that I'd type while he talked. This would give me the basic framework for the chapters. Then we'd sort through the pages of notes, assigning each to its appropriate chapter so I could weave it in later.

"How come you have so many garden gnomes?" he asked, stepping over one.

"My mom collects things."

I dumped all his notes onto the coffee table. Lined notebook paper, paper napkins, Post-its—he'd written whenever the memories arose, on whatever paper he could find at the

time. Many had been written during chemo, on hospital stationery. The pile was huge. "There's a lot of stuff here," I said
worriedly. "How far do you want to get today?"

"To the end." He lay against the back of the couch, his eyelids heavy.

"All the way to the end?" I froze. "Errol?"

"I'm not dying today, if that's what you're thinking. I still
have time. But I just want to finish this. I'm so tired of carrying this story around with me."

Maybe he wasn't dying right then and there, but he sure
looked like crap. His hair used to be perfectly white, but now
gray flowed from his temples.

I looked worriedly at the pile of notes that covered the
coffee table. Errol wanted to finish the story today. "I'll be
right back," I told him.

That's how I ended up knocking on her door. When it
opened, she glared at me with puffy red eyes.

"What do you want?"

"Realm, I need your help."

"He's really dying?" she'd asked me on the way back downstairs.

"Yes. And this is the only thing he wants before he dies. To get his story written."

"I can respect that," she said.

The wind continued to blow, finding its way through cracks in the window frames and drowning out the usual street noise. I set my phone to buzz. "There will be no interruptions," I said. "I promise. We'll work until we get to the end."

Realm sat on the carpet, her legs folded. She didn't complain about having to help with someone else's book. She smiled kindly at Errol and even ate a few Cheetos as she sorted through his notes, starting to put them in order. I set my fingertips on the keypad, waiting while Errol collected his thoughts.

"Where did we leave off?" he asked.

"You'd just put henna in your hair and you were going to introduce yourself to Psyche."

"Right." He took a long breath, then began his tale.

The first time they spoke, Psyche was carrying eggs to market. "I couldn't believe how nervous I was," Errol said. "I told her I was a merchant from a distant island, but the entire time I was near her, I had to hide my hands behind my back because they were shaking. No one had ever made me feel that way."

Psyche was shy but she allowed Cupid to walk with her that day. Many of the locals had tried to court her over the years, but they'd been old men or simple farm boys and she hadn't cared for any of them. But here was a young, handsome man from a distant land, telling her stories about his travels, about places she'd only dreamed of. He filled her head with wonder.

"I courted her slowly," Errol said, sipping some lemonade. "I wanted her desperately, but I wasn't going to force her to love me, not the way the gods had taught me. I wanted it to be real."

"I like the way you're putting yourself into the story," Realm told him. "I do that sometimes, too. It helps me imagine things better."

Errol and I exchanged a knowing look.

To keep the gods from becoming suspicious, Cupid continued to do their bidding, but between tasks he'd rush back to Psyche. He brought gifts from distant lands and kept her family's pantry filled with grain and fresh meat. He learned how to bake her favorite bread, learned how to dance her favorite dance, and how to recite her favorite poem. It was a long courtship and though tempted, he never shot her with an arrow.

While Errol spoke, I typed as quickly as I could. Realm pulled all the notes she could find about the courtship and clipped them together. "Courtship," she wrote on a Post-it.

Then a young, handsome man from a neighboring village showed up and proclaimed his love for Psyche. "I was desperately jealous, so I shot him with a love-at-first-sight arrow while he was standing next to another man's wife. It worked, but another man came, and then another. Word of Psychè's beauty had spread since the wine festival and they started showing up from as far away as Crete. I shot them all."

"Here's a note about one guy who fell in love with his own reflection," Realm said. "And another about a guy who fell in love with someone's grandmother." She clipped them together and wrote "Shooting the Competition" on a Post-it. "This story's kind of sick," she said. "I like it."

An hour passed. Errol's voice grew raspier. I got him some water.

The story went that at the end of the year's courtship, Psyche had truly fallen in love and had agreed to marry Cupid. There was a small ceremony at her father's farm, and then Cupid took her far away, to a remote island in the Aegean Sea. He stole a fortune from one of his lovesick victims and with that, he bought Psyche a beautiful palace at the sea's edge and brought her everything she needed. They were deliciously happy.

In order to keep Psyche safe, Cupid had to set up some rules. First, Psyche could never be seen outside the palace. Venus, the goddess of love, had seemingly forgotten the little Wine Princess. But if Psyche started walking around in public, people would notice her beauty and word would spread. So she began to feel like a prisoner, far from her family, alone for long periods of time when Cupid would disappear to do his work. "As the sea changes its temperament, so too did our marriage change," Errol said.

My fingers started to cramp. Realm put together two more sets of notes: "The Wedding" and "Life in the Palace." She was turning out to be a great help.

"How did your marriage change?" I asked.

"She began to resent my love. No, wait, 'resent' is not the right word," Errol said, getting up from the couch. He walked over to the living room window and looked out at Cal Anderson Park. Branches swayed in the wind and a few pieces of trash skipped down the path. "She started to hate me. A caged animal will always turn on its owner."

"Hey, that's my *Death Cat* story," Realm said.

The marriage fell apart, he told us. Each time he'd return home, Psyche demanded freedom. Though he knew they'd both be in danger if anyone recognized her, he couldn't bear her misery and he finally agreed that she could have some company. So her sisters came for a visit, but they filled her with more resentment. Who is this man to tell you what to do? To hide your beauty from the world? He wants it only for himself. While Cupid was away, they convinced Psyche to go to town without a head scarf. And when people noticed her beauty, the sisters proudly told the story of how she'd been crowned Wine Princess and how many had said she was more beautiful than Venus herself.

Two months later, Cupid arrived home after a long journey to find that Psyche had disappeared.

"Disappeared?" Realm asked.

"She'd gone looking for Cupid," I said. "Mr. Lee told me the story. She thought Cupid had abandoned her so she went looking for him."

"No," Errol said, rubbing the back of his neck. "That's the myth. That's the spin the gods put on the story. She never went looking. They took her. They took her from me." A strong gust of wind shook the panes. "They took her and they entombed her."

"What?" I asked.

Realm sat up real straight. "Entombed? You mean, they buried her alive? Just for being beautiful?"

"Yes." He kept staring out the window.

We sat in silence for a few moments. I shuddered as a horrid image filled my mind. Unaffected by what she thought was merely a plot twist, Realm sorted through the remaining notes. "I don't see anything in here about a tomb."

"It's not there. I couldn't bear to write it."

Realm nodded. "Yeah, I get that. When I had to write the scene where Death Cat chews on her owner's face, it kind of freaked me out for a few days."

Beautiful Psyche had been buried alive. No wonder Errol carried so much grief. No wonder he couldn't face the ending.

"Alice!" Mrs. Bobot called. She hurried into the living room. "Oh Alice, I . . . I . . ."

"What's the matter?" I asked, scrambling to my feet.

"You have a phone call," she said, her voice trembling. "They've been trying to call you but you didn't answer."

I'd set my phone to buzz, hoping for no distractions. It had gotten pushed beneath one of the couch pillows. Mrs. Bobot held out her phone, her face ghostly pale. I knew that Harmony Hospital was on the other end of that call. With all the chaos about the lost envelope, I'd forgotten to call my mother that morning. It was the first time I'd forgotten.

"Hello?" I said. The connection crackled. "Hello?"

"Alice? This is Dr. Merri, the weekend physician at Harmony Hospital. I know this question may sound strange but . . ." She cleared her throat. "Is your mother there?"

"Is my mother where?"

"There. At your home."

"Here? Is my mother here?" Had I heard the question correctly? Mrs. Bobot's hand flew to her mouth. "No, she's not here," I told Dr. Merri.

"We thought not," Dr. Merri said. "There's been limited ferry service today due to the storm and the ferry crew hadn't seen her. But I needed to make certain she hadn't gone home."

"I don't understand," I said, the phone growing heavy in my hands. "Are you telling me that my mother's missing?"

MRS. Bobot grabbed the phone from my hands and pressed the speaker button. Dr. Merri's voice filled the living room. "She walked out the emergency exit and we think she's gone into the woods. We can't find her. We've been looking for three hours."

"Three hours?" Mrs. Bobot said with a gasp. "Did she take anything with her?"

"As far as we can tell she took nothing. Her purse, her coat, all her belongings are still in her room."

Errol stepped up behind me and placed his hands on my shoulders.

"How could you let something like this happen?" Mrs. Bobot cried at the phone. "Is this what you do when a patient can't pay the bill? You let her wander off?"

"Of course not," Dr. Merri said. "We are as upset about this as you are. But the storm has made the search difficult. It's hitting us pretty hard out here. We've had a couple of big lightning strikes and we've lost power. The police and the fire department are helping with the search. I'm sure they'll—" The line went dead.

Mrs. Bobot hit redial but the connection failed. Panic surged through my body. I slid from Errol's gentle grip and started pacing, wringing my hands, looking around. What do you grab when your mentally ill mother is missing in the woods in the middle of a freak storm? A first aid kit, some flashlights, a blanket—what?

"Oh no you don't," Mrs. Bobot said as I snatched my backpack purse. "This is far too dangerous. I will not have you tramping about in the woods in the middle of a storm. You will stay here in case your mother shows up." Then she ran into the foyer and clapped her hands. "William, Archibald, get your coats!"

"Stay here? I'm not staying here," I said, running after her. "I'm going to help look for her."

"What's the fuss?" Archibald said after opening his door. He and the reverend stepped into the foyer.

"Belinda's missing. They think she's lost in the woods. She's been gone for three hours." Mrs. Bobot ran up the stairs, her braid swaying. "I'm getting my keys and some sensible shoes."

"I'm going too," I insisted.

A flash of lighting lit up the foyer. "You listen to me," Mrs. Bobot said. "It is my job to take care of you. I am your legal guardian in your mother's absence and I will not allow you to wander into the woods in the middle of lightning and thunder. You will stay here and keep yourself safe."

"Wanda's right," Archibald said. "Your mother would want you to stay here. We all want to keep you safe."

"But . . ."

Reverend Ruttles thumped his cane against the floor. "Do not argue with Wanda. You will stay here, young lady, where you are safe, and that is the final word."

Archibald hugged me. "I'm sure she's fine. Your mother knows how to take care of herself." Then he hugged me again because we both knew it wasn't true, at least not lately. "The pot roast is ready. I hate for it to go to waste. You and Realm and Errol should go in and eat something. We'll call you as soon as we get there."

And with that, Archibald, Reverend Ruttles, and Mrs. Bobot piled into Mrs. Bobot's car and drove off down the darkened street.

I kicked the back door. "Stay here?" Helplessness tugged at my body, like being caught in a whirlpool. "I can't just sit around and wait."

Back in the apartment I tried calling the hospital. Nothing. "What about a cab?" I asked. "Realm, how much money do you have?"

"Not much, ten bucks, something like that." She tugged at her sleeves. "A cab will cost a fortune. You could take a bus."

"A bus will take forever." I searched through my purse for the credit card, the one that was maxed out, but maybe a cab driver wouldn't be able to tell.

"I think it's ridiculous that they made you stay here," Realm said. "How are they going to search the woods? The reverend can barely walk and my grandmother's ancient. And Archibald will worry about getting his shoes dirty."

I pulled out the credit card. I had to give it a try.

"I'll stay here in case anyone calls or in case your mom shows up," Realm said. She shuffled in place. There were hints of Lily in her softened expression. "And I won't read anything I'm not supposed to read. I won't. I wasn't going to tell anyone about your mom. Really I wasn't. I'm not that mean."

"Thanks," I said. "Realm, I—"

"Let's not do the whole apology thing, okay? Just go find your mom."

I called the cab company. "It's my mother's credit card," I told the woman who answered. "What? But she said I could use it. No, she won't be riding with me. But I don't have my own credit card." Beyond frustrated, I wanted to throw the phone across the room. "What am I supposed to do? I need to get to Whidbey Island and I only have the one credit card!" I yelled at the woman.

Still standing by the window, Errol had been quiet this whole time. But he suddenly called my name and motioned me over. A green Jeep was parallel parking across the street. When the driver's door opened, Tony Lee stepped out, his hair whipping in the wind. I threw open the window.

"Tony!" I called.

He ran across the street and stood under my window. "What a crazy storm. Hey, you never gave me your phone number, so I came by to see if you wanted to hang out or something." His face was back to normal, no blotches, no swelling. But my face was clenched with panic. "Alice, what's wrong?"

"My mom's in trouble. Can you drive me to Whidbey Island?"

"In trouble?"

I leaned out the window. "I need to get to her. Right now."

"Yeah, okay, but I don't know where Whidbey Island is."

"I do."

I grabbed a coat and started to leave but then turned and looked into Errol's bloodshot eyes. "I know I said we'd work until we finished. But I have to go. I'm so sorry, Errol. I'll be back as soon as I can."

He looked away.

"He can tell me the rest of the story," Realm said. "I'll write it down. I can do it."

"You don't need to do that, Realm. I'll write it tomorrow." I touched Errol's arm. "There's still time, right? You said you still had time."

He frowned. "They've got firefighters and police looking for her, Alice. Don't you think that's enough?"

"Maybe." I swung my purse onto my back. "But what if that's not enough? What if something happens to her and I didn't try to help? Don't you get it? I've been trying to save my mother forever but I've never been able to. She just kept drifting farther and farther away from me. But what if this time I can help? I have to try."

I expected anger from him. He'd been stalking me for a week, doing everything he could to get me to help him, and now I was abandoning him just when we were so close to finishing. But he said nothing.

"I gotta go." I started to leave.

"Wait," Errol said. "I'm coming with you."

"You're sick. You should stay here."

"No." He shook his head slowly. "I lost Psyche. I'm not going to lose you too."

"HEY," Tony said, his eyes widening as Errol slid into the backseat.

I didn't expect Errol to apologize for the whole invisible arrow incident. I was kind of hoping he wouldn't bring it up. But Errol didn't say anything. He just folded his arms, then disappeared beneath his hood.

Once we reached the freeway, it wasn't long before we passed Mrs. Bobot's car. Even during a crisis she drove way below the speed limit. Archibald sat in the backseat, Reverend Ruttles up front. Mrs. Bobot gripped the steering wheel, her expression wild with worry. Fortunately they didn't notice me as Tony's Jeep zipped by. I was going to be grounded for an eternity.

"So maybe I should know what's going on," Tony said.

I took a couple of deep breaths, rehearsed my opening statement a few times, then decided to just go for it. "I've been lying to you," I said. "About everything."

A gust of wind pushed against the Jeep. Tony adjusted his glasses. "I'm listening."

I pressed my palms against my thighs and stared straight ahead. "I don't have a cat. I've never had a cat. I told you that because my bag smelled like clams and I was embarrassed. And I'm not going premed. I told you that because I'd been watching you from my window for two weeks and I wanted you to like me." I released a long breath.

He tucked his hair behind his ear. "Two weeks?"

"Yeah." I cringed. Perhaps that part of the confession hadn't been necessary, but I didn't want to pretend anymore. I was who I was, I felt what I felt, and I wanted him to know. Then, and only then, could we move forward. Maybe that meant dating, maybe it didn't.

"There's more," I said as another gust of wind pushed the Jeep. "My mother's not overseas. She's at Harmony Hospital because she's mentally ill. She's been bipolar most of her life. Her publisher and her readers don't know. I didn't tell anyone when I was little because I was afraid that they'd take me away from her. And now that I'm older I still don't tell anyone because we're trying to protect her image."

"That sounds rough," Tony said. "My dad's got a friend who's bipolar. He has to take a pill every day or he can't get out of bed."

"Mom didn't have any pills. She didn't take any medication, so she got worse and worse. Sometimes she'd be gone for days, sometimes she'd lock herself in her bedroom and forget about me. I didn't know what was going on. I thought

I'd done something wrong, you know? I was just a little kid. It was a total nightmare."

For a moment I forgot that Errol was in the backseat. I only felt Tony's presence—his warm brown eyes, his sad smile as he turned to look at me. "I'm sorry," he said. "I'm sorry you had to deal with all that."

I went on. "Then I found her sitting on the bathroom floor." The memories of that day projected onto the windshield like a home movie. The cold tile, the dripping bathroom faucet, her arms curled around her legs, her vacant eyes. "She wouldn't move. She was really out of it. The doctor came and sent her away. That's why I didn't go back to school. I signed up for Internet classes because I needed to stay home and take care of things for her. I've been covering for her, paying the bills, answering her e-mails, writing her letters, all the stuff that needs to be done." There. I'd told him. My shoulders relaxed.

"So what's going on today? Why are we rushing to Whidbey Island?"

"That's where the hospital is. It's surrounded by forest, for miles and miles, and she's wandered off. They can't find her. I don't know what kind of state she's in. If she's out there, in this storm, in some kind of daze . . ." I turned away and looked out the window.

The drone of the tires and wind felt endless. I fought the image that filled my mind—of my mother lying beneath a fallen tree, just like the lumber baron's wife. Was the forest still angry enough to take another life?

Tony reached over and took my hand. "We'll find her," he said.

His understanding should have calmed me. But it pushed something, like the last molecule of air before the balloon bursts. Anger welled up and I couldn't hold it back. "I'm so mad at her for doing this," I said, clenching my hands. "This is so like her to think about no one but herself. To go off and make everyone worry. We always have to stop our own lives just because she . . ." My pulse pounded in my throat. I clenched my jaw. "God! I'm so sick of it."

I turned away, ashamed of my feelings and exhausted by them. Tony squeezed my hand, but then another wind gust hit the car and he put both hands on the steering wheel. I thought about Dr. Diesel's support group. Maybe it wasn't such a bad idea. Maybe they'd understand what it felt like to be totally pissed at someone but love them at the same time.

After a few minutes, I twisted around to check on Errol. His eyes were closed, his hoodie rising steadily. "Errol?" He didn't answer. "He's taking a nap," I whispered. "He's been kind of . . . sick."

Tony's gaze darted to the rearview mirror. "How'd you two meet?"

I may have been done with the lies, but Errol's identity was not my secret to tell. And let's face it—how could I possibly convince anyone that Cupid was sitting in the back of that Jeep, without using another one of those embarrassing arrows? "I had this stupid idea that I could write for my mother," I quietly told him. "I figured that maybe I'd inherited some of her talent, kind of like how you said you'd inherited your mother's talent for science. I've always gotten good grades in English and I've read a million romance novels so I thought it would be easy. And the publisher was waiting for her next book and we needed the money to pay the hospital bill. That's why I was in the library that day checking out those romance-writing books."

"Really?"

"Yeah." I rolled my eyes. "Idiotic, I know."

"I don't think it's idiotic. You were trying to help."

"Well, I didn't help. I didn't get anywhere with her book. I couldn't even come up with a story idea. Then I met him and he said he had this story he wanted to get published. He had all the details from beginning to end but he needed help writing it. At first I thought I could take his story and put my mom's name on it."

"You mean steal it?"

"No. He said she could have it. So I got real excited and we started working on it but then I realized that it wasn't the right kind of story for a romance novel. It didn't fit in with my mother's books. But I love his story and I really want to finish it. And now here we are, and I'm working on a book that won't help my mother at all."

"You shouldn't be so hard on yourself," Tony said as he turned on the windshield wipers. The sky had turned the color of charcoal and rain fell in heavy drops. "It's not your job to fix your mom's life."

That had sounded harsh, and it had stung like a slap in the

face. But it was true. We drove in silence for a few moments. "So I don't get something," Tony said. "How do two people write a book together?"

"I'm writing it but it's his story. I didn't come up with the idea. I'm kind of like his . . . biographer."

"Biographer?" Tony's gaze darted to the rearview mirror again. "But he's our age. Isn't he too young for a biography?"

I looked back at Errol. He'd slumped deeper into the seat, the edge of his hood covering his eyes. In those few days since we'd met at the bookstore, I'd gone from being annoyed and wary of him, to yearning for him, to being angry and suspicious, and finally, to caring about him. But now I felt a deep, sharp pang of regret. Why couldn't we have more time together? Think of all the stories he could tell. All the places he'd been and the adventures he'd had. Meeting Cupid was probably the most amazing thing that would ever happen in my life and there'd barely been time to take it in. When we got back home, I'd ask him to tell me more. I'd write it all down. Before it was too late.

"So that means that you two will be spending a lot of time together," Tony said.

"Maybe," I said. *But maybe not.* "We're friends," I told him. "Errol and I. Just friends."

While the word "friend" reassured Tony of his chances with me, it didn't adequately describe Errol's and my relationship. I'd come to care about him. Not romantically, but deeply. A story had bonded us. I didn't want him to die.

I directed Tony to the ferry terminal. The wind picked up

and rain kept falling. The seagulls that normally hung out on the pilings or circled Ivar's fish and chips stand were nowhere to be seen. "This is the last boat until the storm passes," the ticket taker told us. "It's getting too choppy out there." We were the last car to drive on. Mrs. Bobot and her rescue team wouldn't make it to the island after all.

During the crossing, dizziness washed over me as white-tipped waves pushed the boat side to side. I tried to call the hospital again. I called Realm but there was no news about my mother. "It's still blowing here," Realm told me. "The weather guy said it's gonna be the biggest summer storm to hit the area. Ever. He said he's never seen anything like it. He called it a freak of nature."

What could my mother have been thinking? Why would she have run off into a storm?

I willed the boat to go faster, but the wind pushed against it so it took almost twice as long to cross. A voice came over the ship's loudspeaker. "May I have your attention, please. Due to a power outage at our destination, the passenger ramp is not working. All passengers must go below and disembark on the auto deck."

"It looks like it's the middle of the night," I said as we drove off, though it was only five o'clock. I thought about Archibald's roast, waiting in the slow cooker. About the reverend's ruined sermon. Our normally nice Sunday had turned as dark as the storm itself.

Except for the lone guy directing traffic, the ferry terminal was deserted. And when the few cars had dispersed, the road was deserted too. Our headlights washed over sprays of fir and cedar that littered the roadway. A few times Tony had to maneuver around larger branches. As he drove up the hospital's long driveway, the cracking of a falling tree made me jump.

Errol sat up as we pulled up to the grand lodge. "How are you feeling?" I asked him.

He rubbed his eyes. "Where are we?"

"Harmony Hospital," I told him. "Remember? We're going to find my mom."

"Right." He smiled weakly.

A pair of police cars and a local news van were parked close to the entry. Two people sat in the van's front seats. Tony grabbed a flashlight from his glove box and we all got out of the Jeep. The roar of a generator filled the air. Raindrops smacked into our faces as we hurried into the hospital's lobby. We signed in at the security booth and got our visitor tags. The security guy searched us for cameras. "Can't take any chances. That news crew has been here all afternoon."

Most of the patients sat in the dining room playing games and eating somebody's birthday cake. "We're trying to keep everyone calm," Dr. Merri explained after I told her who we were. "We only have power in the main wing of the hospital so most everyone has gathered here." She ran a hand across her tired eyes, smudging the last bits of her mascara. "We haven't found her yet."

"Who's looking?" I asked.

"The police chief sent a few men out, but he won't let any of our staff help because of the wind and lightning."

Errol stood in a shadowy corner, listening. Tony stood next to me, his arm pressing against mine. I glanced up at the lumber baron, whose painted eyes watched our every move. *Do you know something*? I wanted to ask him. *Do you know where she is?*

Dr. Merri cleared her throat. "Alice, someone leaked this to the press. They know your mother is being treated here and that she's disappeared."

"THE press knows?" I asked, my mind racing.

Dr. Merri folded her arms and stood very straight. "We take the anonymity of our patients very seriously. If we find out who leaked this, we'll have that person fired, I can promise you that."

If my mother's secret wasn't already in print, it soon would be. "Mentally Ill Romance Writer Lost in Freak Summer Storm." That would sell a million papers.

"It's such a shame," Dr. Merri said. "She had such a good morning. She was very talkative."

"What?" My arms went slack and my purse straps slid halfway down. "My mother was talking?"

"Yes. Talking and eating. She even took a shower on her own. The medicine finally kicked in."

"Why didn't anyone tell me?" I said, taking an angry step toward her.

Dr. Merri's cheeks turned red. "She didn't want us to tell

you, not yet. She wanted to surprise you on your Tuesday visit."

Someone yelled "Bingo!" from the nearby dining room.

"Why don't you and your friends go in and have some cake," Dr. Merri suggested, motioning toward the well-lit room. I'll let you know immediately if . . . *when* she's found." Then her pager buzzed and she hurried away.

"It's really dark out there. We're going to need a few more flashlights," Tony said. "I'll see if I can find some."

"Okay." In my panic, I hadn't thought to bring any.

The medicine had kicked in. She'd showered on her own. She'd been talking. I couldn't believe it. What I'd been wishing for had actually happened.

I started toward my mother's room, then, remembering she'd been moved to a shared room, I changed direction. Errol followed me down the dark hallway. Emergency ceiling lights, small and dim, marked each room like dots on a map. I couldn't remember the room number but I recognized the roommate's family photos. The beds were neatly made, the bathroom tidy. My mother's bathrobe and slippers were missing. "Why would she go out in a storm?" I asked. Was it some crazy hallucination? Some kind of manic urge to collect pinecones or fallen leaves? "The medicine is supposed to be working. What is she doing?"

Errol looked out the window toward the forest. Raindrops rolled down the panes. "She's looking for something," he said quietly.

A nurse entered, teary eyed and wringing her hands. I

recognized her from previous visits. "I'm so sorry," she told me. "It's all my fault. I was on duty and I should have noticed her leaving. But one minute she was talking about her next book, and then she was gone. She went out the emergency exit. Our alarms don't work when the power's out."

For a moment I held my breath. "She was talking about her next book?"

"I'm such a big fan. I've read all her books. And I was so happy when she started talking to me this morning. She said she was going to write a book about the lumber baron. She said she'd been looking at his portrait every day and she felt like his love story needed to be told. She asked me to get her a spiral notebook, so I did."

"Did she say anything else?"

"She said that she hated the ending to the lumber baron's story and that she was going to change it and give him a happy ending. When I left to check on other patients, she was writing in the notebook."

I looked around. "Where is it?"

The nurse shrugged. "I don't know. Maybe she took it with her." A pager buzzed at the nurse's waist. "I'd better go." She hurried from the room.

"Oh my God, I know what my mother is doing," I said as Errol sat on the bed. The words flew from my mouth, my lips barely able to keep up. "She's doing research for her story. The lumber baron's wife went for a walk during a storm, right here on this property. That's what my mother's doing. She's doing research, seeing what the forest is like during a storm, seeing the scene from the wife's point of view. That's why she's out there."

"That makes sense." His voice was quiet. I moved close to him, trying to get a better view of his face in the dim light. His upper lip was sweaty and his breathing quick. He suddenly grimaced, as if someone had stabbed him.

"You should have stayed home," I said. "You should be resting."

"I'm sick of resting. I'm sick of being sick."

I sat next to him. "We can go to a different doctor. I'll help take care of you. There's got to be something." I held on to the front of his hoodie as if we were both being pulled under. "I don't understand, Errol. Why can't the gods help you?"

"They have helped me," he said. "They're finally letting me die." He unclenched my fingers then wrapped his icy hands over my own. His gaze moved quickly from my left eye to my right, back and forth, back and forth as if searching for something. Was he confused again, like when he'd held me in his arms and called me his wife? Was he seeing me, or seeing Psyche?

Then he let go of my hands and slowly stood. "Let's go find your mother."

Halfway down the hall we ran into Tony. He'd found two more flashlights in a janitor's closet. Gripping the cold plastic, I traced my mother's steps and opened the emergency exit door. Sideways rain pelted me as I ran my flashlight beam along the edge of the woods. "There," I said, shining the light on a narrow trail. The trail had been marked with yellow tape.

"Looks like the police already searched that trail," Tony said.

I ran the beam along the woods again. "I don't see any other trail and this one's right here, right by the exit. I think she'd take this trail."

The air was humid in the forest, and the trees blocked much of the rain. They blocked the wind, too, but it still whistled overhead. I walked quickly, the guys following, our three flashlights lighting the way. "I think she's in her bathrobe," I said. "It's blue. Perwinkle blue."

After about fifteen minutes the trail ended at a field of stumps. Either the lumber baron hadn't replanted this part of the forest or the trees had been felled since his death. Yellow tape hung at the trail's end. "They searched here too," Tony said.

"MOM!" I yelled into the field. I yelled again and again. A flash of lightning flooded the field in a moment of brilliance. A clap of thunder sounded.

"This is really dangerous," Tony said to me. "I think you should go back to the hospital and wait."

"I agree," Errol said.

But I'd already started across the field, winding around stumps covered in ferns and moss. Without the tree coverage, rain ran down my face and neck. "Alice." Tony caught up to me. "If your mom wanted to go for a walk, why would she turn off the trail?"

"She was doing research for her next book," I told him. I had no idea where I was going, just following a hunch. The police had searched the trail, but Mom wanted to experience the forest. I tried to remember the story. "The wife was killed by a falling tree. And the lumber baron went mad and spent the rest of his life planting trees. Then one night he didn't return and . . ." I stopped. We'd come to a rocky ledge that dipped gradually into a patch of young trees, planted in perfect rows. "His butler found him in a cave. That's what she's looking for." I cupped my hands around my mouth. "MOM!" I yelled. "MOM!" Rain ran down my coat sleeves.

"We should go that way," Errol said, pointing.

"What makes you think it's that way?" Tony asked. None of us had brought coats. His wet T-shirt clung to his chest. Raindrops rolled down his glasses.

"Because it's a natural path," Errol said, aiming his flash-light beam along the ledge.

Tony nodded. "Okay, I see what you're saying."

With Errol in the lead, we followed the ledge. Branches swayed overhead, lightning flashed in the distance, followed by rolling thunder. We climbed down into a creek bed that would have been dry in the middle of July if it hadn't been for the freak storm. Water trickled over the rocks and seeped into my tennis shoes. Rain leaked between my eyelashes and into my eyes. I stumbled on a few loose rocks. The creek cut deeper into the landscape, with boulders here and there. "MOM!" I called again and again. Errol kept the lead with a sudden burst of energy that surprised me. Then he stopped. Tony and I caught up.

"Do you see something?" I asked, almost bumping into him.

Errol didn't say anything. He stood very still, staring into space, blinking away the rain as it dropped into his eyes. His flashlight slid from his hand and cracked on the rocks. Then he looked from me to Tony and back to me. "Errol?" I said. "What's wrong?"

He shivered. I reached out to take his arm but he pulled away. "What are you doing with him?" he asked, his tone as cold as the rain. I recognized the confused look in his eyes. "Why do you do this to me, Psyche? Why do you choose these other men when I'm gone?"

"Errol—"

He glared at Tony. "You don't deserve her," he said, his eyes narrow with rage. "I've protected her. I've taken care of her."

"What are you talking about?" Tony asked.

Errol had drifted back to another time and place. I knew the story, so I could see it in his eyes. The woods had faded away. The rush of the wind became the rush of the ocean. We stood in our palace at the edge of the sea. My tunic blew in the breeze. His white hair glowed the way it used to. He turned to me, his words pleading. "Why do you bring these men into our home? Into our lives? Every time I go away there's another one. Why?"

*These men.* Psyche had taken lovers. He'd kept that part of the story to himself.

"I won't stand for it," he cried. Then his hands flew into their magical dance, folding the air like clay, molding it into an arrow.

"NO!" I yelled as the wind picked up. "Errol, stop it."

"He can't have you," he said through angry tears that mixed with rain. "You're mine. You belong to me."

"Errol." I grabbed his arm again but he flung me aside. Tony caught me as I stumbled backward.

"Hey," Tony yelled at him. "What's the matter with you?"

Errol extended his left arm. He pulled his right hand to his chin and pointed it at Tony. This was not going to happen. Not again. I slid from Tony's hands and with all my strength I threw myself at Errol.

"Please stop," I begged him, trying to release his arms from their frozen pose. But I couldn't move them. How could someone so sick be so strong? "Errol, it's me, Alice. Please don't hurt Tony. Please."

"Hey," Tony said. "I don't know what you two are fighting about but I think I see a cave."

Errol's arms relaxed.

Tony shone his light on a portion of the rock wall that was a bit farther down the creek. I ran. My heart in my throat, I ran to the cave. Its entrance was wide but low. Ducking, I stumbled inside, my hand aching as I clutched the flashlight.

The beam landed on a puddle of periwinkle blue.

BELINDA Amorous, the ex-Queen of Romance, lay in the middle of the cave in her bathrobe and slippers. Her breathing was steady, her eyes closed, her head rested on her arm. At her side lay a spiral notebook.

"Mom?" I could barely say the word, for in saying it I invited a response that I feared with all my heart. Would she be lost to her depression again? Would she be incoherent and confused? Would she stare at me with vacant eyes? I knelt beside her. "Mom?"

She stirred, then raised her head, her blond hair falling around her shoulders. "Alice?" she asked, shielding her eyes from the flashlight's beam. "Is that you?"

I lowered the beam. My hand trembled. "Yes. It's me."

"Alice," she said again, the way she used to say it. Then she sat up and held out her arms. I fell into them. "Alice," she whispered wrapping her arms around me. I closed my eyes and I was three years old again and we were simply on another one of our wondrous adventures.

"You're soaking wet." She tightened the hug. "And you're shivering."

A flash of lightning lit up the world outside the cave. My mother pulled out of the hug and looked sternly at me. "What are you doing here? Don't you know how dangerous it is to walk in a storm?"

"Me?" I said, once again feeling like the parent. "What about you? Everyone's looking for you."

"They are? But I haven't been gone that long, have I?" She rubbed the back of her neck. "I didn't mean to fall asleep but this medicine makes me feel so drowsy." Then she ran her hand over my dripping hair. "You look beautiful. You've got layers in your hair. When did you do that?" I opened my mouth, a million things waiting to be spoken, but my mother startled and looked over my shoulder. "Who are you?" she asked.

Tony had crouched behind me. "I'm Tony," he said. "I'm glad you're okay."

"Tony's my friend, Mom. He helped me look for you."

"You brought him here? To the hospital?" Her face tightened. "Alice? You told him about me?"

I took a deep breath. "He's knows all about you. He knows everything."

"You told him? But . . ."

"I needed his help," I said, looking right into her eyes. "And I don't want to lie anymore. This is who we are." I got to my feet. "Look at us," I said, opening my arms as if I'd just stepped onto a stage and was presenting our little play to an audience.

"You're in a bathrobe and slippers, in a cave, in the middle of a storm. And I'm in a pair of shorts, in a cave, in the middle of a storm." My arms fell to my sides. "You came here to do research for your next book. I came looking for you because I was afraid you were stumbling around the forest like a zombie. I'm the daughter of a mother who does weird things, who's been sick for a very long time but I'm not ashamed. I'm soaking wet but I'm not ashamed."

"You're not ashamed of me?" she asked, looking up at me.

"I've never been ashamed of you," I said. "I've just been confused. And sad. And lonely." My jaw trembled with that last word.

My mother got to her feet. She hugged me again. "I never wanted to be this way. I never wanted you to feel sad or lonely."

"I know," I said, my cheek pressed against the soft blue terry cloth. "I know that now."

"Alice?" Tony said quietly. He stood next to me and ran his flashlight beam around the cave. "Where's Errol?"

There's a moment just before tragedy strikes when you can sense its impending arrival—an unnerving sensation before it swoops down like a bird of prey. I'd felt it just before opening the bathroom door on that morning when my mother was hospitalized. And I felt it right then, stronger than the jolt of Errol's arrow. I stumbled from the cave.

Errol lay on his back in the creek bed.

"Errol!" I cried, flinging myself onto the rocks. "Oh my God! Errol!" Water trickled around his head. His drenched hood was wadded beneath his neck. Tony shone his light on Errol's face and I gasped. His hair had turned completely gray. I put my hand on his cold cheek and his eyes fluttered open.

"I've run out of time," he said.

"No." I shook my head. "No, you haven't. You told me you still had time. You told me—"

"Alice, listen to me." He grimaced.

Tony knelt next to us. "Did you fall?" he asked. "What happened? Is anything broken? Can you move?" He felt along Errol's legs.

I held on to Errol's arm. "You said there was still time to finish. We have to finish your story. And the rest of your stories. I want to hear the rest of your stories. The whole world wants to hear them." Rain rolled into the corners of my mouth.

"Alice—"

"I promised to write your story." I gripped his arm tighter. "You can't die. I want you to read it. I want you to know that it's good and that everyone's going to love it and . . ."

His eyes closed and he moaned.

"What do you mean he can't die?" Tony asked. "What's going on? What's the matter with him?"

I leaned over Errol, blocking the rain from his face. "He's dying. He's got cancer and he's dying."

"Cancer?" Tony said. Understanding spread across Tony's face and he nodded slowly. "That's why you've been trying to get the book finished."

My mother had followed us out. "We need to get him out of the water," she said. "Let's move him into the cave."

Tony slid his arms beneath Errol's and we both helped get him to his feet. Then Tony picked him up and carried him, bearing his weight with slow steps across and out of the creek. Errol's pale face looked almost unnatural next to Tony's tan arm. Once inside the cave, I helped Tony lay Errol on the ground. Tony took my flashlight and set it upright so the light bounced off the cave's ceiling. My mother took off her bathrobe and bundled it up, placing it under Errol's head. Then she wiped his face with the sleeves of her cotton nightgown.

"I'm going to get help," Tony said, wiping condensation off his glasses with his dripping wet shirt. "I'll tell them to bring a stretcher."

"Yes." I nodded frantically. "Bring a stretcher. And some blankets and some . . ." What else did we need? How do you keep a contract of servitude from expiring? I looked desperately at Tony. "Are you sure you remember the way?"

"Yeah. I'm sure I can find the trail. It's not far." He leaned over Errol. "Hang on," he told him. "I'll be back as soon as I can, with help." Then he dashed out of the cave.

*Thank you*, I thought. *Please hurry.*

My mother settled next to Errol. "He's very cold," she said. She moved his head to her lap and placed her bathrobe over him. "Alice, what's going on? How do you know this boy?"

I tucked the bathrobe around Errol's shoulders. "He's my friend," I said. Drenched to the skin, I began to shiver.

"Alice." Errol grimaced again, then opened his eyes. I leaned close. "In the back pocket of my jeans. Get it."

He must have brought his medicine. It would help take the pain away. Rolling his hip slightly, I reached into his pocket but only found a piece of paper. "This?"

"Yes."

Heavy drops of water fell off the ends of my hair as I unfolded the paper. It was the photograph, the one of me and my mother at the romance writers' convention. I must have left it in Errol's room. It was wet along the top edge and the ink had begun to smear. "Um, thanks," I said, shoving it into my own pocket. "Errol, where are your pills?"

"Don't lose it," he said.

"I won't. Errol, did you bring your pills?"

"Be sure to look at it."

Why did he care about a photograph? He was dying. Dying!

A realization came to me, rising out of the panic and desperation. I knew what Errol needed. Not a stretcher, not a blanket, not a doctor or a hospital. "Mom, there's something I need you to do." I reached out and grabbed my flashlight. "I need you to hold this light so I can see what I'm writing."

"Writing?" She hesitated, then took the flashlight.

I crawled a few feet to where the spiral notebook lay. A pen was tucked into its wire coil. Then I sat next to Errol and opened the notebook until I found a blank page.

"What are you—"

"There's not much time, Mom. Please just listen to me. This is Errol and I've been helping him write his story. He wants to finish it before he dies."

"Psyche," Errol whispered.

"That's who the story is about," I told my mother as I pulled the pen from the coil.

"Psyche? The woman who married Cupid? That Psyche?"

"Yes," I said, clicking the pen. "Psyche was Errol's love, his true love. And the mythology books tell the wrong story. They tell that she lived a long and happy life with him. But she didn't. She was killed and Errol wants the true version written so everyone will know. I think it's . . ." I looked down at his still face. "I think it's his way of apologizing to her. He feels responsible for her death. It's his confession."

"Psyche," he whispered again.

"But, Alice . . . ," my mother said, leaning close to me. "Psyche lived a long time ago."

"I know." I bent my knees and set the notebook, open faced, on top of them. My desk was ready, but my mother wasn't. She needed to know. "Errol is Cupid and he's asked me to write his story before he dies." I smiled, sad and joyous at the same time. "Mom, this is Cupid. He's Cupid. The *real* Cupid. And he needs our help with his story."

Who would have judged my mother if she'd laughed? Or if she'd started crying because she thought I was crazy. Or if she'd looked around and asked if we were on some sort of hidden-camera show. But she did none of those things. This was my mother—the Queen of Romance. A woman who'd spent her entire adult life writing stories of love. A woman who'd used her stories as a way to deal with the chaos that swirled around her. If anyone understood the healing power of a story, it was she.

She gently touched Errol's cheek and inhaled a long breath

of dank cave air. "Hello, Cupid," she whispered. Then she aimed the flashlight's beam at the notebook. "How's that?"

"Good." While the rain beat a steady rhythm outside, I gently shook Errol's shoulder. He'd stopped shivering, which struck me as a bad sign. He was drifting away. "You went home and Psyche was gone. What happened then?" I shook him harder, time pressing in on us like the cave's darkness. "Errol, I'm here. I'm here to record your story."

His eyes opened, and though his voice was quiet, it filled the small space the way the reverend's voice filled his church. "I knew they'd taken her." He stared up at the ceiling. "To punish me. I knew they'd kill her." His breathing was shallow. "I went to Venus's temple. No one was there. It was silent, except for the scratching." He grimaced. I wrote his words, my hands trembling.

"They'd built a tomb in the center of the temple. Made of stone walls. The scratching came from the tomb." He closed his eyes. I knew what was coming next and it chilled me more than my rain-soaked clothing. "I called her name. And she answered. She was inside."

My mother gasped.

Errol's eyes flew open. He raised his hands and clawed weakly at the air. "I dug with my bare hands but the stones wouldn't move." His arms fell to his chest. "I went to the village asking for help, but Venus had cast a spell over the villagers and my arrows couldn't sway them." He turned his head and looked at me. "Psyche," he whispered.

"What happened next?" I asked, turning to a new page.

His words were slow, his voice heavy. "I kept trying. I dug until my fingers bled. I used every tool I could find. I begged the gods. One day passed. Then another and another." He kept looking at me. "And then you stopped scratching." He'd gone back to that place and time. The cave became the tomb, and I was Psyche, once again. "Before you died I told you that I was sorry. But you could not hear me."

The flashlight's beam drifted away from the notebook as my mother, caught up in Errol's sorrow, wiped a tear from her eye. I set the notebook and pen aside and lay next to Errol, my head on his shoulder.

"I heard you," I said. "I heard you."

"I told you that I loved you. I promised that we would be together again." His voice vibrated against my ear. "I asked you to forgive me."

I sat up and looked at his face, once so handsome, now slack and frail. "I forgive you, Cupid," I said. "I forgive you." And I pressed my lips to his cheek.

Errol closed his eyes and the cave fell silent. My mother pressed her hand to his chest. "He's still breathing," she said.

"I wrote it all down," I told him, tears spilling out. "I won't change it. I'll write it just like it happened. I won't give your story a happy ending. You don't have to worry. I promise."

"But it has a happy ending," my mother said, stroking Errol's forehead. "It has a very happy ending."

"No, Mom, it doesn't," I said. Couldn't she see what was happening? Psyche was long dead and now Errol was going to die.

"But it does." She smiled down at him. "When he dies, he'll see her again. Just as he promised."

Errol's eyes opened and he turned them up at my mother and smiled—a beaming, brilliant smile, and for a moment his face was young and handsome and strong. And his hair was white and brilliant. He glowed with happiness.

Then he turned his eyes to me. "Thank you, Alice. Thank you for writing my story."

RIGHT after Errol died, the storm abated. The thunder and lightning ceased. The rain stopped falling. A gentle breeze blew outside the cave. My mother and I held each other—the last two women to have known Cupid.

"What was that paper he gave you?" she asked after I'd stopped crying.

I took the photo from my pocket and showed her. "I remember this day," she said. "I was so tired and I signed so many books. You were such a help to me."

I looked at the photo. There I stood, behind my mother at the book-signing table, fake smiles plastered on both our faces. But now I could see what I couldn't see before. Around my mother's head was her sparkling aura and it had reached out and had wrapped itself around me.

It had never gone away.

She'd never stopped loving me.

# SEVEN MONTHS LATER

FEBRUARY in Seattle is usually cold and clear, and so it was that day at Forest Lawn Cemetery, a vast landscape of headstones and rolling hills. Bundled in a jacket, scarf, and mittens, I stood at Errol's grave. The crisp air tickled my nose and some of the guests might have thought I was sniffling because I was holding back tears. But I wasn't crying. I was happy. Okay, so visiting someone's grave on Valentine's Day isn't usually an occasion for happiness, but I had called every-one there for a special unveiling.

My mother, who stood to my left, looked beautiful in her green coat with its white faux-fur trim. She'd come home a few days after we'd found her in the cave, that night when Errol died. And she'd been home ever since. Life as we now knew it, which was very close to normal, meant a pill every day. Sometimes I had to remind her to take it, but that was easy.

Brain chemistry is sort of like one of Mrs. Bobot's

recipes—you never know what you're going to end up with. Add a little of this and you've got a person who can see auras. Take away a dash of that and you've got a person who is so depressed, she can't speak or move. Sprinkle in something else and you've got a person who's in love for a lifetime.

Thanks to the medication, my mother's career was back on track too. Heartstrings Publishers never stopped sending her royalty checks, nor did they ask for the one hundred thousand dollars. It turned out that after my mother held a press conference, during which she acknowledged her mental illness, her book sales went wild. And she got hundreds of letters from readers thanking her for calling attention to a condition that many people suffered from. Her thirty-first book, *The Lumber Baron's Wife,* the story of true love in a Pacific Northwest forest, was scheduled for a May release.

Next to my mother, holding a Tupperware container of cookies and wearing a new crocheted hat, was Mrs. Bobot. Realm and her parents had also come to the unveiling. I hadn't seen Realm since she'd gone away to a center that treats eating disorders. Her hair was longer and she looked a million times better. I'd kept my promise to read *Death Cat.* Guess what? It wasn't so bad. My mom read it too and she called her publisher and Realm got a contract. Everyone agreed that Realm was a much better name for a horror writer than Lily. So the name was staying.

Reverend William Ruttles towered next to Realm in his official collar and robe. Archibald stood at his side in an elegant cashmere coat, a treat he'd bought himself after getting a raise at work. Many members of the Magnolia Community Episcopalian Church crowded behind them. Back in July, a week following the reverend's interrupted sermon about neighborly love, he brought Archibald to church, where they sat together in the front row. Later, during the social hour, he introduced Archibald to as many people as he could find. What Reverend Ruttles did not realize was that the congregation had long been aware of his living arrangements. They secretly adored Archibald, because his arrival had brought a merciful end to the exhausting year following Mrs. Ruttles's death. Even the most well-intentioned church lady has a limit to the number of salmon loaves she wants to bake.

To my right stood Tony and his father, Mr. Lee. Tony looked handsome in his jeans and sport coat. And next to them stood Velvet, in a pink coat and pink hat, along with a few of her salon girls. It was a good thing we'd gathered outside because the combination of perfumes and hair products wafting off the girls was almost toxic.

"Are you ready?" Tony asked me.

"Yes," I said, stepping forward. "Thank you, everyone, for coming here today," I said, smiling at the crowd. "Some of you didn't know Errol, and some of you only knew him for a short time, but I'm grateful that you joined me here. Errol was my friend and as you know, we wrote a book together before he died. *The True Love Story of Cupid and Psyche* will be published this summer, and our royalties will be donated to cancer research, in Errol's name." I nodded at two men in suits who represented a local nonprofit that helped people without insurance get cancer treatment.

"This book was very important to Errol and it's important to me. Writing it helped me realize that this is something I'm good at and I think I'll keep doing it. Maybe I'll even become a romance writer like my mom."

"Well, you've certainly got the right name for it," Archibald said and everyone laughed. Mrs. Bobot took my mother's hand.

I loosened my scarf, my body warm with anticipation. "So, what I'm about to unveil today is just a small way to say thank you to Errol for granting me the honor to share his story."

And to thank him for changing my life.

Here's how a true romance writer would look at it—I'd been kind of like Psyche, stuck with these walls around me and feeling them pressing in. I'd come to believe that I was unlovable, which is the worst thing to feel in the whole world. Errol hadn't been able to save Psyche, but he'd saved me. He'd made me believe in myself again.

"I'd like to thank Mr. Lee and Tony Lee for helping me with this project. It took such a long time because we had to order it from Italy." Then I grabbed the edge of the sheet and pulled.

"Awesome," Realm said.

"That's magnificent," Archibald said.

"It's gorgeous," Velvet said.

Standing over Errol's grave was a statue of a young, handsome man in a toga. The man held a bow and a quiver of arrows. Okay, so maybe I'd gone a bit overboard, because the Cupid statue was even taller than the statue that marked the oldest grave in the cemetery—a grave for one of the men who had founded Seattle. But who would argue that a mere pioneer was more important than the real Cupid, Servant of Love?

"It's a replica," Mr. Lee explained. "The original statue is in Rome."

"I love it," my mother said.

"So do I," Mrs. Bobot said. She handed out raisin cookies and everyone stood around talking for a long time. Then we started down the paved trail, back to the cars.

"How about we all go out to that new Italian restaurant?" my mother suggested.

"That sounds like a very nice way to celebrate Valentine's Day," Archibald said.

I looked over my shoulder. Reverend Ruttles and Mrs. Bobot were still up the path, standing next to the Cupid statue. The reverend was holding Mrs. Bobot's hand. Orange rays shot out of both their heads.

"Alice," Velvet said, her high heels clicking against the pavement as she hurried up to me. "I have something for you." Peppermint perfume swirled around her. She handed me a metal key and a key card.

"What's this?"

"It's for a safe deposit box. It belonged to Errol, and he told me that he wanted you to have it." She smiled. "Oh, I know what you're thinking. You think he left you some treasure."

That's exactly what I was thinking.

"Well, not quite." She pulled a tube of gloss from her pocket and ran it over her lips. "It's just a box of old notebooks. One time when he came in for a shave, he told me he'd written a bunch of stories, about all these things that had happened to him over the years. Now they belong to you." She closed the tube, then gave me a hug. "I love the statue. It looks just like him."

I wrapped both hands around the key. More stories. For me. Amazing.

*Thank you, Errol.*

"I got you something for Valentine's Day," Tony said, opening the back of his Jeep. The box was big and tied with a ribbon. I tucked the key into my pocket, then, beaming, I opened the box. "These are for me?" I pulled out pairs of knee and elbow pads.

"Well, you said you wanted me to teach you how to ride a skateboard."

"Yeah, I do. I really do." I took a helmet out of the box. "But do you really think I need to wear all this stuff?"

He laughed. "I think we both need to. We tend to fall a lot."

Then Tony Lee, cute boy with the freckles, leaned forward and kissed me and I knew, not from his aura, but from the way he smiled, that he felt the same way I felt. And it was real.

"Praise the Lord," Reverend Ruttles said, as he and Mrs. Bobot walked past. "What a glorious day!"

My mother, Archibald, and I climbed into the backseat of Tony's Jeep. Mr. Lee sat up front. As Tony drove us out of the cemetery, I looked back at the statue that stood at the top of the hill. I knew I'd visit it a lot. And maybe others would too.

Then I looked at my mother who sat next to me, her warm shoulder pressed against mine. Maybe I wasn't the one who had pulled her from the darkness. Maybe she'd been awakened that morning at Harmony Hospital by the promise of a new story. But that didn't mean she loved me less. She was who she was. And if a story is what had called to her, then so be it. Perhaps that's what calls to each of us, the promise of the next story, right on the horizon.

Or the story skating by the front window.

Or the one beating inside our hearts, waiting to be set free.

From Heartstrings Publishers' sister company,
FIRESTORM PUBLISHING,
comes a refreshing new voice in the horror genre.

# DEATH CAT

by Realm

They put the cat into a cage and took her to the cat show.

It was a small cage, two feet by two feet, and made of metal bars. The woman had worked for many days decorating the cage. She'd added a white shag carpet. She'd sewn a red velvet pillow and had hung red velvet curtains. The man had made a cardboard crown and then tied it to the cat's head with ribbon. When the cat pushed the hat off, the man told her that she was a bad kitty and that she needed to wear her crown. He pointed to a sign on the front of the cage. PRINCESS'S PALACE, the sign said in glittery letters.

All day long, kids stuck their sticky fingers into the cage. "Look, Mom, she's a princess kitty," they said.

The cat narrowed her yellow eyes and crawled under the red pillow. The woman scolded her for hiding and pulled her out from under the pillow. But the cat crawled under the pillow again.

"What's the matter with you?" the woman asked. "Why don't you want to be a princess?"

"She doesn't appreciate anything we've done for her," the man said.

An extralong, extrasticky finger poked the cat's leg and the cat growled. It was there, under the pillow, where she began to formulate her plan. An evil but necessary plan. She wasn't sure if she could pull it off, but she knew one thing. They'd be sorry.

They'd all be sorry.

# CRAIG'S CLAM JUICE

625 Sandbar Way, Tidepool, WA 60543 • 555-564-1000

## A DISCLAIMER

from the manufacturer

of Craig's Clam Juice

We here at the Craig's Clam Juice Company would like our customers to know that we do not, in any way, claim that our product can cure lovesickness. There is no evidence supporting or disproving such a claim.

However, clam juice does contain many nutritional benefits and we highly recommend that it be added to a well-balanced diet.

We appreciate your support.

Please drink responsibly.

*Craig*

**WARNING**: Do not drink Craig's Clam Juice if you have shellfish allergies.

# SOME NOTES FROM THE AUTHOR

Bipolar disorder has been in the news a lot lately, but that's not why I wrote about it. It has long interested me because I suspect that my father suffered from it. Though he went undiagnosed and though he didn't have the extreme bouts of depression, his mania was obvious and often uncomfortable. He self-medicated with alcohol. Knowing what I know now, I wish I could go back in time and help him. Like Alice, I wish I could fix things.

Sometimes life and story collide in an odd way. I wrote the first draft of *Mad Love* in the depths of a Pacific Northwest winter, which tends to be cloudy and dark. I placed my story in mid-July, in the neighborhood of Capitol Hill, during the worst heat wave to ever hit Seattle. I chose a heat wave because I wanted to put my characters into an uncomfortable environment. The only way to make Seattle, a mild and friendly city, uncomfortable was to raise the temperature.

And as it just so happened, when I went to revise the

novel five months later, my daughter was registered for a writing class in Capitol Hill, Alice's neighborhood. So I found myself revising the story while sitting at the Capitol Hill library, in the middle of July, during the worst heat wave to hit Seattle. No kidding. In my story it reached 105 degrees and in reality it reached 106. I like to think I influenced the heavens. I'm not making this up.

Every writer has a story that drives her to the edge. This was mine. It took me a long time to figure out Alice and her world. At times I nearly gave up. I threw away entire chapters. I killed off characters. I changed the voice. But finally it came together and I'd like to thank the people who helped me with the first draft—my writing group members, Sheila Roberts, Susan Wiggs, Anjali Banerjee, and Elsa Watson; my literary agent, Michael Bourret; and my husband, Bob Ranson.

I'd also like to thank LeAnne and David, the owners of Hot Shots Java in Poulsbo, Washington, and their wonderful staff, because that's where I do a lot of my writing. They are always so nice to me. They fuel my creativity.

I'd like to especially thank the two people who went through the subsequent drafts, listened to my worries, and saw the story when I couldn't—my editor, Emily Easton, and my daughter, Isabelle. Thank you from the bottom of my heart.

Kate deVeaux

# SUZANNE SELFORS

is the author of *Coffeehouse Angel* and *Saving Juliet*, as well as *Smells Like Dog*, a middle-grade novel. She held a number of jobs before becoming a writer, including children's photographer, video producer, organic flower grower, and marketing director. She lives in Bainbridge Island, Washington.

www.suzanneselfors.com

IN THIS MAGICAL LAND,
CHOCOLATE IS MORE PRECIOUS THAN GOLD . . .

the
*Sweetest*
*Spell*

SUZANNE SELFORS

Read on for a sneak peek
at Suzanne Selfors's
delicious new romance

# Chapter One

I was born a dirt-scratcher's daughter.

I had no say in the matter. No one asked, "Wouldn't you rather be born to a cobbler or a bard? How about a nobleman or a king? Are you certain that dirt-scratching is the right job for you?"

If someone had asked, I'm pretty sure I wouldn't have answered, "My heart is set on being a dirt-scratcher. I'm really looking forward to a life soured by hunger, backbreaking work, and ignorance. That sounds delightful. Sign me up."

Oh, and I'm absolutely certain I wouldn't have added, "Could you also give me some sort of deformity? Just to make things *interesting*."

The midwife told me the full story of my birth, as much as she could remember. She said nothing out of the ordinary happened that evening. No blinding star appeared on the horizon, the world wasn't darkened by an eclipse, time didn't stand still—the sort of thing that heralds the birth of someone really important. But the midwife boiled the water and counted the beats between my mother's screams, and after I'd been pushed from the womb, the midwife wrapped me in a rag and carried me outside.

"She's no good," the midwife told my father.

"No good?" My father bowed his head and stared at the cracked leather of his boots.

"She's not a keeper." The midwife didn't hesitate. In this time and place, decisions of life and death had to be made. "You must cast her aside, Murl Thistle."

My father ran his callused hand over his face as if trying to wipe away the truth.

"She's got a curled foot," the midwife whispered. She'd whisked me out of the cottage before my exhausted mother could see what was happening.

Reaching ever so hesitantly, my father slowly peeled back the stained rag. Peering at my misshapen foot, sadness settled in his eyes. Learning your babe is not a keeper has to be the worst feeling in the world. He'd seen the deformity before and it sealed my fate. A dirt-scratcher's daughter needed two strong feet. A curled foot would slow me down, would keep me from doing my fair share of work in the fields. I would be a burden, a gaping mouth to feed. I would never earn enough coin to buy myself a husband. No man would want me.

"Go tell your wife the babe was stillborn." The midwife's tone was matter-of-fact, for she'd learned that it was always best to lie to the mother. A mother, once she's laid eyes on her child, will always beg to keep it despite its defects. "I will take her to the forest, Murl Thistle."

A quiet sound, like a wood dove's coo, floated from my mouth. My father didn't look at my face. Perhaps he figured that if he looked into my eyes he would see that they were exactly like his eyes, and he'd want to claim me as his own. My father didn't hold me. Perhaps he knew that if he felt the warmth that ebbed from my tiny body and if he felt the beating of my heart, I would become a keeper. I would become his daughter.

He turned away. "Do what you must," he said. "I will tell my wife." Then, his footsteps heavy, as if his legs were felled trees, he stepped into the cottage and closed the door.

My mother's sobs seeped between the cottage stones as the midwife carried me away. The sun was setting and she wanted to get some distance between the cottage and my fate. She didn't want my parents to hear me cry out. Nor did she want them to accidently stumble upon my tiny bones one day.

Toward the forest the midwife hurried, keeping between the ruts worn into the road by the dirt-scratchers' carts. The day's heat was fading but I was as warm as a stone taken from a fire. Images flooded the midwife's mind of her own warm children tucked beside her at night. She pushed those images away as she passed the first tilled field, then the next. I wiggled in her arms but she offered no soothing words—what would be the point? Death was coming. In the best of circumstances it would be swift and merciful.

She turned off the road and started across a meadow, her skirt swooshing through tall grass. The forest hugged the edge of the field like a dark curtain, hiding the creatures that lived within its depths. The midwife stopped. She didn't dare go closer. She gently set me on the ground. The predators would come. They always did. And it would be as if I'd never been born.

Finding a clean spot on her bloodied apron, the midwife wiped sweat from her neck. Twilight would soon caress the sky and she needed to get home. She slid the rag free, exposing me so my scent would mix with the evening breeze. A brief twinge of pity pulled at her but she stopped herself from looking into my eyes. Pity wouldn't help me.

The rag tucked under her arm, she left me to my fate. That was the end of her story.

The milkman told how he'd found me the next morning. But the in-between comes from my remembering. I know it sounds strange that a newborn babe could remember, but I do. I swear I do. To this day, it's the brightest memory I have.

Four brown milk cows, having grazed in the field for most of the day, were on their way back to their barn when they caught my scent in the air. Usually wary of the forest's edge, they moseyed up to me, their tails flicking with curiosity. Ignoring their instinct to return home, they stood over me, even as twilight descended. Even as the predators began to stir.

And so it was that four pairs of large, brown eyes were the first to look directly at me and I met their gazes with an unblinking fascination. Four pairs of eyes, framed with thick lashes, were the first to acknowledge me and I cooed with appreciation. One cow gently nudged me from side to side while the others licked me clean. As night crept into the meadow, the cows settled in the grass, forming a protective circle. The ground absorbed their heat the way it had absorbed the sun's heat, and warmth spread beneath me. I found a nipple and warmth spread throughout my little body.

And I, the babe who'd been cast aside, lived.

# Chapter Two

The only thing on my mind that morning was the upcoming husband market. It never failed to be the most exciting day of the year, promising passion, heartbreak, comedy, even murder. Aye, murder, because on a few occasions, disappointed women had turned on the highest bidder. Nothing else could compare to the husband market for sheer entertainment. My head swirled with excitement. That's why I didn't notice the cows until Father said something.

"Those creatures are at the window again."

It wasn't a fancy window for it had no glass, but it was a hole in the side of our cottage and I'd drawn the ragged curtain aside to let in some fresh air. Clearly the cows thought this was an invitation, for they stuck their noses through the hole and flared their wet nostrils. One white-faced, the other brown, they snorted for attention.

"I'll take them back," I said, scraping the last mouthful of mashed potato from my bowl. When the cows showed up, which they did now and then, I always walked them home. It was the only way to get them to leave. They'd come to see me, after all.

After licking my spoon clean, I pushed back my stool and waited for Father's permission.

"Go on then," he grumbled, hunching over his bowl. His sharp shoulders pressed at the seams of his threadbare shirt. I hoped he'd look up and offer a reassuring nod, but he didn't. He rarely looked directly at me. But I'd caught him a few times, staring as I stumbled across the field, sadness dripping off him like rain.

Everyone in the village of Root knew that my father had rejected me at birth. But he'd simply done what any other dirt-scratcher would have done. Food and shelter were precious and not to be wasted on those who couldn't contribute. This was the way of my people. Over the generations, countless deformed babes had been fed to the forest. When the milkman found me, he knew I was Murl Thistle's babe because my mother was the only woman who'd gone into labor that week. The villagers said my survival was a bad omen. Some kind of black magic had influenced the cows. It was unnatural. *I was unnatural.* That's why villagers always kept a wary distance.

"I'll be as quick as I can," I said, pulling my shawl from its peg. There were kitchen chores to get to. Socks to wash. A donkey's stall to be mucked out. The sun never stayed around long enough for all the work to get done. The precious time it would take for me to walk the cows back to the milkman's land was sacrificed because my father didn't want to face the milkman's temper.

"I got no time to chase after my cows," the milkman had hollered at my father one day. "They stray, Murl Thistle, because that daughter of yours has unnatural power over them. If she doesn't bring them back, I'll complain to the tax-collector!"

As I hurried from the cottage, the white-faced cow stepped away from the window and greeted me with a soft moo.

"Hello," I answered. The cow dipped her head and I kissed her wide brow. She smelled like grass and dirt and wind. I'd known this cow my entire life and though the milkman never named his cows, I secretly called her Snow. Snow was the only cow left of the original four that had saved me.

A nudge to my elbow drew my attention to the other cow, Snow's daughter. "Hello," I said, running my hand down her back. Five more cows, brown as freshly hoed dirt, waited on the road just below our cottage. "Oh, you brought your friends." I wrapped the shawl around my shoulders. "Well, I'd best get you home. The milkman will be missing you."

Planting season had come to the village of Root. Having finished their noon meal, villagers were at work sprinkling seed into furrows and setting potato tubers into holes. Men and women, boys and girls, young and old—if you breathed and you lived here, you worked the fields. This part of Anglund's kingdom was called the Flatlands, a wide valley wedged between River Time and the Gray Mountains. My ancestors, the red-haired Kell, came to the Kingdom of Anglund as invaders many generations ago but were brutally defeated. The Queen of Anglund took pity on the survivors, mostly women and children. Though we were forbidden to ever again call ourselves Kell, or make or carry weapons, we were given the right to farm the Flatlands. Honestly, no one else wanted the land, which is parched in the summer and soggy in the winter. But after a single generation, the villages of Root, Seed, and Furrow arose and we have lived there ever since.

No one stared at me as I hobbled down the road. They'd gotten used to the sight of me leading the cows, just as they'd gotten used to the strange way I walked, my right side dipping with each step of my right foot. I walked that way because my right foot was shrunken and curved inward so that I bore my weight on its side. A long trek, such as the distance between my father's cottage and the milkman's land, was difficult and painful. But the cows never seemed to mind my slow pace.

My thoughts drifted to tomorrow's husband market. The boys who'd turned eighteen since the last husband market would be up for bid, joined by the men who had yet to find wives or who had been widowed. Flatlander girls saved all their coins for the occasion. The highest bidder got the best husband. Usually.

There was no law forcing a girl to marry, but most did. A husband provided a house. A husband meant that a girl was no longer a child and could speak for herself. A husband meant other things too—things I'd heard girls whisper about.

Everyone knew my fate was to remain unmarried, thanks to my *unnatural* status. I suppose, out of desperation, I could bid on an "unwanted." The unwanteds were the men who rarely got bids, usually because they had frightful tempers or because they had a flock of nasty, bad-mannered children from previous marriages. Or because they were hideous.

No thank you.

The cows' hooves clomped along the road. Soft clouds drifted lazily over the fields. Two robins circled each other in a spring dance of love. I could pretend that my pride would keep me from bidding on an unwanted, but the truth was this—I was also an *unwanted*.

The pain began at the next bend in the road. It started in my curled foot, then shot up the outside of my leg. It would worsen throughout the afternoon as I followed Father around the field, dropping the potato tubers into the holes he'd dug. I fought the urge to slow down, maybe take a rest beside the river. Daylight was precious. Father needed my help. We had a lot to get done if we wanted to take tomorrow off for the husband market.

No way was I going to miss it. Not this year. Not with Root's most popular boy stepping onto that stage. Every girl in the village of Root dreamed of marrying Griffin Boar.

Including me.

And that's why I gasped when he appeared around the bend.

# Did Cupid pierce your heart with Mad Love?

Then don't miss these other heartfelt novels from Suzanne Selfors.

Walker & Company
www.bloomsburyteens.com

# In the mood for more romance?

Here are other great reads
you'll fall in love with.

Walker & Company

www.bloomsburyteens.com